"*Double Indemnity* by Richard Zappa is not a retooling of James N. Cain's pulp novel of 1943. It's a highly entertaining yarn in its own right, a clever crime story that keeps the emphasis on energy and entertainment, continually building suspense as it goes. New Orleans is home for both the good guys and the bad in this intriguing sojourn into greed, corruption, and megalomania. The bad is represented by an insurance company that buys life insurance policies from individuals ... [who] die before they should, thereby allowing the company to stop paying premiums while collecting big payouts.
The good is Jo Crowder, The Big Easy female detective who winds up looking into a series of seemingly accidental deaths, suicides, and more. She's a tough-as-nails cop who is not at all averse to using lethal force when it becomes necessary. She gets teamed with Alex Hill, a special agent with the organized crime unit of the FBI who is smart, savvy, good with his fists when he has to use them, or when one of them is holding his gun. The two eventually find themselves up against some of the worst of the worst. There's the corporation's founder who has a photographic memory but no moral compass whatsoever. There's his head of security who's an ex-military man skilled at special ops, taking no prisoners, and leaving no witnesses behind. In their employ are stone cold assassins who ply their trade with frightening efficiency. As you might guess, before novel's end these sets of opposites will clash with devastating results."

— Jake Bishop, Pacific Book Reviews.

"Zappa is a skilled storyteller, and fans of crime novels will find a lot to love here. As a trial lawyer himself, Zappa brings a sense of authenticity to his plotline as well as to all matters of crime in the novel. The characters are well-drawn and believable.

Crowder's character as a take-no-prisoners homicide detective is convincing, and her work ethic is easy to admire. Despite their unconventional actions—and even illegal ones—Hill and Crowder both prove to have strong moral compasses. The mounting body count and seemingly endless twists and turns in the story create an exciting, rapid pace that keeps the reader focused and interested. The dialogue is easy to follow and rings true throughout the book. Overall, this is a well-written and exciting novel that builds to a satisfying final conflict while also leaving room for another book in the series."

—Jennifer Hummer, US Review.

"Zappa's novel is remarkably eventful, featuring lots of murder, intrigue, and criminal schemes as well as sexual attraction between the two main heroes. The plot is briskly paced, as well, and the author never skimps on action."

—Kirkus Reviews

"New Orleans homicide detective Jo Crowder finds a link between a series of seemingly random deaths and exposes a corrupt insurance company. After piecing together a link between a number of seemingly random deaths, Crowder finds herself unraveling a lethally corrupt insurance company. It's the kind of plot set-up familiar to readers of the Jack Reacher series wherein the hero picks away at a seemingly above board institution and ultimately busts open its rotten core. *Double Indemnity* is reminiscent of the kind of high quality, deceptively simple crime paperbacks of the golden era of American pulps. Though *Double Indemnity* works as a standalone novel, on completion readers will almost certainly want to catch up on Crowder's previous antics in the novels *The Easter Murders* and *Identical Misfortune*. And as long as Crowder can avoid getting herself killed or fired, the series deserves to run and run. *Double Indemnity* is the third Jo Crowder novel and establishes Richard Zappa as a first class thriller writer and his homicide detective heroine as one to watch."

—IndieReader Reviews

DOUBLE INDEMNITY

Richard Zappa

AIA PUBLISHING

Double Indemnity
Richard Zappa

Published by AIA Publishing, Australia
ABN: 32736122056
http://www.aiapublishing.com

Paperback ISBN: 978-1-922329-32-5
Hardback ISBN: 978-1-922329-33-2

For all of you who read my novels

Introduction

I'm worried about Jo Crowder. She insists on putting herself in harm's way. She barely survived her duel of wits with a sociopath in *Identical Misfortune* and her face-off with a psychopath in *The Easter Murders.*

One day my pen may not be able to save her.

Why can't she transition to a different career path? There must be safer jobs out there for a pretty, thirty-six-year-old, educated, athletic, single woman with a unique skill set. Then again, when you put "hunting down murderers and other violent criminals" on your resume as your past work experience, the marketplace narrows considerably.

Why can't she transfer out of the homicide division to a nice desk job in Internal Affairs? Or to community relations, and speak at high schools and homeowners associations about neighborhood watch programs? The Smith & Wesson, handcuffs, and canister of mace can be left in her desk. No need to strap a derringer to her calf as backup. She'd have weekends off. Make friends with people who don't carry lethal weapons. Meet a nice man, get married, have a couple of kids.

No matter how hard I try, my pen will not cooperate.

It's in her blood to confront evil head-on day after day. Jo Crowder would perish from boredom doing anything other than what she does best—pursue the vilest of earth's creatures who pillage, plunder, maim, and murder.

In *Double Indemnity*, Crowder once again shows us the stuff of which she's made. Evil takes on many forms. When it poisons the business practices of a company, the capacity to harm others cuts deep. A corporation is a person in the eyes of the law. Like people—some do good things, some do very bad things. Crowder suspects the latter when she investigates why so many people who have a connection to a company and its owner are dying.

This time she recognizes her limitations in her search for the truth.

This time she will need help if she is to succeed.

Gratitude is deeply owed to my publisher and editor, Tahlia Newland, for her support on this, our third novel together. Special thanks to Rose Newland for another splendid book cover, and to my daughter and transcriptionist, Katie Zappa, who must endure translating my endless babble into a recognizable language. Lastly, my heartfelt thanks to all of you who read my novels. It is for you that I dedicate this novel and the many more I hope to write.

Prologue

The face of a scruffy old coot stared back at him from the mirror.

He'd given up shaving three years ago, the day after he buried Alma, his wife of fifty-two years. Just as his father had done when his mother passed. The only difference, a big one, was that his mother had died unexpectedly from a heart attack in her sleep. Alma, on the other hand, took her time dying. She fought through two years of radiation, chemotherapy, and a couple of experimental treatments first.

Through veiny eyes, he watched himself brush chipped, yellow-stained nubs. The water he cupped in his hand to rinse his mouth did little to blunt the taste of the whiskey he'd drunk. Above thick, untamable eyebrows, the furrows across his forehead were deep. He splashed water on his face and squeezed his beard to drain the moisture rather than dry it with a towel. His skin, tough as cowhide, was as weathered as the pair of old leather boots he'd be stepping into when he awoke in the morning.

Standing there in his pajamas, Cletus Moss saw the face of his father.

The life of a sugarcane grower was hard. He'd lived it every day for as long as he could remember. Just as his daddy and granddaddy had done before him. Three generations of cane produced by the Moss family had made Sugarland Plantation into one of the top growers in Louisiana. Had his son survived his deployment to Iraq, instead of stepping on a land mine on some unnamed road to some godforsaken village in the desert, Clete Jr. would have taken up the mantle for sure.

He'd loved working the farm with his father—a sense of civic duty, though, had lured him into military service. After all, weapons of mass destruction were in the hands of a madman—as the president had claimed—when the country went to war a second time against the Butcher of Baghdad. Now all that remained of Clete Jr. were the memories of a lonely old man. The boy's medal and sympathy letters from his commanding officer and George II remained hidden away beneath a stack of documents in the safe.

~

The large sign read Sugarland Plantation, Est. 1887. It glistened in the illumination of a harvest moon. They'd arrived at their destination. At three in the morning, there was no need for headlights—the ambient light was more than enough for Hawk to see down the asphalt driveway that snaked its way to the main house a quarter of a mile ahead.

The sugarcane stood tall and thick in the fields that covered nearly a thousand acres. Hawk knew it would—it was harvesting season. The report they'd been given inked out the long history of the farm. Homesteaded by Clayton Moss in the 1850s, it supplied cane to both the Union and the Confederacy. Clarence followed in his father's boots through the Great Depression and two world wars. Cletus, the grandson, picked up from there.

Until recently Sugarland Plantation had been luckier than most cane growers. It turned a profit more often than not. But to do that took all the skill of an experienced farmer and some luck. Natural predators abounded: red rot, spider mites, borers, white grubs, wireworms, and weevils could eat into the stalks, as well as the profits, of even the most experienced grower. Too little rain. Too much rain. Unexpected heat waves and cold spells. Climate was a grower's fair-weather friend. Global market conditions played their part too. A five-year-straight decline in yield per acre, and foreign competition, had brought Sugarland Plantation to the brink of bankruptcy.

It was all there in the file they'd been given—along with aerial photos mapping out the geography and buildings. The farmhouse sat just beyond two large wood-frame, tin-roof barns that housed the tractors, cultivator, sett cutter, stubble shaver, and the all-important combine harvester. In the distance, three large cabins served as barracks for the seasonal farmhands who lived there rent-free while earning minimum wage during planting and harvesting seasons.

"The old fool told me he didn't need the security alarm system I wanted to sell him because his loaded twelve-gauge, double-barrel shotgun by his bed was all the protection he needed," Hawk said. "The migrants won't be arriving for another week. Satellite images show no human activity other than the target on the property."

Wolf, sitting next to him, put on tight-fitting black leather gloves, then pulled out a handgun and loaded a full clip.

Hawk drove their rental car with the stolen out-of-state plates around the back of the barn closest to the house and parked it there. He shot a quick glance at his Casio G-Shock watch—the kind used by Special Forces. "I want to be in and out in under twenty minutes."

The earthy smell of uncut crops hung heavy in the humid air. Only the distant hum of the tree cricket's chirp and the great horned owl's hoot disturbed the quiet stillness of a pre-dawn Louisiana morn.

Dressed entirely in black, with matching ski masks, the duo appeared like ninjas at a door in the rear of the house. Hawk activated the timer on his watch and nodded to Wolf, who picked at the door lock until it released.

Wolf entered first, gun drawn. Hawk followed in his partner's steps through the pantry, scented with the sweet smell of spices, and into the kitchen. Unwashed dishes lay in the sink and an uncapped empty bottle of Jim Beam sat on the counter. They made their way to the staircase and slowly ascended the steps. Their rubber-soled shoes absorbed the creaking of the risers like sponges soaking up spilled milk.

With no one else living in the house, Hawk knew that the bedroom door of the target would be open. Predictably, the doors of the three other bedrooms were closed.

Hawk, six feet three inches tall, stood behind Wolf, a half foot shorter, giving both an unobstructed view into the room. A man lay on his back on one side of a four-poster bed, a white sheet pulled up to his chin. A straggly, salt-and-pepper beard stretched almost to the folded hands that rested upon his chest. The uneven sound of his snoring telegraphed his restlessness—he could be easily awakened.

Wolf walked to the foot of the bed, the gun pointed at the target's mid-section. Hawk went bedside, pausing only long enough to reach for the beaded chain of a lamp that sat on a nightstand beside a King James Bible, a pair of wire-rimmed spectacles, and an empty glass.

The moonlight beamed through a window just enough to allow Hawk to see the old man's shotgun leaning against the wall next to the bed and easily within arm's reach. He picked it up with a gloved hand as the light came on.

Moss instinctively reached for his gun, but soon saw its two barrels pointed at his face.

"Easy, old man," Hawk warned. "Cooperate and we'll be out of your life very, very soon."

"W-What do you want from me?" Moss stammered, the wide-eyed, open-mouthed look of terror on his face a familiar one to the intruders.

Hawk cocked a hammer on the shotgun. "Speak only to answer my questions. Move only when I tell you to move. Where's the safe?"

Moss's gaze darted from one trespasser to the other before replying, "Downstairs in my office."

"I want you to go to your office and open the safe," Hawk said.

Hawk liked giving orders, making demands, and telling people what to do. He enjoyed watching them twitch, sweat, even piss and shit themselves, when he told them to do something they knew was wrong—like betray a comrade or their country, or breach a moral code they believed was inviolate. The price of refusal could be dangerous—even fatal.

Like being made to spin the barrel of a revolver loaded with a single bullet, put it to one's head, or the head of someone else, and pull the trigger … and then, if someone's brains weren't splattered on the ground, to do it again. Or being made to run through a minefield. Or playing a water sport that required a cloth hood and a hose. Or, forget the gamesmanship, either cry uncle or take a bullet in the head—their choice.

Hawk had done those things and worse—in Iraq, Afghanistan, Syria, and Somalia—in search of a cache of weapons, an enemy's hideout, or information about planned terrorist attacks and assassinations. Hawk took his special skill set with him when he left government service to become a privately-retained independent contractor.

So did Wolf.

The man rose slowly from the bed and stood beside it. "I have nearly twenty thousand in cash. Take it and get out."

"And your wife's jewelry?"

"What little I have is in the safe. I gave most of it to my daughter when my wife passed away. Her wedding band was on her finger when I buried her." The old man sighed as he spoke. "What's left has only sentimental value."

Moss shuffled barefoot out the bedroom while Wolf menaced with the handgun from behind. Hawk uncocked the hammer of the shotgun, returned it to its place against the wall, and followed them out.

The floorboards squeaked under the sweaty feet of a slump-shouldered old man as he led them to the safe. Hawk found a table lamp when they entered the room and turned it on. Flanked by his captors, Moss's hands trembled as he removed a faded reproduction of *Whistler's Mother* that hung on the wall and placed it on the floor. He rotated the dial of the lock from right to left and right again until it clicked open. He perspired so much his pajama top stuck to his back.

"Move away," Hawk demanded, wary that Moss had a loaded handgun in the safe if the need ever arose for him to use it.

The need arose … but not the opportunity.

Hawk opened the safe and found a pistol resting on the top shelf. On the shelf just below sat several piles of cash bound with rubber bands and a lidless box of costume jewelry. He pulled a cloth bag from a jacket pocket and put the money and jewelry in it. Deeds, mortgages, a will, and other documents lay beside the cash. Hawk removed them from the safe and, with a passing glance at each one, threw them on the floor. A medal and two letters followed next.

"You got what you came for … now get out and leave me alone," Moss pleaded. Beads of perspiration dotted his forehead.

Hawk moved away from the safe and stood beside Wolf. "A last request and we'll be finished with you, I promise. I want you to reach inside the safe and bring me your pistol."

Moss's face had the pallor of a corpse. He showed a reluctance to move away from his desk. He wiped his runny nose and the drool from his mouth with a sleeve. Wolf waved the barrel of the gun in the direction of the safe to coax him on. He lumbered over and reached in the safe for the gun.

Moss turned around to face his intruders.

Two shots rang out. Both from the same gun. A couple of 9mm slugs. One entered Moss's chest slightly left of center. Another blasted a hole in his forehead.

The old man, his face frozen in terror, collapsed to his knees with a thud and tumbled forward. Blood quickly puddled on the floor.

Hawk went to Moss, who still had the gun gripped in his hand, and knelt beside him. He manipulated the gun in the dead man's hand and fired a shot into the wall in the direction where Wolf had stood when Moss was shot. Their work completed, the intruders left the room, walked to the kitchen, and left through the door they had entered.

Hawk returned to their vehicle and waited.

Wolf found a first-floor window and punched out the pane closest to the lock, exposing the latch. With the window raised, Wolf pulled out some blades of grass and pinched some mulch from a flower bed, and sprinkled the particles on the floor below the window.

When Wolf returned, Hawk drove to the entrance to the farm, stopping just long enough for them to unmask and for him to stop the timer on his watch. As he proceeded onto the main road, he turned to Wolf and said, "Nineteen minutes, thirty-two seconds."

A half hour later, Hawk stopped the car on Highway 90, midway across the Vintage Bridge. Wolf unholstered the gun used to shoot Moss, took the bag with the loot that lay on the seat, and got out of the car.

Hawk watched as Wolf tossed the gun over the railing and dumped the cash and jewelry into the muddied waters of the East Pearl River.

Chapter 1

The call came over the police radio while Crowder and Steele were on their way to the coroner's office. Their meeting with the chief medical examiner was to discuss the results of his autopsy of a badly decomposed body discovered by several Boy Scouts who'd wandered away from their campsite during a weekend outing. The meeting would have to wait.

The call came from O'Malley.

Frank O'Malley was head of the Violent Crime and Homicide Division of the New Orleans Police Department—the position had come with his promotion to captain more than a decade ago. A tough job in a tough-to-live-in city of a million-and-a-quarter people of diverse religious, ethnic and cultural backgrounds—a city famously known as much for Mardi Gras, music, and merriment, as it was for muggings, mayhem, and murder.

"Crowder, I want you and Steele over to 2712 Landsdale Lane for a domestic dispute in progress," he said in his usual no-nonsense manner.

Detective Lieutenant Jo Crowder, a muscularly toned, five-foot five-inch, one-hundred-twenty-five-pound, thirty-six-year-old woman with short raven-black hair and intensely inquisitive honey-hazel eyes, was O'Malley's diamond in the rough. Fourteen years on the force, she had degrees in criminal justice and criminal forensics, was well trained in weapons, martial arts, and crime scene investigations, and she was the best damn homicide detective on the force. She was tenacious, could be impetuous and impudent, and occasionally insubordinate. But, in the end, she was O'Malley's go-to detective in the most difficult homicide cases.

"What's Homicide doing responding to a domestic?" Crowder asked, knowing O'Malley had a good reason for overriding the police dispatcher and contacting his detectives directly.

"Someone at probation and parole fucked up, and the wrong Michael Hopkins was released. The one they let out was only three years into his life sentence for murdering the guy the former Mrs. Hopkins was sharing her bed with."

"Let me pick up on the narrative," Crowder interrupted. "The first thing he did was to make a beeline to his ex's house to finish what he'd started."

"He's holed up in the house, threatening to kill her and the kids."

"Kids?"

"Four. All under twelve. With him in the house."

"The ex-wife?"

"Rope-tied to a tree on the front lawn."

"Who's responded?" Crowder asked.

"A couple of black-and-whites. State police. They have the house surrounded."

"Crisis negotiator?"

"Samuels is on his way … Crowder?"

"What?"

"It could get real ugly out there today if Samuels can't sweet-talk Hopkins into ending this without bloodshed."

Several blocks from their destination, Crowder told Steele to cut the siren.

Detective Sergeant Sid Steele, early thirties, was Crowder's physical opposite—a lanky six feet three with shoulder-length, densely curly, chestnut-brown hair pulled back in a ponytail. He'd been her partner the last three years—ever since Crowder's previous partner had taken two bullets in the chest in a shootout. He'd have taken more had Crowder not put two slugs between the eyes of the shooter. She saved her first partner's life that day but couldn't save the lung he'd lost or his career as a homicide detective.

Crowder had never forgotten that day.

She'd relived it every time she attached her gold shield to her belt.

A day filled with regret.

Regret in not insisting that she approach the suspected meth lab from the front and that he provide the cover. But being the more experienced and senior officer, her partner always insisted on being the one most in harm's way, like an overly protective big brother.

Crowder felt the same way about Steele. She'd trained the former undercover cop when he came over from Vice, just as her previous partner had trained her. She was now the experienced, senior detective and the one expected to call the shots—just as her previous partner had done. And as he'd done, she'd do whatever was necessary to shield Steele from harm.

She had never allowed Steele to be the first one in.

And she never would.

"Pete's on a losing streak," Steele said, referring to Pete Samuels, the department's crisis negotiator—the third in eight years. "A jumper he couldn't talk down, and that disgruntled hardware-store employee who shot the bullhorn out of his hand and two coworkers before turning the gun on himself."

Crowder understood the roller-coaster ride of a crisis negotiator. She'd gotten drunk with a few of them after they'd worked a scene together—for better and for worse. Euphoria came with saving someone who'd lost everything in the stock market or at the casinos and avowed to do a swan dive off the roof of a high-rise, or appealing to an abductor's inherent goodness and persuading him to release a hostage unharmed. But when the guy jumped, or a bullet sent a hostage to the afterlife, a profound sense of failure, dissatisfaction and regret punched you in the gut and took your breath away.

The bipolar world of a crisis negotiator required thick skin, icy blood, and titanium nerves. Burnout was an occupational hazard.

"Let's hope his luck changes," Steele continued, interrupting Crowder's reflections.

"I have a bad feeling about this one, Sid."

"Why so?"

"A guy who's already serving a life sentence for murder has little to lose," she explained. "If he kills someone today and lives through his ordeal, he'll have a lethal injection to look forward to." She paused a moment, assessing the situation further. "Another thing—he's a very angry man. He was angry enough to kill his wife's lover instead of opting for a simple divorce. He could have used his get-out-of-jail-free card to go into hiding and plan a new life. Instead, he returns home to exact revenge on his ex-wife in a public display that guarantees he'll be caught. He has no intention of giving up and returning to his cell to sleep on the same lumpy mattress and eat the same shitty food for the rest of his life."

"I see what you mean. Samuels has nothing to offer him, nothing to bargain with."

"Precisely. Hopkins is putting on a show. He wants the ex-wife to suffer. Not just physically, but mentally and emotionally, like he's suffered the past three years. So he ties her to a tree for all the neighbors to see her terror, feel her humiliation, and witness her execution."

"Cap's right." Steele sighed. Cap was what most of the detectives in the homicide division called O'Malley. "It could get real ugly out there today."

On their way over, Crowder accessed the NOPD database on the police vehicle's mobile data computer to locate Michael Hopkins's criminal history. She wanted to know as much as possible about him before they squared off. The trial judge's remarks at sentencing gave the most reliable perspective—it was the epilogue of a murder case.

The judge's comments about the killing were telling but not unexpected: cold-blooded, premeditated, vicious, and senseless. Chilling was his description of Hopkins during an unhappy marriage: bully, wife-beater, abuser, mean drunk, and a wife's worst nightmare. The judge admonished him for being unrepentant and remorseless, and deserving of life without parole.

Hopkins had no moral compass then.

He'd be no different now.

The detectives arrived at what looked like a neighborhood block party featuring a live outdoor theater production. Lights from police cars and rescue vehicles flashed like disco strobes. Reporters, with cameramen in tow, mixed among the spectators who'd gathered on both sides of 2712 Landsdale Lane—all jockeying for the best views of the drama unfolding on the front lawn. The house, a cookie-cutter, white-clapboard, two-story home with a weathered asphalt tile roof and uneven gutters, appeared as a background might on the set of an outdoor stage.

All that was missing were ushers handing out playbills and vendors selling refreshments during intermission.

Cops and paramedics huddled in pairs, all talking but not looking at the persons to whom they spoke. Like the others in the audience, their stares fixed on the main attraction—a woman tethered to the bough of a mature silver oak tree in the middle of the lawn. A few onlookers raised cell phones to take a photo and prove they'd experienced something unique—like a solar eclipse or the tail of a comet streaking through the sky.

Steele navigated around a cable news van and parked on the lawn of the house next door, scattering a cluster of nosy neighbors. Crowder overheard their chatter when she exited the vehicle. They spoke of the gruesome murder Hopkins committed three and a half years ago. Crowder had seen it described in the sentencing report on the way over. Three slugs in the chest of the forty-year-old divorce lawyer his wife was seeing on the sly, and two more in his testicles for emphasis—the message delivered in the lawyer's office. Hopkins saved the remaining bullets in his handgun for his wife, but police apprehended him a block from his home.

Crowder surveyed the scene. The house was about sixty feet from the sidewalk. The tree was dead center. The eyes of the crowd were like guns aimed at a single target—a plain-looking woman in her late thirties with streaky gray hair, who hung by her arms from a tree limb, the rope around her hands so taut that her feet barely touched the ground.

The woman's face was severely bruised, her lip split open, one black eye swollen shut. She whimpered like a wounded animal. Two things stood out that captivated the crowd—the woman was naked, and she had the letter A spray-painted in red on her back.

Crowder handed one of the two Kevlar police vests she'd

gotten from the trunk to her partner. She put hers on as she walked over to Pete Samuels, who stood beside a state trooper and a couple of NOPD patrol officers. Crowder recognized one of the patrol officers, Jake Tolliver.

"Jake, what do we have here?" she asked.

"The next-door neighbor heard the woman screaming and called it in." Tolliver nodded in the direction of a woman standing outside the front door of her home. "She was tied to the tree when I got here. The neighbor says there's an arsenal of guns in the house. Hopkins was a big-time Second Amendment guy, NRA member, and hunter. The ex-wife never thought it would be important to get rid of his weapons."

Crowder stepped closer to Samuels. "Pete, have you made contact with Hopkins?"

"Just got here," he replied. "Things were quiet. I thought I'd wait until you showed up."

"Any shots fired?"

"Not yet," Tolliver answered from behind Crowder, an ominous tone in his voice.

As if on cue, shots rang out from an open window and blew out the windshields of the two patrol cars closest to the house. Neighbors scattered in the direction of their homes like mice chased by an alley cat. Police sought refuge behind vehicles not shot at, guns raised and pointed in the direction of the gunfire.

"I guess it's time to make contact," Crowder said to Samuels.

Samuels stood behind a patrol car, but he could still see the front of the house clearly. He spoke into his bullhorn. "Michael Hopkins. My name is Pete … Pete Samuels. I'm unarmed. While we're talking, no one, and I mean no one, will take any action against you. We will not move toward the house … as long as we continue to talk. Do you understand what I've said, Michael?"

Only the mumbling of distant onlookers could be heard

above the eerie hush.

"Michael, are any of your children hurt?" Samuels continued. His amplified words reverberated as he spoke. "Do any of them need medical attention? We're here to help them … and you … in any way we can. Will you let them out of the house so they can be safe while we talk?"

This time even the mumbling ceased. A morbid silence blanketed the airspace … broken only by the distant sound of a barking dog.

Hopkins broke the silence. "The woman's a whore," he yelled through the open window. "She was fucking every guy around, not just the one I shot. These kids, how do I know they're mine?"

The woman tied to the tree screamed out: "Michael, they are *our* children. Please believe me." The woman's trembling voice weakened as she continued, "Please let our children leave the house. Please don't hurt them, Michael." Her head drooped into her chest, making her last words barely audible.

"What's left for me?" Hopkins shouted back. "I'm paying the price for what you did to me, and now you'll pay the price for what I must do to *your* children."

"Our children, Michael … our children," the woman, suddenly revived, cried out hysterically.

"They're not my children. If they were, you would've brought them to see me in prison. Not once did you bring them. It's been so long; I don't even know who they are."

There was a creepy pause in the dialogue between Hopkins and his ex-wife.

Another shot rang out, this time striking the tree just above the woman's head, splintering the bark. Terrified, she squirmed like a hooked fish dangling from a line.

Samuels moved away from the car just enough to allow Hopkins to see him from his position by the window. "I'm coming out, Michael, so you can see me. I have no weapon, only this bullhorn. I'm asking you to send out your children one by one so they can walk to me and be safe while we continue to talk."

"You move any closer to the house," Hopkins said matter-of-factly, "and you'll be the first one I shoot … and then these bastard kids and the bitch, in that order."

Crowder had bad vibes. The situation was deteriorating. She'd been present at other crisis negotiations and learned that the tone of voice of the perpetrator was as important as his words. When the words were uttered with uncertainty and nervousness, there was room for negotiation and compromise. But Hopkins spoke with conviction and a steely resolve to do what he'd set out to do.

Crowder was convinced—it was about to get ugly.

Chapter 2

Crowder spoke to Samuels in a voice that only he and Steele could hear. "Pete, talk to him, but don't move any closer. Keep him engaged. We're going in. When you hear shots, drop to the ground."

Samuels talked about how the children were innocent of any wrongdoing, how they had their whole lives ahead of them, and how they could grow up and do great things—if he would just give them the chance. He spoke, too, of how Hopkins had the opportunity to choose good over evil, love over hate, and life over death. He articulated his words softly, like a preacher delivering a sermon.

Crowder understood men like Hopkins. Men who'd killed in cold blood—with malice aforethought. Exposing his wife's adultery to public scorn, having her wear the scarlet letter he'd painted on her back, and terrorizing their children wouldn't be adequate penance for her sins. Her punishment needed to fit the crimes she'd committed against him. In control for the first time since he was arrested, he had the power to decide whether someone should live or die.

He'd ignore Samuels's pleas for mercy.

In the end, he'd choose death.

It all played out in Crowder's mind. Something would spark in Hopkins's brain. He'd go on autopilot. With the calculated resolve of a paid assassin, he'd shoot the children first. Four shots in quick succession. He'd want his ex-wife to know her children were dead, and that he'd exacted his revenge.

Next, he'd fire downrange at the target hanging from a tree limb. He might take the time beforehand to reload a full magazine and riddle his ex-wife's body with bullets before turning the gun on himself. Then again, wife-beating bullies like Hopkins were cowards—afraid to face up to their shortcomings and inadequacies—who reveled in the misery of others. He just might keep blasting away. Kill as many as he could before being subdued and put down like a foaming-at-the-mouth, rabid animal.

Crowder was sure of one thing—once Hopkins started shooting, he wouldn't stop until his wife and children were dead.

The words of her deceased father, a career lawman, came to mind. "Hesitation in the face of imminent danger," he'd warned her when she received her badge, "strips you of control and allows luck to determine your destiny."

Crowder had to act quickly while Hopkins was still distracted by Samuels's pleas to show mercy. She looked at Steele and nodded so that he'd know to follow her. They moved stealthily from behind patrol cars to the neighbor's front door. The neighbor had gone into her house when shots were fired but came out when the detectives appeared.

Safely out of Hopkins' sight, Crowder asked, "Ma'am, have you been inside the Hopkins home?"

"Many times," she replied, wiping away tears from bloodshot eyes with a hanky. "Miriam and I have become quite close since Michael did what he did and was sent away."

"Tell me about the layout of the house. What rooms face the front?"

"When you go in, the living room is on the left and the dining room is on the right."

"What's underneath the bay window in the dining room?"

"Nothing. The cabinet and hutch are against other walls."

"Are there any windows in the living room that look out the side of the house?"

"There are t-two windows," the neighbor stammered.

Crowder saw a motorcycle parked in the carport of the woman's home. "Whose bike?"

"My son's," she replied. "He's a reservist away on weekend drills."

Crowder walked to the bike and took the helmet that rested on the seat. "I'll need to borrow this," she said. A long-handled shovel leaned against a wall in the carport. She pointed at it. "Sid, take the shovel and go around the back of the house to the side window—the one farthest from the street—and smash it with the shovel. Then step away from the window and empty your weapon into the ground. Space the shots a couple of seconds apart. He'll instinctively turn toward the window and fire into it. Leave the rest to me."

To remain out of Hopkins's crosshairs, Steele, shovel in hand, took the longer route around the back of the neighbor's house. Crowder strapped on the helmet and pulled out her eight-round, semi-automatic pistol. She drew back the slide, loading the chamber, and went to the corner edge of the neighbor's house.

Nothing obstructed her view of the dining-room window about sixty feet away. She gripped the weapon firmly in her hand. To avoid an accidental discharge, she left her finger off the trigger. She crouched down in a sprinter's stance—and waited.

Samuels was still speaking.

Hopkins was still listening.

A vision flashed in Crowder's brain like the illumination that followed a lightning bolt. She saw Steele standing beside the window with the shovel in his hands pulled back over his shoulder. A recollection flickered next. For a moment, she saw herself at bat that day on the softball diamond, with the score tied in the League Championship game. It didn't matter that the count was 3 and 0 and the take sign was on. The pitcher put one over the plate. She swung and knocked the ball over the centerfield fence.

She played being a cop the same way. For Crowder, when the opportunity arose and the odds were in her favor—and sometimes even when they weren't—she seized the moment. High risk, high reward.

Carpe diem.

A surge of adrenaline rushed through her when she heard the glass break. She sprinted across the lawn as fast as she could—torso raised and straight, shoulders relaxed, arms pumping and uppercutting through the air like a prizefighter.

Halfway there, she heard them—one quick blast after the other. The shots were still being fired when she reached the flower bed below the bay window in full stride. With all the athletic skill she could muster, Crowder catapulted her body forward, right shoulder first, helmeted head tucked into her chest.

The sensation of free falling overwhelmed her—like she'd just jumped off a cliff or fallen into an abyss. She missed her mark, but was still high enough to strike the protruding bow of the window. The glass shattered inward. She landed on the floor on her back with a thud in a spattering of glass. Her helmet banged so hard against the thinly carpeted wood surface that her brain rattled, dazing her momentarily.

The momentum from her lunge caused her to roll over a

half-turn. She stopped abruptly, face down on her stomach. A few ticks of a clock later, her finger was over the trigger of her pistol, and she was on her feet headed into the hallway. Hopkins, his back to her, was shooting his rifle into the side window when she entered the family room.

"Weapon down … now," Crowder yelled, shaking off her syncope.

The shooting ceased. Hopkins stood frozen, his back still to her. She kept her pistol pointed at the middle of his back so her aim would be center mass if he decided to turn and shoot.

Crowder's peripheral vision scoped out four children. They sat on the floor with their backs against a wall—hands, feet and mouths bound with duct tape. Unable to move, unable to scream, their popped-out eyes were their only means of communication, and they cried out in terror.

Hopkins didn't immediately drop his rifle. Instead, he raised it above his head with his left hand.

Crowder felt and heard a distinctive thumping in her chest, a sure sign that something unexpected—and usually bad—was about to happen. "Lower the rifle and drop it to the floor," she said, her inflection denoting a sense of urgency. "Then put your hands behind your back and slowly, and I mean slowly, kneel down."

Hopkins's hesitation in complying gave her the cold sweats.

She couldn't see his right hand.

"Don't shoot. Please don't shoot," the man pleaded, as he spun around to face Crowder.

She saw the pistol in his right hand a second before shots rang out, two striking her in the chest. In the bedlam, Crowder managed to get off three shots of her own as the impact from being struck knocked her backward to the floor.

The family-room ceiling spun out of control. It was the last thing she saw before her eyelids dropped like stage curtains.

The air left her lungs.

~

The onlookers had run for cover when the shooting started. They returned when things quieted down.

Steele slipped into the family room through the shattered window, his gun raised—a new full clip in it. Hopkins and Crowder were both on their backs, neither one moving. Hopkins's blood-soaked shirt was proof that Crowder's shots had hit their mark.

But what of Crowder?

"Jesus, Jo. Are you all right?" Steele cried out as he passed Hopkins's dead body, kicking it just to be sure.

Crowder lay sprawled out on her back. Steele holstered his weapon, knelt down, and stared into his partner's face. Her eyes were pasted shut. He felt for a pulse. As he pressed his fingers against her carotid artery, Crowder's eyes flew open, and her hand shot up to grasp Steele's wrist in a vice-like grip. A raspy cough followed. A deep inhale and slow exhale later, she stuttered between uneven breaths, "I-I think I-I've bruised, maybe broken a couple of ribs. Help me up."

Steele gave his partner a shoulder to wrap an arm around and helped her to her feet. She removed the helmet and her police vest and dropped them to the floor, wincing in pain as she did. "Check on the woman," she huffed, as she stumbled over to Hopkins's children.

The acrid smell of burnt sulfur lingered in the room.

Four sets of panic-stricken eyes watched her every movement when she knelt to release the oldest child from the bondage of tape. She conscripted her to do the same for her younger sisters.

Crowder went to the youngest child, a boy about five years old, and gently removed the tape from his mouth, hands and feet. "Mommy, I want mommy," the boy cried out, tears streaming down his cheeks.

The jabs of pain that knifed through Crowder's chest became tolerable as soon as the boy put his arms around her neck and she felt the warmth of his breath on her cheek. "Mommy's outside waiting for you," she whispered in the boy's ear. "I'll take you to her, I promise."

Miriam Hopkins lay on a gurney covered by a blanket, in the care of a paramedic when Crowder came out the door with her children. As she walked across the lawn to reunite them with their mother, she thought how lucky she'd been—how insanely fortunate all of them were.

So many things could have gone wrong.

Her leap into the glass window might not have shattered it enough to allow her to tumble through it, leaving her partially impaled by the shards of glass that remained embedded in the window frame. Hopkins might have heard the commotion in the dining room and had his rifle turned on her instead of the side window when she entered the family room. He might have gotten lucky with one of his shots and blown a hole in her face, rather than gotten them lodged in the ballistic gel of her body armor. The shots she'd gotten off might have missed their mark entirely if fired a split second later.

Her reflections were interrupted by the sound of someone clapping. The one became several, and before long there were whistles and shouts of "Way to go!" But the adulation she received from those who'd witnessed what she'd done brought Crowder little satisfaction.

She was angry—majorly pissed off.

A man lay dead—someone she'd killed. A woman had been

publicly humiliated in front of her children and her neighbors. She'd wear the emotional and psychological scars of the ordeal long after the painted A was washed from her back.

Four children had front-row seats to the spectacle. They'd witnessed firsthand what their father had done to their mother. They'd heard him cry out that she was a whore, that he wasn't their father, that he was going to shoot them one by one. They'd sat ringside and watched him shot dead—to relive the horror every time they walked into the room where their father had bound and gagged them, and every time they passed by the tree where their mother had been hung by a rope like a piñata at a child's birthday party.

Horrible things that didn't have to happen. But they did happen—because of stupid mistakes of people not doing their jobs. At that moment, Crowder could only speculate—a court clerk providing the parole office with the social security number of the wrong Michael Hopkins, the parole office not checking Hopkins's file to be sure his sentence had been fully served, a warden not questioning why a man serving a no-parole life sentence was being released after three years.

Stupid mistakes with tragic consequences.

Crowder left the crime scene as she had many others—ambivalent, asking herself … why did it have to happen?

Chapter 3

Crowder took a pass on meeting up with Steele, Samuels, and other off-duty detectives at Benny's Sports Bar. Located in downtown New Orleans, Benny's was the local watering hole for cops, prosecutors, and beat reporters looking for a scoop.

By most anyone's standards, there was cause for celebration—one perpetrator killed, five lives saved. No one played the *minus-sum* game better than Crowder. In a standoff with guns and multiple hostages involved, there were usually only losers. The only uncertainty was the number of body bags that would be needed at day's end—and who'd be in them. For one day at least, body bags had been kept to a minimum.

Celebrating wasn't on Crowder's agenda. She had more pressing matters—like the statement she'd be giving to Internal Affairs at ten the next morning, and the hearing before the Police Review Board that would follow later in the week. She'd been placed on paid leave—routine in all cases where a cop used deadly force in the line of duty. She'd need to be cleared of wrongdoing in Hopkins's death before she could return to work with her weapon. A technicality. She'd be back at her desk tomorrow.

A year ago, the review board hearing would have been a business-as-usual exercise—a process to appease the public that a police killing was justified. But this case wasn't routine—it involved Jo Crowder, whose record of using lethal force topped all detectives' since she'd received her gold shield eight years ago at the age of twenty-eight—the youngest detective ever out of the select minority of women whose job was to hunt down murderers and other violent criminals.

No one disputed Crowder's unparalleled results. She'd solved over eighty percent of her cases. In first-degree-murder prosecutions of her investigations and arrests, she had the highest conviction rate. Of all the detectives in the department, she had the fewest cold-case files.

But statistics don't lie. To some, and Ron Santoro in particular—the first-ever civilian member of the review board—Crowder's kill numbers painted a picture of a rogue cop, who used her badge as a license to kill. Crowder had killed four men in the line of duty before Hopkins became number five. Five in eight years put her in first place by a wide margin over the runner-up, who had three kills in a career spanning twenty-six years. Her kill count could easily have been more—a lot more—had she not been a crack shot with her pistol, delivering carefully placed non-lethal bullet wounds to a half dozen other suspects who deserved worse.

Public perception of law enforcement had changed. Crowder sensed it as each year passed. An increasing reluctance from the community to report crimes and come forward as witnesses. A criminal justice system viewed by many as one-sided and discriminatory. Public outrage over the use of excessive force in several highly publicized cases had led to protests in cities throughout the country. Progressive politicians pushed through police reforms that banned certain neck holds, mandated sensitivity training, and required civilian oversight when police confrontations resulted in serious injury or death. Some initiatives led to the defunding of police departments, layoffs, and fewer resources to solve crimes.

The New Orleans Police Department fell in line with many others. Ron Santoro was the result. He'd successfully lobbied for the newly created civilian position on the review board. He pledged to keep his finger on the pulse of the NOPD and not only root out corruption but also trigger-happy cops with a shoot-first philosophy of law enforcement.

Crowder wasn't overly concerned because in every wounding—and death—she'd been cleared by the review board. The shootings had always been necessary to defend herself or protect the lives of others.

So far, at least.

Still, a good case could be built on the statistics. Her kill numbers didn't just furrow a few brows, they contorted a fair share of journalists' faces. Editorials criticized the NOPD's lack of sensitivity training and shoot-first mentality—one op-ed referred to Crowder as "Dirty Harriet," another as "law-woman Jo-sey Wales."

When Crowder arrived at district headquarters, it was after seven in the evening. O'Malley was sitting in Crowder's chair with his feet on her desk, arms folded across his chest, eyes closed. The noise she made when she approached startled him out of his catnap.

Two fleshy palms rubbed the sleep from his eyes. He leaned forward, placed his elbows on the desk, and rested his chin on the knuckles of his folded hands. "I hear you took a couple to the chest. How are you feeling?"

Crowder removed her jacket and empty shoulder holster, grimacing as she did, and laid them on her desk. She got close enough to her boss to smell the menthol in the cough drops he sucked on to soothe the perpetual hoarseness in his throat and resulting gruff voice he was noted for. She eased into the chair in front of her desk and rested her shoulders against the back of it, doing her best to muffle a groan. "Cracked ribs. Bruises. Nothing serious."

"The review board meets on Wednesday at two."

"Why the rush?"

"The mayor wants to put the Hopkins mess to rest as soon as possible. He's expecting Miriam Hopkins will sue."

"I don't blame her," Crowder said. "We give a murderer the jailhouse keys, and he walks out and terrorizes, and nearly executes, his family on national TV."

"It could have been worse, a lot worse. What made you go in? You could have waited to see how things played out … or punted and called in a SWAT team."

"Too little time. Too much risk. If he'd seen them on site, he'd know it couldn't end until he killed as many of his family as time permitted."

"At least one review board member might not see it that way," O'Malley warned.

Crowder didn't need him to identify who.

~

The review board meeting began a few minutes after two in the afternoon. Three deputy police superintendents, a police captain who served as chairperson, and its newly appointed, first-ever civilian member, Ron Santoro. They sat at a conference-room table with the chairperson on one side, flanked by two members on his right and left. Crowder, the only person scheduled to testify, sat in a chair on the other side. A stenographer sat in a chair to her left.

After putting some preliminary information on the record, the chairperson began the questioning. "The board members have reviewed the report of Internal Affairs and the sworn statements of your partner, the department's crisis negotiator, and several others with knowledge of the facts and circumstances surrounding the death of one Michael Hopkins, date of birth, August 4, 1980, late of Orleans Parish, Louisiana. Have you reviewed the report and statements, Lieutenant Crowder?"

"Yes, sir. I've reviewed them."

"Do you dispute any of the factual statements made by the persons interviewed by Internal Affairs or by the witnesses who provided sworn statements?"

"No."

"The statements you've made during the course of the investigation, were those statements true and correct to the best of your knowledge?"

"Yes, sir."

The chairman shot quick glances at the other board members and asked if there were any questions. Having been through the process before, she was expecting the usual soft lobs over the plate—nothing accusatory or controversial. Two deputy superintendents were more concerned about her injuries than Hopkins's death. The third lauded her bravery in the line of duty.

Business as usual in a clear case of justifiable deadly force. So Crowder thought. But it was Santoro's turn to ask questions. The manila folders on the table in front of him signaled to her that he'd pulled the files of her previous review board hearings—her other kills.

"Lieutenant Crowder, I was appointed to the Police Review Board to be sure there is public oversight of police actions involving the use of lethal force." He paused with a smug look on his face. "Do you agree that police officers should only use deadly force when absolutely necessary and as a last resort?"

Crowder wanted to bitch-slap the self-righteous look off his face. Her response was surprisingly measured. She recited the passage from the page of her training manual like a Sunday school student reciting one of the Ten Commandments. "Deadly force shall be used only when there is an imminent danger of death or serious injury to the officer or another person."

"Do you agree that Michael Hopkins posed no danger to you until you broke through the window and confronted him in the family room of his home?"

His home? What a crock! A man who is imprisoned for life without any chance of parole has only one home—a one-room, state-owned condo with a front door of reinforced steel. She didn't mind Santoro's question; it was his arrogant tone she didn't much care for. She'd control the sarcasm. "True," she replied, an edginess in her voice. "But he posed an ongoing threat to others—his ex-wife, for one, who he'd strung up to a tree and used for target practice, and his children, who he'd disowned and threatened to kill."

"But you stormed his home before giving any warning of your intentions. You never gave Mr. Hopkins the opportunity to give up before you took actions against him, correct?"

Crowder muffled a chuckle. "I thought it best not to forewarn him that since he'd shown no intention of giving up, I'd be smashing through his dining-room window and coming after him."

So much for controlling the sarcasm.

"But didn't the crisis negotiator promise Mr. Hopkins that no one would take any action against him while they were still talking and working things out?" Santoro asked.

"A conversation that was decidedly one-sided," Crowder

replied. "No one could see what he was doing while Samuels was speaking. No one knew what he was planning to do. What we knew for sure was that a convicted murderer, with intentions of killing again, had discharged his weapon three times—one shot came within inches of his ex-wife's head."

"That's just my point. He didn't shoot anyone. He shot out two windshields of police vehicles no one was occupying, and shot into a tree. If he wanted to kill the woman, he could have put a bullet in her very easily, but he hadn't."

Crowder's back stiffened. "Hopkins was playing with us," she shot back. "He was buying time. Time to enjoy terrorizing his ex-wife before shooting her and his kids. We were sitting on a time bomb that was going to blow up at a time only Hopkins knew. I had to disable the clock while it was still ticking."

"When you broke through the glass window, you knew that Hopkins would resist, didn't you?" Santoro asked aggressively, like a prosecutor cross-examining someone accused of a crime. "After all, the plan was for your partner to create a diversion—that he was coming through a window—while you gunned Hopkins down from behind."

"I gave him a chance to surrender. He chose to turn and shoot."

"But we have only your word on that," Santoro said scornfully. "Your partner wasn't in the room at the time. You didn't have your body camera on. So we have no corroboration of your account of what happened."

"The camera came off my vest when I crashed through the window," Crowder explained. "I found it on the floor afterward."

"That's one possibility," he countered.

Why not show some balls and simply say you think I deliberately took it off my vest?

Crowder was emphatic in her response. "That's the only

possibility as far as I'm concerned."

"Oh!" Santoro feigned surprise by her response. "Then let me paint you another scenario on the canvas. You precipitously, some might say recklessly, busted into Hopkins's home, gun blazing, endangering four children and surprising Hopkins, who instinctively turned to shoot at someone who was shooting at him. You had the protection of body armor; he had on the cloth shirt he left the prison in that day."

Crowder wanted to take Santoro's paint brush and shove it up his ass. She allowed herself a deep breath instead. "You can paint any picture you want," she said defiantly. "But that's not what happened. I made the call on what to do. A woman and four children were in imminent danger of being systematically executed by Hopkins. I had to act to save lives even at the expense of Hopkins's life—or mine."

"But you're here and Hopkins is dead—just like the four other men you shot and killed in the line of duty." Santoro paused to pick up the four files and drop them on the tabletop. "Are you aware of the number, Lieutenant Crowder? You've killed four … no, five … men in eight years. These are hall-of-fame-worthy numbers. No law enforcement officer in the state of Louisiana has shot and killed more than three people in the line of duty in the last half century. And of the nearly three hundred fifty law enforcement agencies in Louisiana that employ more than eighteen thousand police officers, ninety-eight percent have never even fired their weapon in the line of duty."

"Sir, ninety-eight percent of our police officers aren't involved in arresting violent criminals who are armed and dangerous."

"The statistics show your use of lethal force seems to follow you like a devoted pet. Any thoughts on why that's the case?"

"Just doing my job."

"Just doing your job? You are a phenomenon—an outlier.

Five times you've shot it out with a suspect, and five times you've emerged alive and the suspect dead. You are one lucky individual."

Crowder looked at Santoro. Her eyes shot out like daggers. If a stare could disembowel, Santoro's internal organs would be in a pail and fed to farm animals. She took a slow, deep breath, grinned, and said, "I'd much rather be the lucky one in a gunfight."

Santoro paused his questioning.

The chairman shrugged. "Have you completed your questioning of Lieutenant Crowder, Mr. Santoro?" he asked.

Santoro rustled through some papers on the desk as if he was looking for more things to quibble over.

"I do have several questions for the lieutenant," the chairman said, not waiting for Santoro's response. "Would you consider yourself proficient in the use of firearms?"

"Yes. I learned to shoot rifles and pistols at an early age."

"Who taught you?"

"My father."

"Tom Crowder. I knew him. An exemplary career in law enforcement. A tough, fair-minded cop in the opinion of everyone who worked with him." The chairman removed his eyeglasses and sat back in his chair. "How many times have you been injured in the line of duty, lieutenant?"

The answer was in front of him—in her personnel file. He was covering her ass, coming to her defense. "Three times," she replied. "Twice in the shoulder, once in the leg."

"Why didn't you include the rib fractures when Hopkins shot you twice in the chest?"

"Sir, I understood your question to be serious injuries."

"Well, no need to be modest, Lieutenant. We track those things. You've been injured eight times in the line of duty where treatment was required, five involving hospitalizations. Of the five persons you've shot and killed in the line of duty, were you ever the person who initiated the gunfire?"

"Never."

"In each case, were you apprehending a known violent criminal?"

"All five were responsible for the murders of one or more persons; in some instances, the victims were children."

"Was your use of force in all cases for the purpose of repelling deadly force against you or others?"

"In all cases, I had no other choice."

"Lieutenant Crowder, if you had the day Hopkins was shot back again, would you do anything differently?"

"Just one thing," she replied.

"What's that?"

Santoro moved up in his chair as if she was about to make a damaging admission he could use against her.

Crowder looked directly at Santoro and said, "I'd have taken the day off."

Chapter 4

"What bullshit," Martin Goldman said halfway through the magazine article he was reading. Alone in the back seat of the company limo, he could speak freely.

Goldman was the chief financial officer and in-house legal counsel for Heartland Insurance. He was also the best friend of Jared Finch, the person featured on the cover of the latest issue of Forbes magazine. They'd been roommates at MIT their freshman year and later shared an off-campus apartment until they graduated with honors in computer science and mathematics.

Goldman admired Finch. He was the founder and CEO of one of the most successful start-up companies in recent years, and Goldman had been by his side every step of the way.

Heartland Insurance was Finch's brainchild. An insurance company in name only, its business model was a simple one—buy people's life insurance policies and collect the proceeds when they died. The cash payments the persons received while they lived were a fraction of what the policies would eventually pay out when they died—more so if they died earlier than expected.

Goldman chuckled when he resumed reading the article and came to the part where Finch spoke of the benevolent mission of his company. He'd told the journalist who interviewed him, "We help elderly people in financial need."

Goldman knew otherwise.

Companies like Heartland Insurance preyed on vulnerable people who needed immediate cash. They targeted the elderly with inadequate retirement savings, the chronically sick without funds to pay the high cost of institutional care, the terminally ill looking for organ donors and last-chance experimental cures, and business owners who needed capital to save a dying enterprise.

Finch saw the upside potential right from the start. The more desperate people were for money, the more likely they were to sell their insurance policies quickly and cheaply. The only downside with the scheme was that the longer the person lived, the longer the cash payments had to be made—and the longer the company had to wait to collect the insurance proceeds.

But Finch had a solution for the problem—one he didn't reveal to the journalist.

Goldman remembered like it was yesterday, not eight years ago, when Finch's fledgling company went a year and a half without a dollar of revenue and then suddenly blossomed into a cash cow that made Finch a multimillionaire. Heartland Insurance's success was grounded on its ability to buy life insurance policies from people who for various reasons were unlucky—the ones who died earlier than expected from heart attacks, strokes, and accidental injuries. When that happened, the company's obligations to pay periodic cash payments immediately ceased and the company was paid the proceeds in full. The earlier they died, the greater the company's profits. It was that simple.

To improve its chances of selecting the *unlucky* ones, the company reviewed healthcare records, required a medical examination, and performed diagnostic testing. It formulated an algorithm that could predict the probability of death with greater accuracy than the life expectancy tables used by government agencies and life insurance companies. The algorithm gave Heartland Insurance an enormous edge over its competitors, who had to pay out more and wait longer to collect on the policies.

The company launched television and internet advertising campaigns promising substantial cash payments to persons with at least one million dollars in life insurance. Its marketing slogan—*the bigger your policy, the bigger your payments*—encouraged healthy people in their sixties to insure their lives for millions of dollars in the hope of having their policies purchased by Heartland Insurance. What these people didn't know was that they were selected because the company's algorithm had determined that they would be dead within three years.

The algorithm was responsible for tens of millions of dollars of profits annually. It was so revolutionizing that its existence was known only by Finch and his inner circle of trusted company officials.

Goldman was one of the inner circle.

Goldman returned to reading the article. He smiled when he came to how Finch described his childhood as the only child of a blue-collar dad, who taught him the trades and the importance of working hard, and a stay-at-home mom, who made sure he did his homework and taught him the value of a good education. Finch rattled off a variety of manual labor jobs he claimed he had worked to pay his college tuition—always sending some money home to his parents. More bullshit.

Goldman, more than anyone, knew the truth. He knew why Finch was successful—he was cunning, calculated, and opportunistic. It helped that he had a genius IQ and a photographic memory that he'd put to good use while they were both earning their degrees at MIT.

Goldman came from a well-to-do Jewish family, who paid his tuition and living expenses. Finch wasn't so lucky. His father was an alcoholic and mostly unemployed tradesman. His mother was a diner waitress, who served dessert in customers' cars in the parking lot on her breaks. With money scarce, Finch hustled for every penny he could get on his own. He delivered newspapers on a bike he'd stolen. He looted the poor boxes at the churches in his neighborhood, and pilfered students' lockers for cash and coins.

Even with the academic scholarship he'd been awarded when he graduated valedictorian of his high school class, Finch required student loans to cover most of his expenses. But he disliked owing anyone anything. To help solve his financial problems, he put his mastery of computers to good use by hacking into the university's secure computer systems to obtain professors' passwords, which he then used to access quizzes, mid-terms, and final exams.

Finch didn't need to cheat. He aced his exams without help. But he needed to know the test questions in advance in order to tutor other students, including Goldman, who paid handsomely for his services. Only Goldman knew the truth of the subterfuge; the other students thought that Finch was a gifted clairvoyant.

Goldman understood early that Finch was special and would be successful in any business venture he set his sights on. Finch's brain operated like a high-speed computer—always collecting and analyzing data. He took no notes. He kept no calendars. He required no calculator. Everything was stored in organized files in the recesses of his mind and was instantly retrievable.

Because schoolwork came easily, Finch had time to spare. He studied up on casino gambling, learning strategies that would give him the upper hand in card games of chance. One game was particularly easy for him—blackjack. His photographic memory made him a natural card counter at the casinos. He could predict to a high statistical probability the cards the dealer would pull from the deck.

With the confidence he could beat the house, Finch used the money he'd earned from tutoring to rent a car and drive five and a half hours to Atlantic City where he won a thousand dollars in two hours at the blackjack table at one of the casinos. He slept the night in his car and came back the next afternoon and tripled his winnings at a different casino. After that, Finch made frequent weekend jaunts to Sin City, hitting three different casinos each trip. He'd always cashed in his chips before his winnings reached the amount on which a casino was required to withhold taxes. Whenever asked to complete a tax form, he gave a phony name and social security number. Finch told Goldman he had no intention of declaring his winnings on any tax return.

When he'd won enough money, Finch bought a used Ford Mustang convertible for cash. He began staying overnight in decent hotels but never at the casinos where he'd bet. By the time he graduated from MIT with honors, he had no student loans, and had enough money saved to pay his first year's tuition and living expenses at Harvard.

As Finch explained it later to Goldman who subsequently studied law at Yale, the big money came while he was earning his MBA at the Ivy League school. He'd researched his classmates, singling out the ones from wealthy families by hacking into the admissions director's computer and finding the ones whose parents could easily afford the quarter-of-a-million dollars it cost to earn a Harvard MBA.

He prepared a short list of ten prospects, concentrating

on the risk-takers whose backgrounds involved dangerous avocations and hobbies like sky diving, rock climbing, white-water rafting, scuba diving and survival training—people who needed excitement in their lives. Finch needed people who lived every day like it was their last. He then staged chance meetings with all ten until he selected a group of five whose lives would revolve around a single weekly event—a poker game.

Finch organized the games, promising an exciting and challenging evening away from the doldrums of studying, a respite from the boredom of academics—and the chance to win a large pot of money. With the money he'd banked from his card-counting casino sprees, Finch rented a suite at the Four Seasons in Boston's historic district for the weekly games. Initially, he allowed the others to win, gradually upping the ante and increasing the size of the raises. With players from families who measured their net worth in millions of dollars, pots were soon worth thousands of dollars.

Finch called the group the "million-dollar boys' club." By the time the two-year master's degree program had concluded, Finch had twice the winnings of the second luckiest card player. Even the losers enjoyed the weekly ritual—more so when Finch provided catered room service and female companionship from a local escort service. The participants gladly contributed to the tab equally. Finch made certain to double the amounts; he kept the overage as his commission for handling the arrangements.

Goldman saw his boss as the consummate con man. He'd convinced his poker buddies to play card games he knew from the beginning were slanted in his favor. Then he'd used that same skill set and swagger—of a fast-talking carnival barker, slick snake-oil salesman, and tent-preaching evangelist—to con the boys' club members into financing his company.

He started with the weakest link in the group—the club member who'd lost the most money. He figured he'd be the one most likely to back a proven winner and erase the stigma of being a loser. The other members of the club soon fell like dominoes. Each loaned Finch two million dollars. In return, he guaranteed to pay them ten percent annual interest with full repayment in five years, and a twenty-percent penalty if he defaulted—deals too irresistible to pass up.

Finch conscripted Goldman's help to create a phony investment portfolio that showed Finch's net worth exceeded seven million dollars, which he pledged as collateral to secure the loans. With ten million dollars of other people's money, Finch had Goldman incorporated his limited liability company, Heartland Insurance. Goldman prepared fraudulent business records falsely listing the company's creditors as shareholders and their loans as capital. The bank salivated over providing an equivalent line of credit to such a well-endowed company.

Finch used the bank's line of credit to make the monthly interest payments to the boys' club members. The money he'd borrowed from them he used to fund his company's operations. The con had worked to perfection. Finch had raised nearly twenty million dollars. He'd put up not a single dollar of his own money.

Finch paid off the boys' club's loans in three years. By then the company's annual revenues exceeded fifty million dollars. Three years later, revenues had doubled, and tens of millions of dollars were made in distributions to Heartland Insurance's sole shareholder—Jared Finch.

Goldman was well paid for his collaboration. A salary of two million dollars, plus millions more in profit sharing each year, was lucrative compensation for having aided and abetted the enterprise.

Goldman closed the magazine. He'd read enough about the fairy tale Finch had spun for the journalist.

The limo pulled into the gated home of Jared Finch.

It was time for Finch and Goldman to leave the world of make-believe and return to reality.

Chapter 5

Finch joined Goldman in the company limo. "Revenues for the quarter?" he asked, his eyes fixed on the flat-screen television tuned to a business news station presently analyzing NASDAQ's performance for the week.

"Up ten percent," Goldman replied without a moment's hesitation. He sat next to the luxury vehicle's built-in bar, his eyes also locked in place, but not on the TV screen. They fixed on the lean, tanned legs of the pretty young beauty in the lavender Valentino evening dress, who sat beside his boss.

"And our profit margin?" Finch probed.

"Nearly fifty percent of revenues."

Finch cracked a rare smile. "That rivals the top tech companies," he bragged. "I want to call a meeting to discuss our performance for the third quarter."

"I'll talk to the others and tell them to have the data for you by Thursday," Goldman replied.

"Tell them I want it by Tuesday," Finch shot back.

"Must you discuss business every waking hour?" the young woman asked while sipping Dom Pérignon from a crystal flute. A hint of exasperation laced her voice. "Most of the men I know talk about their sports cars, yachts, and golf handicaps."

"Christine, most of the men you know are underachieving bottom-feeders living off trust funds," Finch said dismissively.

Christine Benchley Finch was the perfect trophy wife—young and beautiful with a lust for the good life. An only child, her blue-blood American father was a Wall Street banker. Her British-born mother, a renowned artist, had studios in the Chelsea district of Manhattan and on the river Thames in London's South Bank.

Raised in a multimillion-dollar co-op overlooking Central Park West, Christine spent her school years in the most exclusive private boarding schools. She earned a degree in fine arts from Brown University where her admission to the Ivy League school coincided with a sizable gift her parents made to the school's endowment fund. Too much partying and too little studying led to her barely passing grades. An artist with mostly wasted, above-average talent, her works hung on display at her mother's studios, but persons not related or beholden to her parents seldom purchased them. Finch bought many of them to furnish the offices of Heartland Insurance. But seldom did he stop to appreciate his wife's paintings ... or compliment her on her creative expression.

Christine Benchley had more than her fair share of faults.

A spoiled rich kid who cavorted with other spoiled rich kids, she redefined the euphemism "a handful to raise." Her father had a lawyer on retainer to deal with the possession charges, DUIs, and disorderly conducts that required the assistance of counsel. She even came close to doing serious jail time when she left a bicyclist she'd clipped with the bumper of her sports car for dead on a shoulder. Instead of rendering aid or calling for help, she thought it prudent to go home and sober up. When she showed up at the police station the next day with her lawyer, her explanation was that she thought the thing she struck was a deer.

Instead of standing trial for manslaughter, her thousand-dollar-an-hour lawyer worked out a plea bargain—Christine pleaded no contest to leaving the scene of a personal injury accident. Her father paid two million dollars to the teenage boy who survived the incident. But he'd spend the rest of his life navigating the world in a motorized wheelchair. She, on the other hand, served a three-month sentence of home confinement at her parents' summer estate on Martha's Vineyard.

Goldman refilled Christine's glass without her asking, and poured himself another.

Goldman believed that Finch's wife suffered from PMBS—post-marital boredom syndrome. Once the glow of her quarter-of-a-million-dollar wedding dimmed and she took up residence at Finch's Georgian mansion in the Garden District of New Orleans, she pouted like the bratty teenager she'd been growing up. Ten years younger than her husband, marriage did little to domesticate her. She found the laid-back Cajun lifestyles of the city's iconic rich and famous too provincial, and spent more time with her clique of jet-setting friends in the Big Apple than with her husband in the Big Easy.

Finch never objected to Christine's sojourns away from the marital home. He'd shared with Goldman that he found her circle of friends to be clones of his wife—effete elitist snobs. He'd also shared with Goldman the reason he married Christine Benchley—she was the best lay he'd ever had, and he'd had his fair share of paramours to provide him with the necessary sampling to judge.

So had Goldman.

What Goldman didn't share with Finch was that … he agreed with him.

"The governor and Senator Tipton have only us dining with

them at their table," Goldman said, his stare no longer on the lower limbs of the drop-dead-gorgeous femme fatale, but on the nearly perfect doll-like countenance of the most beautiful woman he'd ever known.

Goldman couldn't help himself.

He remembered like it was yesterday. The Finch-Benchley wedding, the highlight of the summer's glitziest events covered by the never-sleeping city's paparazzi. He'd stood at the altar no more than six feet from Christine—at the place reserved for the groom's best man—his dick hardening as he pretended to be Jared Finch when the vows were exchanged. He knew then that he had to have her.

She was an obsession of which he was no longer in control. An irresistible impulse to be with the only woman with whom he'd ever been smitten had overcome his free will. The spoiled, bratty, childlike nymph had cast her spell over him, as if a cauldron-boiling witch had concocted a brew and ordered him to drink it. Such had been the tortured life of Goldman, his love unrequited.

Over time, that had changed.

"How much do they want this time?" Finch asked.

"One hundred thousand … each," Goldman replied.

Finch let Goldman's words hang in the air while he used the remote to switch to a different business news channel. After a moment he said, "As usual, always looking for handouts."

After her second glass of wine, Christine tapped a polished nail against the crystal to communicate to Goldman her readiness for a refill. "You mean bribes." She pouted. "If you'd just given them briefcases full of unmarked bills last week, we could've avoided another boring political fundraiser tonight."

Finch caught Goldman looking at Christine while reaching for the bottle of champagne. He cleared his throat to gain his attention, and shook his head, nixing more wine. "Call it what you want, Christine, but remember this—one man's need is another man's greed. We need the senator to put an indefinite hold on some federal legislation that's before his committee, and we need the governor to veto a similar state bill that's sitting on his desk."

"I know, darling—money talks..." His wife sighed and didn't bother to complete the sentence. "Who have I heard say that before?"

Finch continued, "It's the way of the business world, my dear. It's in the Bible. Proverbs, Chapter 17, Verse 8: 'A bribe is like a magic stone in the eyes of the one who gives it; wherever he turns he prospers.'"

Goldman chuckled. "The cost of doing business in the twenty-first century." He reached into the inside pocket of his tuxedo jacket, brought out two envelopes, and handed them to Finch.

Finch nodded. "And entirely legitimate. The checks from Heartland Insurance to the Committee for the Defenders of Liberty will help fund negative ads against our friends' opponents."

~

The fundraiser was being held at the Essex House in downtown New Orleans. When the limo arrived at the entrance, the driver got out and opened the double side doors of the vehicle. Finch exited first, not waiting for his wife. Goldman stepped onto the sidewalk and offered his hand to Christine, who took it and followed him out. The three then made their way into the hotel to the Grand Ballroom.

When Christine stumbled on the carpet in the hotel lobby,

it was Goldman's hand that reached out to grab her outstretched arm and prevent her from falling.

"Thank you, Marty," Christine said with affection.

Finch looked over his shoulder in time to see Goldman and his wife share an intimate gaze. It wasn't the first time he'd noticed such exchanges between them.

When the cocktail hour was over, the Finches and Goldman took their seats at the governor's table. By then Finch's checks were in the governor's jacket pocket behind a couple of smuggled-in Cuban cigars and in the greasy hands of the senator's campaign manager. But not before assurances were given that there were not enough votes in the legislature to override his veto. The senator had given a similar guarantee: "The proposed federal regulations will never see the light of day on the Senate floor."

The colonel's text message came to Finch as dinner was being served. *We have a problem and need to talk.*

Can it wait until tomorrow? Finch texted back.

Nein, the colonel replied. *It's best taken care of over the weekend.*

Finch knew the colonel's background well. A third-generation German American, his grandmother fled Germany after the Second World War pregnant with his mother. His grandfather, an officer at one of the Nazi death camps, would have stood trial for war crimes had he not put a bullet in his head the day before the camp was liberated.

The colonel's grandmother changed her name from Schmidt to Smith. His mother's marriage to an American career army officer named Hanratty assured that her son, James, would have his family's sordid association with the Third Reich buried with his grandfather. He followed in his father's footsteps. During his twenty-year military career as a commanding officer in the Delta Force—the world's most elite fighting unit—he'd had extensive tours in both Gulf Wars and in Afghanistan.

Finch needed a director of security whose loyalty to him was unequivocal—someone who would do whatever was necessary to protect his company's operations and trade secrets. Most of all, he needed someone who followed orders.

He found that person in Colonel James Hanratty.

Finch texted back—*My office in an hour.*

For twenty minutes Finch listened to the governor and senator brag about their political accomplishments, then he excused himself to take care of an urgent matter back at the office. As he'd done on other occasions, he put Goldman in charge of Christine—no easy task controlling the behavior of a bored, free-spirited socialite with a penchant for reckless behavior.

That Goldman undertook such assignments eagerly did not go unnoticed by Finch.

Chapter 6

Finch Tower was unique among skyscrapers in New Orleans. Located just outside the central business district on the east bank of the Mississippi River, it not only had easy access to Highway 90, the main thoroughfare through the city, but its upper floors had a majestic view of the New Orleans cityscape. Importantly, it was relatively isolated in a sprawling, cluttered metropolitan area.

Finch had bought the building for pennies on the dollar when the previous owner went bankrupt. One man's loss, another man's gain—an opportunistic business philosophy that Finch knew well. It would be home for the business offices of Heartland Insurance. Finch renovated the building for hybrid uses that allowed him to lease the space to businesses and condominium dwellers in search of upscale accommodations. Finch's company occupied the top three floors of the thirty-story building.

Owning the building was essential to Finch. Security was his top priority. An owner didn't have to deal with meddlesome rental managers, landlord inspections, and nosy maintenance workers. He hired his own people—from the office staff to the cleaning crew. The offices of Heartland Insurance were in a building within a building. The company had segregated underground parking, a dedicated lobby entrance with private security, and three high-speed elevators in the main lobby. Finch had exclusive use of the helicopter pad on the roof.

Secrecy shrouded the company's operations. Background checks, signed confidentiality agreements, and random drug and polygraph tests were a condition for employment. The clerical workers and support staff were prohibited from bringing laptops, mobile phones, cameras and recording devices of any kind to work. Security officers were all former military who used state-of-the-art detection equipment to screen employees coming to and leaving work. The slightest breach in security meant immediate termination.

Finch sat on a sofa in his penthouse corner-office suite on the thirtieth floor. He'd just finished reading documents collected in a dossier prepared by the colonel marked CONFIDENTIAL—*for Jared Finch's eyes only*. The documents included charts, graphs, and memoranda about the company's performance and revenues.

The colonel stood by the floor-to-ceiling windows of Finch's office. There, he had an unobstructed view of the Mighty Mississippi on his left, and on his right, the city's business district glittered under a dark, moonless sky. He poured himself a bourbon from the bar, an amenity Finch reserved for others. Finch didn't drink alcohol, smoke, or use illicit drugs. Never had. Never felt the need to. He got his high watching the steady upticks in his net worth.

Finch wished he could say the same for others, including Goldman and his wife. Both required a daily intake of alcohol and a more than occasional line or two of blow.

"What do we know about this"—Finch paused to look at the photos on a driver's license and an employee identification badge—"Brian McManus?"

"Twenty-eight. Single. Lives in a Mid-City one-bedroom rental. He works with our chief actuary. Hired a year ago."

"Background check?"

"The usual. No criminal record. No drugs. Smart guy. Top of his class at his state university."

"Looks like he's too smart for his own good," Finch said. "Parents, siblings?"

"Parents were killed in a car crash when he was ten. He and his eight-year-old sister were raised by their maternal grandparents, who live in Utah."

"Friends?"

"I've had a tail on him for the past week. No roommate or live-in girlfriend. Keeps to himself. Plays video games at night."

"Social media?"

"Facebook. Family, some high school buddies—nothing regular or consistent."

Finch cracked an uneven smile. "Good. He keeps a low profile and won't be readily missed. Has he leaked what he's found to anyone?"

"Not yet," the colonel replied. "We're monitoring his office computer and personal laptop. He's gathered information from a number of in-house sources but so far he hasn't sent anything to anyone."

Finch watched the colonel move to the bar and pour himself another drink. "The algorithm—is it safe?"

The colonel walked across the room, sat in the chair closest to Finch, and sipped his drink. "He has enough information to know that it exists, but not enough to know how we use it in the field."

"Looks to me like he's on the cusp of discovery," Finch said. "If he were to figure things out, he could use the information against us, or for his personal gain."

"We've blocked him from sending what's on his desktop computer to anyone. Transmissions from it and his laptop are intercepted, diverted to us, and only delivered after I've screened them."

Finch winced. "Even if he hasn't sent the information to someone else's computer, the knowledge is in his brain. He can write it down and share it with someone else when he leaves the office."

The colonel looked down into an empty glass. "That's why we're having this meeting," he said. "I've had his cell phone tapped for two weeks. Nothing. But, after he left work today, he sent a text message to a burner phone just after seven this evening. It's a communication that should concern us."

"What was the message?"

The colonel tapped his cell phone and looked down to read from it. "It said, *I'm afraid to dig deeper. We need to meet. When and where?*"

"Who did he send the message to?"

"Burner phones are hard to trace. But the owner needs cellular service to receive text messages. We hacked into the account of the service provider."

"And?"

"The billing statement for the phone number is in the name of Alex Hill."

Finch leaned forward on the sofa to close the distance between them. "And who is this … Alex Hill?"

The colonel leaned forward as well and spoke in a low voice as if the office might be bugged. "A special agent of the organized crime division of the FBI."

Finch sat back, took a deep breath, and let it out slowly. He reopened the dossier, located Brian McManus's identification badge, and studied the face of the soon-to-be former employee of Heartland Insurance as he spoke: "The consequences for violating the employment agreement he signed when he was hired are spelled out clearly, 'An employee who violates any provision of this agreement, whether intentionally or unintentionally, shall be immediately terminated.'"

The colonel didn't need to be reminded.

Finch returned the badge to the dossier, resealed it, and handed it to the colonel. "You know what you need to do."

~

The colonel sat at his desk in his office at the opposite end of the corridor and pulled out his cell phone. He navigated to Contacts and tapped the screen. He'd placed the same call many times before.

After two rings, the call was answered, but the person on that end of the line said nothing.

Only the colonel spoke. And he said only one word:

"Proceed."

Chapter 7

Crowder knelt beside the body of an elderly man shot dead in his home. In an outstretched hand, his fingers gripped the handle and trigger of a half-century-old, single-action .45 Colt revolver. He lay there, belly down on the floor a few feet from an open safe, his head turned to one side in a puddle of congealed blood. The pupil of the visible bloodshot eye was fixed and dilated, and his open mouth revealed a gold-crowned premolar.

A six-inch diameter, maroon-colored stain on the back of his light blue pajama top and a bindi-sized dark dot in the center of his forehead revealed to Crowder that Cletus Moss had been shot twice—once through the heart and once through the brain.

Outside, a CSI technician scoured the property for footprints and anything the intruder had left behind. Inside, a forensic team dusted for fingerprints, looked for fibers, and photographed the scene and body.

Crowder used a ballpoint pen to lift the pajama top enough for her to see the exit wound from the shot through the torso. "How long has he been dead?" she asked the chief medical examiner's crime scene investigator and autopsy assistant, who knelt beside Crowder.

"Judging from his color, the degree of rigor mortis, and the amount of bloating, three to five days," he replied. "We'll know more precisely when we take a look inside."

Crowder turned to look at the wall behind the body. "From the location of the exit wound, the bullet passed through his heart, probably lodging in that wall." She walked over and inspected the knotty pine wood paneling until she found a small indentation about five feet above the floor. "Was there an exit wound from the head shot?"

"At the base of the skull above the hairline—left of center."

Crowder ran the fingers of her right hand over the paneling until she found another indentation lower and to the left of the first one. "The bullet through the heart passed mostly through tissue, so it didn't deflect much when it exited. The bullet into his forehead deflected off hard skull bone, which is why it entered the wall lower than the one through his chest."

Steele entered the room as Crowder walked back to the body. "The daughter found the body around noon and called 911," he said. "She drove over from her home in Lake Charles when her father didn't answer her calls last night and this morning."

Crowder asked, "Did she touch anything?"

"According to the patrol officer first on the scene, no."

"We'll want to speak to her today before she leaves the house."

"She's waiting for us in the kitchen."

"Any sign of forced entry?"

"A broken pane of glass in an open living-room window," Steele replied. "Glass and some dirt and grass on the floor below the window."

Crowder put on a pair of latex gloves. She removed the revolver from Moss's hand, sniffed the barrel and looked in the chamber. "He got a shot off." She looked in the direction Moss would have been facing when he was shot. No blood marked the floor between the body and the wall. She walked over and located a pockmark in the paneling—the spent bullet embedded in the wall about seven feet above the floor. "His aim was too high to do him any good."

Crowder did a quick assessment. The safe was empty. The thief had looked at the documents in it before tossing them on the floor. "He was in no rush," she deduced. "A light had to be on for Moss to open the safe, and for the killer to deliver two well-placed shots. He remained calm after murdering the old man and turned off the light on his way out."

Her work in the room complete, Crowder made her way into the kitchen. There, a teary-eyed, forty-year-old, married mother of two teenage boys gave her account of how she found her beloved father, three years a widower, shot dead in the farmhouse where she'd grown up. She described a man who was a respected business leader in the farming community, a deacon in his church, and so kind and generous a friend that he was known as "good neighbor Clete."

Crowder learned little from the daughter she hadn't already suspected.

No one held a grudge against her father or had an ax to grind with him. Cletus Moss was a good and honorable man. He had no enemies. Nobody who would have wanted to kill him.

Unless it was for the money he had in his safe.

Too often, good and honorable people ended up dead during the commission of a robbery—most of them because they resisted like Moss. He should have given over the money and been thankful to be left bound and gagged after being roughed up a little. Crowder could remember only one bank robbery where someone was shot and killed in Louisiana since Bonnie Parker and Clyde Barrow ran amok in the thirties. Bank personnel, even the armed guards, were trained to be compliant.

The mortally wounded were almost always the defiant ones. The store owner who reached for the gun under the counter instead of turning over the $135 in the cash drawer. The businessman in the suit who bled out from a knife wound to the gut because he tried to talk the robber out of taking his wallet with two twenties and a half dozen easily replaceable credit cards. Even the gray-haired old lady who played tug-of-war with a purse snatcher ran the risk of suffering a fatal subdural hematoma from a knock on the head by a pipe. Crowder had seen those and too many others she didn't care to remember.

When there were no witnesses or physical evidence at the scene to identify the perpetrator, the police maxim was "There are no suspects and an endless list of them." It was well known in the community that Moss kept a lot of cash around to pay field hands during harvesting season. Anyone needing quick cash was a potential suspect—the guy who lost his six-figure salary job with an overdue mortgage and college tuitions to pay, or someone who needed the dough to support a drug habit or make good on a gambling debt, or someone with the irresistible impulse to rob and kill an old man who lived alone on a secluded farm—simply because he knew he could get away with it.

"Ma'am, your father tried to defend himself during the robbery. Did he keep any other weapons in the house?" Crowder asked.

The woman sniffled into a hanky. "He kept a shotgun in his bedroom."

"Did your father follow a bedtime routine?"

"What do you mean?"

"He was in his pajamas. Did he go to bed around the same time every night?"

"Like clockwork. A farmer's schedule. In bed at dusk, up at dawn."

"I'd like to see his bedroom. Where is it located?"

"Dad's bedroom is"—the woman paused a moment, squeezed her eyes shut, and corrected her tenses—"*was* on the left at the top of the staircase."

Crowder and Steele went to the bedroom for a look.

"His shotgun's against the wall," Steele said, "so he must have been downstairs when the robber first confronted him."

Crowder walked over to the bed and stood next to the nightstand. "No—it was here in the bedroom."

"How so?"

"The bed's been slept in." She sniffed the empty glass. "He'd finished what was left of the bottle of whiskey I saw in the kitchen—his substitute for a sleeping pill ever since his wife passed away." She looked down at a pair of slippers by the side of the bed. "He wasn't wearing his slippers. So he was most likely in bed and awakened by the intruder." She picked up the shotgun and opened the barrels. "Loaded. If he'd been awake, he most likely would've heard the sound of breaking glass or someone roaming about the house. The first thing he'd do after he stepped into his slippers would be to grab his shotgun and go confront the intruder. It was here to protect him and his home."

"Why not use it when he was confronted in his bedroom?" Steele asked.

"Because he was asleep when the intruder entered. He'd finished his whiskey. His Bible is closed on the nightstand with his reading glasses on top. So he'd finished reading and turned off the light. The intruder, armed with a weapon, caught him completely off-guard. If he'd reached for his gun, he would've been shot here in the bedroom. Instead he was forced at gunpoint to go to the safe and open it. Given the chance, he reached for his revolver, got off an errant shot, and was gunned down for resisting."

"The old man should've known better than to shoot it out with someone with a gun pointed at him," Steele said.

Crowder walked to the doorway and turned for a last look. "And who was an excellent marksman—each shot was nearly instantly fatal."

~

Crowder sat at her desk the next morning, finishing up her preliminary report. Forensics had come up empty. Moss's prints were the only ones found on the gun, the documents, and the safe. The only evidence the killer left behind were size-nine shoe prints in the soil outside the broken living-room window. The one-way direction meant the intruder exited the house through a door that locked when it shut.

Crowder concluded it was a well-executed, garden-variety break-in, robbery, and murder. Even the money, in small denominations, was untraceable.

No witnesses. No suspects. No leads.

A crime likely to end up as a cold-case file.

Chapter 8

Hawk set the timer on his watch for twenty-five minutes. Wolf was first over the six-foot high wall.

Hawk followed.

Both scaled it easily.

They made their way through a garden of irises, Mexican heather, lantana, and butterfly bush. The flowerbeds looked better maintained in the glow of moonlight. The daytime video in the file they'd seen showed the soil covered by clover. The dandelions outnumbered the blossoms. In the dark the untrimmed sculptures of the topiary they passed looked more like letters from a calligraphy alphabet than the animals they supposedly depicted. Two giant magnolias stood sentry on the front lawn. But they went unnoticed—the intruders had approached from the rear.

The double cellar doors were padlocked shut as Hawk knew they'd be. Wolf had little difficulty picking the lock. The architect's schematics recorded with the zoning board a decade ago, when the kitchen was renovated and the patio extended, gave them the layout of the house. The security system only signaled an alarm when a first-floor door or window was breached. The surveillance cameras targeted the front and rear entrances, missing the cellar doors located out of view on the side of the house.

Once inside, they used their pencil lights to navigate around a chifforobe, a chest of drawers, a hope chest, and a clothes rack full of dresses. The musty odor of old things permeated the stagnant air. One didn't need an acute sense of smell to catch the underlying scent of mothballs.

The staircase to the first floor was by a wine closet—its door ajar, the empty racks inside occupied by cobwebs. Wolf easily opened the lock on the door at the top of the steps, using a thin blade from a tool that resembled a Swiss army knife. They entered a dark hallway—a timer on the strategically placed table lamps in several of the first-floor rooms had tripped off an hour before they arrived.

Their pencil lights revealed the lavish accoutrements of the mansion: thick oriental carpets on stained hardwood floors, period antique furniture, the obligatory baby grand piano, an eclectic collection of art on wainscoted walls, sculptures on pedestals, a tapestry, and crystal chandeliers in the dining room and main parlor.

A home for the rich and famous.

A mansion that had aged as gracefully as its occupant.

A semi-circular staircase in a cavernous foyer led to the second and third floors. Their journey ended one floor up. The target lay asleep in the master suite. Their lights no longer needed, they moved through the darkness with the ease of cat burglars. Hawk waited by the door, while Wolf approached the elderly woman lying in the middle of a queen-sized bed. In the shadow of moonlight that streamed through the windows, the heart-shaped, velveteen-covered headboard gave the bed the appearance of having wings.

They knew she'd be asleep—the file had her daily prescriptions, including the sleep medicine she took at bedtime. She lay in a fetal position, her right cheek resting comfortably on the end of a pillow. Her breathing was restful, her appearance angelic.

The woman's left eye opened just as the chloroform-soaked cloth Wolf held in a hand covered her mouth and nose. She squirmed for a few seconds, then went limp. Hawk found a table lamp and turned it on. The pungent smell of the chemical quickly overwhelmed the pleasant aroma of perfume, facial creams, and body talc.

Wolf pulled down the bed cover, revealing the slender figure of an attractive sixty-eight-year-old woman in a champagne-colored silk nightgown. Wolf pulled her legs out from under the sheet and put the pair of slippers that lay beside the bed on her feet. Hawk held the woman upright while Wolf put her in her robe and tied it in the front.

The intruders moved about with the urgency and skill of trained stagehands removing props between scenes. Wolf went quickly to the nightstand for the tray with the bone-china tea set and the plate with a half-eaten scone on it—remnants of the target's bedtime snack—and walked out the door to the top of the staircase. Hawk followed his partner, carrying the woman in his arms, and stood behind Wolf waiting his turn.

Wolf took one step down and upended the tray. The teapot, cup, saucer, creamer, plate, and silverware bounced down the risers, settling here and there, and splattering tea on the flowered wallpaper and carpeted steps.

Wolf stepped back.

Hawk moved to where Wolf had been. Adjusting his hold on the woman, he stood her upright, her feet dangling above the first step down. Suddenly, her slack body stiffened, her eyes fluttered open, and she began to mumble. Just as she opened her eyes wide and regained possession of her faculties, Hawk flung her down the staircase.

Instinctively, the woman stretched out her arms and hands to brace herself when she landed on the staircase. She tumbled forward in a double somersault, struck her head against the wall along the way, and came to rest at the foot of the steps. She lay there motionless, her arms and legs contorted.

Wolf scurried down to the body and felt for a pulse, then looked up at Hawk who asked, "Is our work complete?"

Wolf's head shook no. Wolf then took hold of the woman's head in both hands and, with one quick twist, broke her neck.

Hawk heard the vertebrae crack and smiled.

Now their work was complete.

~

Crowder looked down at the dead woman lying on her back, twisted like a pretzel, at the foot of the staircase. An evidence technician dusted the banister for prints; another photographed the body and the broken china and other debris on the steps.

A rookie female patrol officer summarized the facts for Crowder. Olivia Hartman. Sixty-eight. Singer. Dancer. Actress. Did some Broadway in her early years, a few movies afterward, and nearly two decades as head nurse Libby Gordon on *Doctors and Nurses,* the third longest-running soap opera on national television at the time of its cancellation. Multiple marriages. As many divorces. Hadn't worked professionally in nearly ten years, except for some commercials in which she played a happy resident of a retirement community, and a pain-free elderly woman on an arthritis medication. A fading star doing her best to maintain a grandiose lifestyle on royalties and an annuity.

"My mom missed maybe one or two episodes," the rookie cop said. "Even when she was in the hospital for her operations, she demanded a room with a television and refused treatment when the show was on. She cried for a week when the character Hartman played died."

Crowder didn't watch much television, but she recognized the name. "Who found her?"

"Her personal assistant. A graduate student working on her doctoral thesis. She was sort of a companion to Hartman. Had the night off. Returned this morning around eleven and called it in."

"So Hartman was alone last night?"

"Looks that way. The security alarm was on when the companion got home."

Crowder looked at the staircase. Her mind recreated what probably happened. Olivia Hartman fell down the steps while returning the tray she was carrying to the kitchen. The autopsy would determine if she died from a broken neck or head trauma. The obvious arm and leg fractures were not life-threatening.

Crowder's cell phone pinged. It was a text message from Steele. *4302 Goddard Street, Apartment 4. Likely overdose. Meet you there.*

Crowder closed her phone. "Have the personal assistant do a walkthrough, particularly the bedroom. Check the windows and doors. See if anything looks out of place. She'd only been away one night. Things should look pretty much the same if no one other than Hartman was here."

"Will do," the patrol officer said. "It looks pretty clear that she stumbled and fell down the steps, don't you think?"

"Looks that way," Crowder concurred.

"Funny thing, though ..." The cop chuckled, a curious look on her face.

"What's that?"

"The nurse she played on the show died after being pushed down a flight of stairs by a doctor whose incompetence she believed had killed a patient."

Chapter 9

Beverly McManus sat with her arms folded tight against her chest, rocking back and forth on a sofa. "My brother wasn't some drug addict. He never even smoked a cigarette. He was a vegetarian and a health food fanatic. We both are."

Steele stood in front of her, jotting down the important words in his notepad. When he finished, he said, "Ms. McManus, what we found in the apartment tells a different story."

"I don't care what you found here, he was no druggie," she protested.

Crowder, who'd just arrived, walked over to them. Steele introduced his partner, and Crowder took a seat on the sofa beside the agitated woman. "Can I call you Beverly?" she asked softly.

She looked at Crowder through glossy, bloodshot eyes. "Y-Yes … y-yes," she stammered.

"We're here to find out what happened to your brother. We won't come to any conclusions until we've completed our investigation. You are just one part of that investigation, but an important part. Will you help us, Beverly?"

The sister wiped her runny nose on her sleeve. "You don't

think Brian was a drug addict, do you?" she asked.

"I didn't know Brian. That's why we're here—to find out the truth."

"Of course I'll help," she said.

Crowder planned to take over the questioning, but she wanted to look over the scene first. Steele led her into the kitchen. There, a young man in blue pin-striped boxer shorts and a white undershirt sat slumped over the kitchen table with a needle stuck in his left forearm, an elastic cord fastened snugly to his bicep. A tablespoon lay beside a packet of white powder and a cigarette lighter—the paraphernalia of a heroin addict, the scene of a drug overdose.

"He didn't even have time to release the tourniquet," Crowder said, knowing that its release just before infusing the heroin was the preferred way of mainlining. "Either he bought some very powerful stuff or he exceeded the recommended dosage."

An evidence technician emerged from the bedroom and entered the kitchen.

"What did you find?" Crowder asked.

"Some residue of cocaine on a hand mirror on the dresser and in a waste basket," he reported. "A couple of ounces of weed and a pipe in the drawer of the nightstand."

Crowder looked down at McManus's left forearm. Other than a purple circle the size of a dime at the site of the injection, there was no evidence of other puncture marks. She turned over his limp right arm. It showed no evidence of past use. "Looks like he did a couple of lines first to get up the courage to take the next step."

"One and done," Steele said with the cynicism that came with having worked as an undercover cop in the drug unit for three years.

"What do we know?" Crowder asked.

Steele referred to his notepad and summarized what the sister had told him. "He was twenty-eight. She's twenty-six. Parents died when they were kids. Raised in Utah by their Mormon grandparents. She works as a teller at a bank in Mississippi. Her brother worked as an actuary for an insurance company here in New Orleans. He was as straight as an arrow according to her. When he hadn't responded to her calls, she took the day off and came over from Biloxi to check on him."

"When was the last time she had contact with him?"

"A week ago on Facebook. They were back and forth about their plans to drive to Utah and spend time with their grandparents."

"Anything else?"

"That's it, so far."

"Let me talk to her."

The detectives regrouped in chairs next to the sofa. "Beverly, today's Thursday," Crowder began. "Do you know what your brother did this week?"

"I assumed he was working," she answered. "Until I received a call on my cell phone at work yesterday afternoon."

"Who called?"

"A woman from Human Resources for the company he worked for."

"What company?"

"Heartland Insurance."

"What did the woman tell you?"

"That Brian hadn't been to work this week and that he would be receiving a letter explaining his employment status with the company. She wouldn't tell me anything else. I was concerned that Brian might get fired. I came over when he didn't answer my calls and texts last night.

"Did you check his mailbox?"

"Before I came into the apartment. The mail's on the kitchen counter. When I saw Brian, I got sick to my stomach and threw up in the sink."

A look from Crowder was all she needed to get Steele to bring her the mail. He'd placed the letter from Heartland Insurance on top. After getting the sister's permission, Crowder opened the letter and read it to herself.

Dear Mr. McManus,

You have been absent from work for two consecutive days. These are unexcused absences. Unexcused absences from work violate section 12c of the company's employee manual and are grounds for immediate termination.

Please be advised that your employment at Heartland Insurance is terminated effective the date of this letter. A check in the amount of your unpaid vacation and personal days, and your personal effects, will be delivered to your address on file with the company within 48 hours of the date of this letter.

Very truly yours,
Jessica Hightower

After Steele read the letter, Crowder gave it and the remainder of the mail to Beverly McManus. The dead man's sister sat back on the sofa and held the mail addressed to her brother firmly to her chest as if she were holding him in her arms.

She closed her eyes, lowered her head and burst into tears.

Chapter 10

The autopsy reports, stacked four high, sat on Crowder's desk next to a cold half-full Styrofoam cup of black coffee. She didn't get to them until six in the evening—when she normally wrapped up a day's work in the office and headed to the gym. She always reviewed the reports in their entirety—first line to last—even when the cause and manner of death were as clear as the bodies were dead.

Careful to a fault.

Not a pebble left unturned.

The first report was a pedestrian death. Hit and run. Some homeless vet crossing the street with his bag of earthly possessions in one hand and a *will-work-for-food* sign in the other. Going sixty, the teenager who'd hot-wired a car with a friend blindsided the poor bastard and dragged him a full block before a rear tire crushed his skull. *Cause of death: multiple blunt force trauma. Manner of death: Homicide (Vehicular).*

The second report was on "good neighbor Clete." Crowder scanned the report looking for something she didn't already know or suspect. Key words and phrases caught her eye, confirming that 9mm bullets entered Moss's heart and brain, exiting cleanly, but leaving behind organs that stopped working in less than a minute. *Cause of death: Gunshot wounds to chest and head. Manner of death: Homicide.*

The third report was on the soap opera star. Met her death the same way as the head nurse she'd played for so many years—broke her neck from a fall down a staircase. Only this time she wasn't pushed. *Cause of death: Complete vertebral fractures at C2, C3. Manner of death: Accident.*

The last report was on Brian McManus. Crowder focused on the lab work. Heroin and Fentanyl was found in the blood and liver. Enough narcotics to kill him twice over. *Cause of death: Overdose on heroin laced with fentanyl. Manner of death: Accident.*

Routine stuff—until she read what the chief medical examiner had written in the physical examination section of the autopsy report: *Muscular development indicates a left-hand dominant male.*

Crowder brought up the crime scene photos on her computer. They confirmed what she remembered. McManus had injected the drugs into his left forearm, something that a right-handed person would do. It was unlikely he was ambidextrous. There would've been an imperceptible difference in muscle mass. Here, there was an observable difference.

She scrolled down to contact information for next of kin and called Beverly McManus. When the call ended, she texted Steele and then headed over to the apartment building where Brian McManus had lived the past year. It was after seven. By the time Steele met up with her, those who lived there would likely be home.

The building had eight apartments, four on each of two floors. Crowder took the first floor where Brian lived in apartment four.

Only two residents responded to Crowder's knocks on

their door. Neither one knew McManus other than to see him occasionally coming or going. Neither heard or saw anything unusual the week of his death. Nor did they smell anything that suggested McManus smoked marijuana in his apartment. They described him as a pleasant, shy young man who kept to himself.

Steele found nothing noteworthy from the three residents who responded to his inquiries.

The detectives huddled up outside the apartment building.

"So what's your thinking on this?" Steele queried.

"The sister says they're both left-handed. Brian's nickname was 'Little Lefty' when he pitched on his little-league team."

Steele was unconvinced. "Still, his prints were on every piece of evidence from the syringe on the kitchen table to the rolled-up dollar bill and empty gram bag of coke found in the waste basket in his bedroom."

"But he'd have been chancing fate, injecting himself with his right hand," Crowder argued, resting her back against the door of her four-year-old pickup truck. They'd driven there in their private vehicles, as they usually did when working investigations in the evenings. Steel would be heading home in his pride and joy, a restored '68 VW Beetle. "Something else is off," she continued.

"What?"

"There was twice the amount of a usual fatal dose of heroin in his blood. The syringe he used was bigger than what most addicts use in order to avoid an accidental overdose. He took care of himself and had no history of drug use. Yet he shoots up for the very first time with enough heroin to kill two sumo wrestlers."

"So you're saying someone staged the overdose?"

Crowder opened the door of her truck and got in. Before she closed the door, she turned and looked at her partner. "I'm not saying anything, yet. I want to talk to his coworkers and supervisor. See if they noticed anything that suggests he was a user."

Steele still had his doubts. "Jo, it wouldn't be the first time someone overdosed on his maiden voyage and went down with the ship."

But something in Crowder's gut told her otherwise.

Chapter 11

"Do you have an appointment?" the security guard asked. The man, early thirties, sat behind a desk in the lobby of Finch Tower. His black uniform looked more like the tactical dress of a SWAT team member. His form-fitted shirt showed off a sturdy physique. Short hair. Clean shaven. Definitely ex-military.

Odd—no name tag.

Crowder took an instant dislike to the jerk. She didn't mind the question when she showed him her badge and asked to see Jessica Hightower. It was his insolent tone, and the fact that he hadn't turned his head away from the computer monitor he'd been looking at. Not being able to see his eyes behind his dark sunglasses didn't help his cause.

"Don't need an appointment when I'm here on official business," Crowder said, trying her best to control her temper.

"Why do you want to speak to her?" he asked, still frozen in place.

"That's between her and me."

"No appointment, no entry. She'd want to know why you're here before she'd authorize me to let you through security. It's that simple."

Crowder was half-tempted to fake a call for backup and let him hear her say that she was about to arrest someone for obstructing a criminal investigation. But he just might call her bluff. She'd take a safer route instead. "Inform Ms. Hightower that I want to talk to her about a former employee."

"Does this employee have a name?" the wise guy goaded.

Crowder hoped her face wasn't the shade of pissed-off red. She wouldn't want the prick to know that he was finally getting under her skin. "Brian McManus. He worked here as an actuary."

The guard turned his head for the first time. "You'll need to enter your information in the terminal over there." He pointed at a monitor about ten feet behind her, near the only piece of furniture in the lobby, an uncomfortable-looking hardwood bench. "If you'll take a seat in the lobby, your information will be processed in due course."

Crowder had no choice but to comply. Another armed guard, who could've passed as his younger brother, stood at parade rest beside a body scanner. But if they wanted her gun, she'd tell them to fuck off. This wasn't White House security, and she wasn't a private citizen carrying a weapon into a government building. She was an on-duty homicide detective there on official business.

A tap on the screen brought up the company name and logo—a sinister-looking black bird resembling the infamous Maltese Falcon. The portal asked for name and residential, business, and email addresses. One of the required fields was *reason for visit*. The extent of the detail required became known to Crowder when she typed in *police matter.* A warning in a red box popped up indicating *insufficient detail.*

A deep breath later, Crowder added *to discuss employee Brian McManus.*

The final directive was for visitors to scan their driver's licenses.

What, no blood and urine tests?

Crowder provided the information—and sat down.

A text from O'Malley came to her cell ten minutes later: *Some asshole at a company, Heartland Insurance, wants to know if you are there on official business. I said you were, of course. Some fucking nerve.*

Crowder smiled. O'Malley's skin was as thin as hers.

Another ten minutes passed before a tall, well-built man in his mid-to-late fifties appeared in the lobby. He had short, neatly trimmed, slowly graying black hair and wore a business suit. He smiled as he approached. "Jim Hanratty, Director of Security for Heartland Insurance. If you'll follow me to the elevators, Detective Crowder, we can talk in the privacy of my office."

Crowder liked the red-carpet treatment, but why the sudden change?

She followed Hanratty into the street-level lobby of Heartland Insurance. He bypassed security and the body scanner and led her to a vestibule with three elevators, two on one side and a single, much wider one on the other side. When they passed through the lobby, Crowder thought it strange that there was no directory or signage anywhere. Just marble walls and a floor of polished charcoal granite. *Mausoleumesque.* He chose the single elevator, gaining access to it by inserting a keycard in a scanner.

The austere surroundings evaporated as soon as the elevator doors opened. The elegance of the interior chamber befitted an elevator of a posh hotel. They stood on thick-pile, gold carpeting in an elevator at least twice the size of those in most office buildings. In the center the initials HI were carved in ebony in a circle the color of desert sand. The walls were sky-blue fabric bordered in white. Recessed ceiling lights created a soft amber glow, and when the elevator lifted off, the sheen off the interior doors gave the illusion of ascending into heaven.

The private compartment moved effortlessly to the penthouse without a shudder or a squeak. The doors opened into a large foyer. Furnished with expensive-looking furniture, a grand piano, and four crystal chandeliers, it resembled a miniature ballroom. The absence of a reception area meant that only its inhabitants nested there and that outsiders were only a select few. Crowder suspected that visitors, when allowed, were personally escorted to destinations within the inner sanctum—just as Hanratty was doing with her.

They exited the elevator and took the corridor on the right. Original artwork adorned the walls, creating a sophisticated, yet intimate, residential warmth. They journeyed down the corridor before coming to Hanratty's office. It, like the several others they passed on their way, had no signage on the door.

When they entered Hanratty's office, Crowder did a quick survey of the interior. Much could be learned about people by what they put in their offices. Her reasoning? If you spent most of the week in a single room, you were likely to put things in it that mattered most to you —the diplomas, certificates and awards in gold frames, the obligatory family photos, a portrait of an ancestor, artwork that pleased your taste, and the photo of you with a politician of your party of choice.

To her surprise, Hanratty's office was as sterile and unfeeling as the lobby entrance. The walls remained undecorated except for large mirrors that reflected the floor-to-ceiling windows. Crowder felt a weird sensation of being suspended in space. The furniture was a spartan mix of chrome and glass, and ordinary-looking chairs and tables one might see on display at a discount furniture store. The only amenities were a wall-mounted flat-screen television and a well-stocked bar in a corner. The TV remote lay near the sink beside some glasses and bottles of liquor.

Crowder concluded that she'd learn nothing about James

Hanratty other than what he wanted her to know. So far, the only glimpse into his life he permitted was that he wanted immediate access to the national and local news, and that bourbon was his liquor of choice.

"Please have a seat," Hanratty said, waving his hand at the single chair in front of his drawer-less desk.

The uncluttered appearance of the man's workstation intrigued Crowder. No landline phone, desk lamp, or bins to accumulate correspondence and reports—and no secretary or administrative assistant to scan and file them. The lighting was all recessed. A desktop computer and a laptop lying close beside it occupied the tabletop. The absence of cabinets and a waste basket suggested an entirely paperless environment. Not a shred of paper on his desk other than a white envelope that lay at the center.

They faced each other. She sensed that her undersized, lower-to-the-ground chair was purposeful. Looking up at the head of security could easily be intimidating to some—particularly employees who might be under investigation and who'd been ordered to appear and show cause.

Crowder wasn't intimidated. She went on the offensive. "Sir, I was expecting to meet with Jessica Hightower, is she unavailable?"

"Her presence at our meeting is unnecessary," Hanratty replied dismissively. "I understand you are here to discuss Brian McManus whose employment was terminated on Wednesday of last week. No one knows more about the circumstances of his hiring and discharge than I."

"He worked here as an actuary," Crowder shot back. "He must have had coworkers and a supervisor. I need to talk to them about his behavior here at work, and outside the office if they socialized with him."

"I assume this is about his use of illegal drugs?" Hanratty said in the tone of voice of an overly strict high school disciplinarian.

That Hanratty knew McManus died from a heroin overdose didn't surprise Crowder. It was in the police blotter and reported in the newspaper over the weekend. But how many employers check police blotters or look for a two-paragraph story about a drug overdose buried in the local news section? "Yes, it is. I need to know whether anyone saw Brian use drugs, or suspected he was a user. His sister says he never experimented with drugs. She was caught completely by surprise by the way he died."

"We have a very strict policy about illegal drugs. You use them, you are terminated."

"That's just it, sir," Crowder said, figuring that Heartland Insurance probably drug-tested McManus before they hired him. "Brian must have tested negative to get hired. So we know he wasn't a drug user a year ago. Do you randomly test employees during the year?"

"We do, but McManus wasn't among those tested during the past year."

"He'd be taking quite a chance, don't you think, to use the drugs he appears to have been using and work for a company that does random drug testing?"

Hanratty's eyes pierced Crowder's like lasers. "Once you're addicted, your willpower is compromised," he said authoritatively. "In his case, it was obviously lost completely. For an addict, job security is not on his list of priorities. Getting high is his first and only priority. We would've found out eventually. As it turned out, his unexcused absences did him in before it came to that."

"I'd like to see his workstation?"

"I'm afraid that's impossible."

"Why so?"

"It no longer exists. His personal things were cleared out last Wednesday and delivered in a box to his address on record with the company." Hanratty paused to look at the screen of his laptop computer. "It was left at the door to his apartment on Friday of last week. Beverly McManus, his sister, signed for it."

"I spoke to the sister. There was nothing in the box that suggested he used drugs."

"It's what *wasn't* in the box that should concern you."

Crowder frowned in confusion. "I don't understand."

Hanratty looked down at the envelope on his desk. Crowder followed his gaze. "I saved what's in that envelope when the articles were found in a paper bag in the bottom drawer of his desk behind some hand sanitizer and a box of tissues. I saved them in case there was an investigation that brought someone like you to the company where he worked."

Crowder reached for the envelope and opened it. She didn't need to study the contents very long. She'd seen drugs and their paraphernalia before—a mostly used-up gram bag of blow, a rolled-up dollar bill and a razor blade. The stuff an addict needed to get through a difficult day.

Crowder had her doubts. Something about snorting cocaine at work didn't fit most cocaine users, least of all someone with McManus's profile. "I'd like to speak to the person who found the drugs."

"You are," he said bluntly. Hanratty stood to signal an end to their meeting. "Now, if there isn't anything further you need from Heartland Insurance ..." he said, not waiting for a response as he walked to the door.

Crowder put the envelope in an inside pocket of her blazer and followed Hanratty, who accompanied her all the way to the security guard's desk in the lobby. Before he turned to walk away, Crowder asked for his business card.

"I've never felt the need to print them," he said. "You know how to reach me."

Crowder thought it peculiar that she'd not seen or heard anyone other than Hanratty in the offices of Heartland Insurance. It was as if the floor they'd been on was completely empty.

Chapter 12

The inner circle gathered in Finch's office, sitting in seats around the conference-room table like a pack of thirsty desert animals mustering at a waterhole. The design of the two-hundred-and-seventy-degree circular, black-walnut tabletop served a purpose. Finch sat where the arc ended in a straight edge, with Goldman to his right and Hanratty to his left. Heartland Insurance's medical director—responsible for medical screenings and evaluations—and the company's procurement director—responsible for selecting those whose life insurance policies they would purchase—occupied the two remaining seats.

Finch had hand-selected his inner circle. Goldman, his closest ally, had been with him from the beginning. Together, they found the directors—each with special talents and indispensable roles.

Grayson Gladstone was uniquely qualified to collect and analyze the data needed to select the insureds whose policies they purchased. Finch first met him when he transferred from Caltech to MIT, where he and Finch graduated *magna cum laude*.

Finch learned his computer hacking skills from Gladstone, who had the knowledge and practical experiences to teach him.

Gladstone had been secretly expelled from Caltech for hacking into the university's endowment donor list and diverting funds from elderly alumni's cash accounts to an offshore account. When one of the donors found out that her account had been breached, the university hired a cybersecurity expert to set a trap. They caught Gladstone the next time he hacked into the accounts—but not before he'd transferred more than half a million dollars from unsuspecting donors.

Gladstone had the same kind of ballsy confidence as Finch. He had proved it when he refused to return the funds unless they agreed not to prosecute and to allow him to transfer to an equally prestigious university. Fearing a scandal, the university's board of directors approved the deal, but not before they had agreed to Gladstone's final demand—a twenty-percent finder's fee for the return of the money he'd stolen.

Finch needed Gladstone. The business of selecting the unlucky ones began with knowing who owned the larger life insurance policies that the algorithm identified were age-appropriate and selectable. Gladstone supervised a staff of computer hackers who breached the computer systems of life insurance companies nationwide in search of people in their sixties and seventies who had insured their lives for at least one million dollars. They also hacked into the records of healthcare providers in search of the least healthy ones—those with high blood pressure, diabetes, cardiovascular disease, and other underlying health conditions. Afterward, the company's sales representatives took over—offering potential candidates insanely generous lifetime settlements that would never be paid.

For Finch, Grayson Gladstone was the perfect fit.

In selecting Dr. Maximilian Litchman, Finch had recognized and seized upon an opportunity. Heartland's medical director needed to be a medical expert with negotiable allegiance to the

Hippocratic oath. He also needed to have the necessary education and expertise to create the algorithm that would identify who they would select and when they could expect them to die.

Educated at the finest universities in Germany, Litchman had risen to become an esteemed professor of molecular biology and medicine at the University of Heidelberg. His research led to the engineering of an anti-cholesterol lipoprotein that could be infused in the blood stream and cause the liver to produce less LDL cholesterol, the *bad* cholesterol that collects on the walls of arteries and blood vessels. Its potential impact on healthcare was to eliminate the need for anticoagulant therapies, and dozens of widely used cholesterol drugs and cardiovascular procedures to address problems of arterial blockages. His *good protein* was predicted to revolutionize cardiovascular medicine.

Litchman was hailed as a leading expert in the prevention of heart disease and stroke, two of the leading causes of death worldwide. He was nominated for the Nobel Prize in medicine. But Litchman was more interested in money than in fame. His goal was to market his discovery as quickly as possible. In his rush to cash in, Litchman bypassed safety protocols and conducted clinical trials that led to an inordinate number of deaths. It turned out that his *protein* caused the HDL cholesterol, the *good* cholesterol in the blood, to rise to levels that negated its ability to control the bad cholesterol. Many died from heart attacks and strokes within a year of receiving the protein.

Litchman was demonized by his colleagues and the pharmaceutical companies whose pocketbooks would have been hardest hit if his protein had worked. Big Pharma hired medical specialists who wrote articles attacking Litchman's scientific methods and ethics. His nomination for a Nobel Prize was withdrawn. He was pressured to resign from his tenured position with the university. Civil lawsuits for wrongful death were filed. Rumors circulated that he would be criminally indicted for manslaughter.

Litchman's fall from grace was both professional and personal—and nearly complete. He lost most of his personal wealth and filed for bankruptcy. He became depressed and drank heavily. His wife divorced him. With nothing left for him in Europe, he fled Germany for the United States, taking a position supervising a small private laboratory facility in upstate New York.

Finch read about Litchman's troubles. The more deeply he delved, the more certain he became that Litchman was another perfect-fitting puzzle piece at Heartland Insurance. He met with Litchman in New York City to discuss his new company and the need for someone with his unique skill set to create the algorithm. He offered Litchman one million dollars to develop a reliable *mechanism of prediction* and, if he succeeded, a position with the company, a substantial salary, and a share of the profits. Within two years, Litchman's algorithm was making tens of millions of dollars for Heartland Insurance.

He was rewarded with a seat at the table of the inner circle.

Finch placed his hand on the table over a square piece of glass. As soon as his handprint was recognized, a computer screen and keyboard unfolded on the table in front of him. He typed in a password. The screen lit up. When he tapped *unlock and allow access,* computer screens unfolded on the table in front of the other members of the inner circle.

Finch located the chart he wanted to discuss—*Actuarial Performance – 3rd Quarter.* It consisted of six columns with abbreviations at the top of each column. From left to right: *UN* for unit number, *AP* for age at purchase, *AD* for age at death, *CD* for cause of death, *FVP* for face value of policy. Some had an asterisk above the face value of the policy. None of the insureds were identified by name.

The reports tracked the company's revenues and had been prepared every quarter of every fiscal year since the company began buying life insurance policies eight years ago. Finch remembered the reports during the first year and a half—six consecutive quarters of no revenues. Heartland Insurance had to wait for the insureds to die before it could collect on the policies, and they weren't dying. Money went out, nothing came in. The boys' club loans and line of credit kept the company afloat.

The revenues dribbled in until midway through the third year when deaths began occurring with increasing frequency and predictability. By the end of the third year, Finch could predict the company's revenues a year in advance.

He scrolled down the columns, comparing the ages when they'd purchased the policies to the ages when the insureds had died. The algorithm had accurately predicted that all would die within three years. His gaze focused next on cause of death. Twenty-three of the insureds had died from either heart attack or stroke. The remaining three had died from accidental and unintentional injuries.

Fifty-three million dollars of anticipated revenues for the quarter.

Finch looked up from the screen and then at Litchman, triggering his report. Litchman described how the changes he'd made to his algorithm two years ago lowered the life expectancy of the insureds from 2.5 years to 2.3 years. On average, the insureds were now dying two months earlier.

Finch interrupted Litchman: "Max, how difficult would it be to bring the 2.3 years to under two years?"

"The algorithm was designed to select insureds who could be expected to die between two and two and a half years after their policies were purchased," Litchman reminded Finch.

"But if the average life expectancy is under two years, many of the third-year annuity payments can be avoided," Finch argued.

"Jared, industry-wide actuarial averages are five, six times ours," Litchman countered. "If it should ever get out that we're getting our revenues ten to twelve years earlier than expected, it could lead to an investigation."

Finch gave Litchman an icy stare. "Heartland Insurance is a privately owned company. No one knows anything about the algorithm, or anything about our averages."

"There's always the chance of a leak, no matter how careful we've been in setting up firewalls," Litchman warned.

"We're equipped to handle attempted breaches in security," Finch countered, shooting a glance at the colonel who moved uneasily in his chair.

Goldman interjected himself in the discussions. "Jared, I may have a solution that addresses your concerns. Suppose we begin offering lifetime settlements that pay larger payments but make them payable every eighteen months instead of every twelve months."

This piqued Finch's interest. With his computer-like brain functioning like a calculator, he followed through on the practical effect of Goldman's proposal. "If we offered payments that are twenty-five percent larger, on a typical one-million-dollar policy of someone in their mid-to-late sixties, we pay an initial payment of $125,000 instead of $100,000 and make the second payment eighteen months later. By the time the third payment is due, the insured will be deceased, as predicted by the algorithm, and we pick up another $50,000 on the policy."

Finch turned to Goldman. "Martin, have our advertising and sales departments ready to go on this by the end of the year." To Gladstone he said, "What are we doing to keep our stable of life insurance companies from becoming suspicious?"

"A diversified portfolio has been the game plan from day one," Gladstone replied, speaking like an investment adviser. "We now select from more than one hundred life insurance companies. Our insureds reside in more than thirty states. By spreading the policies out with so many insurers, we lessen the risk that any one of them will see the actuarial anomaly the algorithm has created—people dying ten or more years earlier than standard life expectancy tables predict."

"Is there a chance the well will run dry?" Finch asked.

"Not for a long time. There are more than seven hundred and fifty companies to select our insureds from. The key is not relying too much on any one of them."

"Can we improve the redemption time?"

"It depends on the circumstances of the death," Gladstone explained. "If the manner of death is in question and there's an inquest, it can drag on for weeks before we get a certified death certificate and can redeem the policy."

"And if the police are involved?"

"If there's a criminal investigation, getting our money can take months."

Finch noticed that the colonel became restless again and asked, "Colonel, is everything under control on your end?"

The colonel hesitated before answering. His eyes diverted to the entries on the chart that had asterisks. "Yes," he replied. "Everything is under control."

"Then I guess today's business is concluded," Finch said, tapping *lock and deny access* on the screen. When he did, all the computer screens folded into the table in unison.

Litchman, Goldman, and Gladstone departed. But when Hanratty approached the door to leave, Finch said, "Colonel, stay back a moment longer."

Hanratty closed the door, walked over to the bar, and poured himself a drink.

~

Finch and the colonel sat in their usual chairs around the chrome and glass coffee table. Hanratty downed what remained of the bourbon in his glass.

He knew he was drinking too much. But he'd known that for years. The time he spent on missions for the CIA had taken its toll. The things he'd seen … and done. His operatives in the field were accountable to no one but him. He had called the shots—all of them.

The CIA official who recruited him and assigned the missions had the code name Falcon, the colonel's was Eagle. Communications between them had always been in person. In all the years he'd worked black ops, Hanratty had never been in the CIA's offices in Langley, Virginia, or met anyone who worked there other than Falcon. Only Falcon knew Eagle's true identity and background. The names of the operatives Eagle recruited were known only to him. Payment for services rendered was made to an offshore account.

The traditional training CIA agents received at The Farm—the agency's field operations training center at Fort Peary, Virginia—was unnecessary. The colonel and his recruits were all former members of the Delta Force. No soldiers were better trained in weaponry and martial arts, including Krav Maga—the deadliest of all self-defense skill sets. They could turn most objects in their surroundings into lethal weapons: shoestrings or a necktie, bra, or belt to strangle with; restaurant cutlery or a broken plate or water glass to stab and slice with; a pen, pencil, coat hanger, or a sliver of wood to blind an eye or puncture an artery. Or … a simple swiftly delivered thumb strike to the heart to cause a fatal arrhythmia.

When missions were assigned, Falcon personally delivered the top-secret dossiers to Eagle. The dossiers included identity documents for members of the team, abundant cash in US dollars and the currencies of the countries where they'd be working, and a mission statement that always began, "By any means necessary ..."

In his five years of service, Eagle had successfully completed twelve of fifteen missions in ten countries in the Middle East, Eastern Europe, Africa, and Central America. The targets shared a common bond—all were persons or organizations who the CIA perceived to be a threat to the United States' political, economic, or national security interests.

It wasn't the failed missions or the collateral damage from the successful ones that led to the team disbanding, or their last mission—a bomb planted in a diplomat's vehicle exploded and killed not only the foreign official but his entire family who had unexpectedly come along for the ride. They were acceptable incidental losses. Falcon's forced retirement ended the missions. The new CIA director had a different moral compass than the one that guided his predecessor.

Hanratty stood, walked to the bar, and poured himself another drink.

When he returned, Finch said, "I noticed you hesitated before speaking when I asked if everything was under control."

"A private detective has been snooping around, questioning family members about some of the policies we bought," the colonel said.

"Is that unusual?"

"It happens. A family member is suspicious of the cause of death and hires someone to investigate."

"Then why be concerned?"

"These were multiple policies issued by different companies," the colonel explained. "The chances of the same private investigator investigating more than one of our claims at the same time are like the chances of the same spectator catching multiple foul balls off the bats of different players at the same baseball game."

"Then should we be worried?"

"Like I said before, everything is under control."

"One other matter. What do we know about this homicide detective who's been investigating that employee's drug overdose?"

"Thirteen years with the NOPD, eight with the homicide division. The employee's sister made a racket about her brother never using drugs. The cop's looking into his past use of illegal drugs. Don't worry. It's been taken care of."

"She shouldn't have been allowed in our offices," Finch admonished.

The colonel didn't like being interrogated or scolded. He looked up from the bottom of another empty glass. "She was with me the entire time," he said emphatically.

"Have we seen the last of her?"

"I gave her the drugs from his desk at work. That should satisfy her."

"Good. But keep your finger on her pulse."

The colonel didn't bother to respond. When McManus's prints showed up on the evidence he'd given Crowder, she'd have no choice but to close out her investigation.

Chapter 13

It was nearly noon when she completed her testimony at the suppression hearing.

Defense counsel had her on the stand for an hour-long cross examination. He questioned the scope of the search she'd conducted of his client's home. The state's murder case rested on the evidence seized—a .44 Magnum uncovered under the floorboards in the defendant's bedroom—found with nearly a hundred thousand dollars in cash and a kilo of cocaine. Ballistics matched all six slugs removed from the chest, stomach, and head of the victim—a drug dealer underling who'd been skimming off the top—to the gun with the defendant's prints on it. It was the defendant's lawyer's desperate attempt to keep the state of Louisiana from injecting an IV full of day-of-reckoning chemicals into his client.

Finally, the judge ruled from the bench. Crowder had brought Barney, the department's drug-sniffing German shepherd, with her to the defendant's home. Barney loved the smell of snow—the kind that melts in a hot spoon. Although the search exceeded the parameters of the warrant, the canine's nostrils gave her probable cause to search for what was hidden under the floorboards. The search was constitutional. The evidence was admissible at trial.

All in a day's work.

Crowder accessed her text messages when she left the courtroom. A text from O'Malley, succinct as usual, said, *Call me ASAP.*

Crowder called from the courthouse lobby.

"What do you know about Nathan Helmsley?" O'Malley asked.

"Owns some apartment buildings and a couple of strip malls in the Lower Ninth Ward. Massage parlors. Laundromats. Havens for drugs and prostitution. The feds investigated him for money laundering a few years back. Nothing came of it. Why?"

"They pulled his Mercedes out of the Manchac Swamp yesterday."

"Body?"

"What's left of it was found this morning a half mile downriver. The wife's on her way over to the coroner's office to try and identify the body."

"I'd like to talk to her. Hear what Sessions has to say. Take a look at the car."

"I thought you might. The car's been impounded. I'll have the wife wait until you arrive."

~

When Crowder arrived at the coroner's office, Dr. Sessions's longtime administrative assistant greeted her in the usual bitchy manner: "Girl Monday through Friday, at your service." The woman believed she was overworked, underpaid, and underappreciated since the day she was hired. "The body's in the basement. The ME's in his office. The *grieving* widow's in the conference room."

Crowder sensed the aide had more to say about Mrs. Helmsley. "And?" she prodded.

"The woman has some nerve. She telephoned and asked me if I could fax over a photo of her husband's dead body. She has a salon appointment this afternoon and said it would save her a trip into the city."

Crowder chuckled and headed to the conference room to meet a grief-stricken widow in mourning.

Bridget Helmsley, a flashy, attractive woman in her forties, had platinum-blond hair teased high and an excessive amount of rouge and eyeliner painted on a foundation-caked face. She wore red leather pants that clung to her like pantyhose, and a white pullover V-neck sweater revealed a bulging cleavage enhanced by a pushup bra. Her thick lipstick color-coordinated with her retro, strappy high heels—in blood-red.

Nathan Helmsley was in his late sixties, so Crowder figured this was wife number two or three. After introducing herself to the widow and getting permission to record their interview, Crowder's questioning revealed that Bridget was wife number three. The previous marriages ended in divorces filed by his wives. They'd met in Las Vegas where she worked as a part-time showgirl. They married two years ago. Mrs. Helmsley candidly admitted to having hired a lawyer to file for divorce number three.

"When was the last time you had any contact with your husband?" Crowder asked.

"Let's see," she said, cracking her chewing gum. "Four, maybe five days ago. I woke up around ten and passed by his bedroom. He was gone."

"Were you concerned when he didn't return home?"

"I was relieved," she said, impatiently tapping one hand of

red acrylic nails on the table.

The woman's cavalier attitude led Crowder to ask, "I take it that you were estranged from your husband at the time of his disappearance."

"That's putting it mildly. I couldn't stand the creep."

"Your candor is appreciated, Mrs. Helmsley. But was there ever a time in the last four or five days that you thought about calling the police to report him missing?"

"No," she answered bluntly.

"I understand that your husband's body was largely mutilated. Were you able to identify him from the remains?"

"Oh, that's him all right. He's never looked so good."

Crowder had to keep from breaking out in laughter. The woman's callousness was as blatant as her candor. Clearly, she had only married Helmsley for his money. But Crowder explored further the basis for the bitterness. "You sound resentful. Was your husband abusive to you?"

"Abusive? The fat slob's very existence was abusive to me. When I married him, he promised me a life of luxury and to take care of me when he died. What I got was his constant bitching about me spending too much of his money, particularly after his partner split with half of the properties they owned. He told me he had trouble leasing his properties, and put me on an allowance. Then I found his will a year ago. He'd just redone it. Left everything to the daughter by his first wife. I was to get nothing."

"Did he have any life insurance?"

"He cashed the policies in more than a year ago. Even the one he had naming me the beneficiary. He said he needed the money for his businesses and to pay off gambling debts. The jerk was nearly broke."

When the interview concluded, Bridget Helmsley raced

off—she had an appointment for a massage and manicure to keep.

Crowder went down the hall to see Dr. Sessions and found him in his office dictating his autopsy findings. He waved to her to sit in the only other chair in his office.

On one side of his desk lay a pile of autopsy reports, stacked unevenly. A desktop computer sat on the other side with dictation equipment and a phone within arm's reach. Several pathology textbooks lay open in front of him, paragraphs highlighted in bright yellow. Behind his desk two microscopes sat side by side—boxes of autopsy slides on either side of them.

Medical licenses, diplomas, and family photos covered the walls. A tree coat rack stood sentry on one side of the door through which she'd entered. On its branches hung identical blue blazers, a Spurs jersey, an Astro's ball cap, and an umbrella. On the other side stood a full-size skeleton with a *Rest in Peace* sign dangling from its neck, the name of Sessions's predecessor etched on it. When she'd first entered the office eight years ago, she'd deduced it belonged to a devoted husband and father, an avid sports fan, and a busy, educated man with a sense of gallows humor.

Sessions handed her the autopsy photos. She'd seen photos of men and women whose dead bodies had been bitten and eaten by alligators before. Not a pretty sight. Limbs partially or completely torn from the body. Flesh ripped off. Internal organs gone. What the gators didn't get, the crabs feasted on. It wasn't unusual to require DNA testing to identify the body.

After four or five four days in the Manchac Swamp, it was impossible to visually identify the face or body as that of Nathan Helmsley. For Bridget Helmsley, her positive identification was nothing more than wishful thinking and the urgency of an impending salon appointment. The proof would be in the DNA.

Bridget's wish had come true—it was him.

Sessions read from his autopsy notes: "By history provided in primary care physician's notes of most recent physical exam, Nathan Helmsley was a five-foot, five-inch-tall, 312-pound Caucasian male with underlying health conditions, including cardiovascular disease, high blood pressure, non-insulin-dependent diabetes, and morbid obesity." He paused to take an audible breath. "I'm afraid there wasn't much to autopsy other than the brain, which was intact."

"Cause of death?" Crowder asked.

"He wasn't found in the car. So he was able to get out of it. He most likely drowned. Because the lung tissue was minimal, I couldn't reliably determine if there was the kind of alveolar injury we see in drowning cases."

"What about the brain?"

"There's cerebral edema. That's certainly consistent with drowning."

"What about blood alcohol?"

"Not detected in the peripheral blood because the blood loss was nearly complete. But analysis of brain blood strongly suggests he was intoxicated."

"So—bottom line?" Crowder asked.

Sessions put his notes in a folder and placed it in a basket on his desk marked *to be filed*. "Bottom line," he replied, "accidental drowning complicated by alcohol intoxication."

~

Crowder found Helmsley's vehicle in the police compound.

She walked around it. The silver Mercedes sedan had no visible exterior damage, so he hadn't been forced off the road and didn't strike anything before driving into the water. The seatbelt was unlatched, the driver and passenger's front windows down, and the sunroof open.

Escape routes.

The police report had Helmsley's remains found a quarter mile downriver from where the car had sunk in twelve feet of water.

Crowder sat in the driver's seat and latched the seatbelt. She reconstructed the accident in her mind's eye. Intoxicated, Helmsley dosed off or got disoriented driving too fast around a curve. His car ended up in the river and floated to the deep water in a matter of seconds.

With windows down, the car would quickly flood. With Helmsley's situational awareness impaired by alcohol, he may have had difficulty unlatching his seatbelt. If the water wasn't pouring through his window, he might have tried going through it. If it was, his only other way out was the sunroof. Either way, he'd have struggled to get his bulky frame through, perhaps swallowing some water in the process. He would have gotten out just before the car sank to the bottom. Unable to stay afloat, he drowned.

The gators did the rest.

Accidental drowning complicated by alcohol intoxication.

Just like Sessions concluded.

Crowder turned her head and stared at the opened window. Could Helmsley have squeezed through it? She'd give it a try. She put both hands through the window and then her head. She rolled over on her back, grabbed the roof's edge and wiggled her upper body through the window, kicking at the console to propel her slender hips out. One foot slipped off the seat, slowing her progress, but she finally pulled herself through.

"You might try opening the door. I hear it's a lot easier," Steele said, laughing as he walked over to his partner.

"And I had time to plan how I'd exit, wasn't drunk, and didn't weigh three hundred pounds."

"He'd have gone through the sunroof," Steele deadpanned.

"I know … if he was clear-headed enough to figure out that was his best escape route. That's the second part of my experiment."

Crowder returned to the car and fastened her seatbelt. She white-knuckle-gripped the steering wheel as Helmsley would have done when he hit the water, and pictured his surprised look as the car floated out to the center of the river. She waited ten seconds to give Helmsley time to gather his senses and figure out that his best escape route was the sunroof, then she very coolly unbuckled the seatbelt and reached up with her hand. With one foot on each seat, she stood up and lifted her slim frame through the sunroof.

Crowder sat on the roof with her lower legs still dangling in the vehicle. "If the accident happened at night, he would have been disoriented."

"So where does all this lead?" Steele asked.

Crowder pulled her legs from the vehicle and slid off the roof. She turned to face him. "If the wife wasn't so credibly honest and Helmsley so pitifully broke, I'd say she might have hired someone to drown her husband and stage the accident."

Chapter 14

Steele showed up with two coffees. He put one on Crowder's desk, sat in the chair in front of it, and turned it sideways so he could stretch out his long legs and cross his feet. He took a sip of coffee. "Spoke to the last tenant in McManus's apartment building," he said. "She just moved in and doesn't know anyone."

Crowder took the plastic top off the Styrofoam cup and blew on the coffee before taking a sip. Her gaze quickly returned to her computer screen. "Did you know that you can sell your life insurance policy and pick up cash payments while you're still alive?"

"I thought you had to be dead before the beneficiary received the proceeds."

"That's still the case. But companies like Heartland Insurance pay you cash to make it the beneficiary."

"Maybe I'll sell the one I have with the department. I could use the cash."

"You won't qualify. You need to be in your sixties or seventies. It all depends on your health and life expectancy."

"How so?" Steele asked.

"If a company's going to give you cash for your life insurance, they want you to die when you're supposed to die."

"What if you live longer?"

"With Heartland Insurance, you get a yearly payment for life. So they take a hit if you don't die as expected." Crowder paused to snicker. "So these companies cross their fingers … and their hearts … and hope *you* die."

"So what did his employer tell you that we don't already know?"

After summarizing her encounter with Hanratty and the evidence of McManus's drug use at work, Crowder said, "I'm having forensics look for prints on the envelope and what was in it."

"Why the envelope?"

"Hanratty's office was as sterile as an operating room. He never touched the envelope on his desk when I was in his office. If he found the paper bag in McManus's desk like he said, he would've touched the items when he removed them from the bag. Beverly McManus read me the inventory of things in the box that was delivered to her brother's apartment—everything from rubber bands and paper clips to a half-eaten box of raisins. Why didn't he just throw the bag in with everything else?"

"Sounds to me like a lot of work in a straightforward drug overdose case."

"Maybe. But I owe it to the sister who had to explain to her grandparents that their grandson died from an overdose of heroin. If Hanratty's prints are on what's in the envelope as well as McManus's, I'll be able to close out the case in good conscience."

"What about Helmsley? Cap wants to know why you haven't signed off on accidental death. Sessions called it an accidental drowning. We have no concrete evidence to suggest otherwise."

"The geometric truth is that Helmsley was too fat to escape the vehicle."

"Cap thinks it's all speculation on your part. He had Al Munson, who's a good 270 pounds, squeeze through the window and sunroof of Helmsley's Mercedes. He got stuck in the window but was able to get through the sunroof."

"But Munson spreads his weight over a frame that's eight or nine inches longer than Helmsley."

Crowder had no choice. She'd close out the investigation. But it bothered her that things didn't fall into place.

The phone rang. It was the desk sergeant. "There's a man on the line. He wouldn't give his name. He wants to speak to the detective in charge of the Moss case."

"Transfer him," Crowder said.

When the call connected, she said, "This is Detective Crowder. Do you have information about the Cletus Moss case?"

"Maybe," the man replied.

"What do you know that might be important?"

"Moss ... Hartman ... Helmsley." The man paused a moment between each name. "They have something in common."

"Sir, are you referring to Cletus Moss, Olivia Hartman and Nathan Helmsley?"

"I am."

"What do they have in common?" Crowder was thinking but didn't say ... *other than being dead.*

"It's best we talk in person. I can come to New Orleans tomorrow. Can I see you in the afternoon?"

Crowder checked the calendar on her cell phone. She had a preliminary hearing in a manslaughter case in the morning. "How about two o'clock?"

"I'll be there."

Crowder wanted a name and contact number. "Sir, who am I speaking to and how can I reach you?"

"I don't want you contacting me. It's safer that I meet

you there."

"Then tomorrow at two." The phone call disconnected on his end. Crowder held the phone by her ear a moment longer.

Safer? What was that all about?

~

Hawk approached the man from behind. Though maskless this time, Hawk's gunmetal-gray eyes hid behind a pair of dark aviator sunglasses. He'd trimmed his head of dense, almost-white hair, had had a clean shave, donned khaki slacks and a white-collared shirt to cover his rock-hard, muscular physique, then added a blue-striped tie—all appropriate for the occasion.

The person in Hawk's crosshairs, a thickly built, middle-aged man in a rumpled blue suit, had worn the same suit to work the entire week, always with a white shirt and a blue-and-gray-striped tie. The man routinely parked his Prius in a space on the uppermost level of the indoor garage of his office building, even when there were spaces available on other levels.

A creature of habit.

It made the mission easier—only one security camera lens for Wolf to redirect.

Wolf had noticed the pattern a few days into the week. The man's job didn't need him anchored to a desk. He left the building several times each day but always returned to his office before going home.

The man's car's headlights flashed, and the locks clicked open as he approached it. By then Hawk stood directly behind the target with a syringe full of anesthetic in his hand. Just as the target reached out to open the door, Hawk delivered the dose into the man's carotid artery. He collapsed into Hawk's arms.

Wolf, also maskless, lay in wait in a white rental van with

stolen out-of-state plates. The side door was already open when it pulled up and stopped alongside the Prius. Hawk lifted the unconscious body into the van and dropped it on the floor. Wolf waited with duct tape.

Hawk returned to the Prius with the man's suit jacket, wristwatch, car key and briefcase. He got into the car, put on the man's jacket and watch, and drove from the lot using the keycard that lay on the console.

Wolf pulled into an empty parking place and waited until several vehicles had passed by and had exited before she drove from the lot. As on previous days, she paid the garage attendant in cash.

Hawk and Wolf weren't wearing gloves. They didn't need to. This time it didn't matter if they left prints behind.

~

Mystery Man was a no-show. At half past six, Crowder left word with the desk sergeant to phone her if he showed up at district headquarters or called in.

Crowder mulled over what might link the three deaths. Moss, a farmer, was robbed and murdered. Hartman, an actress, fell down steps and broke her neck. Helmsley, a businessman, was drunk when he ran off the road into a river and drowned. Three individuals who didn't know each other and shared nothing in common other than bad luck and an unexpected demise.

Why the cloak-and-dagger prelude to the meeting? Why not give his name? Why was it safer for her not to contact him? What was he afraid of?

For now, Crowder had only questions.

She could do nothing other than wait until he called or showed up.

Chapter 15

The blue-and-white flying machine cut through the thin air like a warm knife through butter. More than three miles up, the mechanical bird soared at nearly two hundred miles an hour. Jared Finch always demanded that his Eurocopter AS350 fly at maximum operating altitude and speed.

He expected nothing less than top performance from everything—and everyone—he owned.

Finch had learned to fly four years ago. He hired a private instructor and flew nearly every day until he accumulated enough hours to be an instrument-rated certified flight instructor. He paid two million dollars for the helicopter the day he was certified. It came equipped with a state-of-the-art computer and navigational and radio systems, and could carry four passengers—large enough to fly the inner circle more than three hundred miles on a single tank of gas.

Owning a helicopter was a much-needed amenity. Flight plans weren't required by any federal or state agency. The aircraft could be flown anywhere as long as there was a flat surface to land on.

Finch could travel in secrecy.

He made one trip regularly, to a secluded building outside the rural southwestern Alabama town of Hanson, infamously known as a stronghold for Klansmen, Neo-Nazis, and Proud Boys. On thirty acres of woodland, the unassuming concrete-block, one-story building was formerly a government research laboratory. Constructed in three months in 1942 while a world war raged on three continents, it had a single purpose—to secretly develop chemical biological weapons for possible use against the Axis powers if they used similar weapons against the Allies.

The Doomsday Lab, as it was known to those who'd worked there, had been second only to the Manhattan Project in the covertness of its apocalyptic mission. Located at the back end of the property, which bordered a river, the building's façade had a harsh, uninviting appearance. It didn't matter. It was never intended to be seen from the roads that passed by it. Fenced and gated, only a select few and those who had worked there knew about the myriad nerve agents, toxins and poisons that had been developed and stored there. After the war ended and the facility was closed, the EPA discovered that chemicals buried in the ground had leached into the river. Even with its environmental cleanup efforts, the government couldn't give the property away.

Finch bought the land and building from the federal government at a fire-sale price. Title was taken in the name of a shell company that traded as the Kratos Research Laboratory, a research facility, ostensibly for the development of synthetic grains.

In a matter of months, the laboratory was equipped with electron microscopes, stereoscopes, incubators, centrifuges, cell separators, cryogenic freezers, pharmacy refrigerators and liquid nitrogen storage tanks. The operations were as top secret as those previously conducted.

Finch replaced the rusted barbed wire that encircled the property with an electrified perimeter fence. The guard station remained—this time manned by a private armed security force. The technicians who worked there signed confidentiality agreements and affidavits of loyalty as conditions of employment. Identification badges served as keycards that limited workers' access only to the sections of the facility where they performed their work.

Finch descended to an altitude of a thousand feet. The amber glow of a setting sun mellowed a darkening sky behind him. A pale crescent moon hung like a claw above the eastern horizon. A familiar scene to Finch when he visited that time of year.

He'd radioed ahead of his imminent arrival. Security knew to illuminate the helipad.

Finch circled the facility for a visual inspection of the grounds and building before landing. While hovering over the landing platform, he saw the man responsible for operating the laboratory facility standing on the tarmac. The man's clothing and hair flapped under the gust of the rotor blades as Finch made a soft pinpoint landing. Standing there to greet him when he shut down the engine and got out of the aircraft was Max Litchman.

It was there that Litchman had created the algorithm.

~

The colonel, on an errand for Finch, sat in a café across the street from the Hotel LeBlanc. He took the table closest to the window and waited.

The hotel was a good choice—reasonably upscale, with valet parking, and only a forty-minute drive from New Orleans on Interstate 10. The colonel got there sooner than expected—

but only because the high-end, late-model luxury SUV he was tailing made the trip in a half hour.

A month ago, Finch had borrowed Christine's Porsche convertible, a $150,000 birthday present, and found a valet parking receipt in the console's cup holder. The receipt, from a hotel in Slidell, a city on the northeastern shore of Lake Pontchartrain in St. Tammany Parish, piqued Finch's curiosity.

The colonel understood Finch's concerns. Finch shared confidences with Goldman—his best friend and a charter member of the inner circle. He conditioned membership on a strict unwritten code of silence, secrecy, and service. The mafia called it *omertà*. Finch called it a pledge of allegiance. Its violation was punishable by more than expulsion—a lot more.

Finch would never reveal the secrets of the inner circle to Christine.

But would Goldman?

Twenty minutes later, a white convertible with its top down—taking advantage of the warm day—screeched to a stop at the hotel's front entrance. The driver's hair was neatly tucked under a red beret that perfectly matched the color of the red leather seats. The woman paused only long enough to remove her head covering. With a shake of her head, wavy golden locks fell over her shoulders. The designer sunglasses did little to disguise the identity of the vivacious young beauty.

Chapter 16

When Crowder arrived at district headquarters, the forensics report lay on her desk. Only McManus's prints were on the drugs found at work. Oddly, there were no other prints—not even a smudged partial print of the person who sold him the gram bag of heroin—and Crowder's prints were the only ones found on the envelope. Her only explanation was that Hanratty wore gloves when he gathered the evidence and put it in the envelope.

The report did nothing to alter the indisputable facts—McManus's prints were on every piece of incriminating evidence at home and at work. Crowder picked up the phone to call Beverly McManus. It was time to bring closure to her brother's death. When the call ended, she focused her attention on the man who had contacted her three days ago.

Had he gone missing?

She looked up missing persons reports that had been made in Louisiana since the day the man called. There were four reports—two involving teenagers, one involving an elderly woman with Alzheimer's disease, and one involving Robert Marshall, a forty-six-year-old man who disappeared three days ago.

Crowder contacted the Baton Rouge Police Department where the missing person report had been made by the man's wife. When Crowder called Sara Marshall and identified herself, the woman cried out, "Have you found my husband? Have you found Bob?"

Crowder answered the question directly. "So far, Mrs. Marshall, no one has contacted us to say he's been seen." She paused a moment to allow the woman to bring her sniffling under control. "I called you because I received a call last week around the time your husband went missing."

"Was it Bob who called you?" she asked excitedly.

"I don't know. He wouldn't leave his name. We were supposed to meet last Friday afternoon at two. He didn't show up."

"My husband's been missing since Thursday evening."

"Where does your husband work?"

"Marshall and Maron here in Baton Rouge."

"What does he do there?"

"He and his partner are private investigators."

"Did he have any reason to be in New Orleans on Friday?"

"Not that I'm aware of."

"Did he ever mention Cletus Moss, Olivia Hartman or Nathan Helmsley?"

The woman was quiet for a while, then asked, "Is Olivia Hartman the actress who just passed away?"

"Yes. All three died recently. The man who called wanted to discuss their deaths with me."

"He never mentioned them to me."

"Mrs. Marshall, do you know anyone who would want to harm your husband?

"The people he investigates have occasionally made threats. One had been fired for stealing evidence my husband uncovered. Another was a man he proved was cheating on his wife, who then divorced him. But nothing ever came of their threats."

Crowder sensed the woman was about to cry for the umpteenth time since her husband had gone missing. If she knew the statistics, she'd have good reason to cry. Nine times out of ten, someone with no reason to vanish, who'd been missing for as long as Robert Marshall, was either found dead or never found. With little more to be gained, Crowder ended the call.

She reflected on what she'd learned about Marshall. He was a private investigator who went missing the evening of the day the call was made. If he was the one who called her, it had to be because he was investigating the deaths of Moss, Hartman, and Helmsley.

But why?

~

Robert Marshall has been found in Mississippi. Report to follow.

The text message came from the sergeant in the missing persons unit who had given Sara Marshall's contact information to Crowder. A week had passed since Marshall had gone missing. A half hour later, the report she was sent told her why.

The report read:

> *A 2018 Prius Prime registered to Robert Marshall, DOB: May 25, 1975, 3918 Beaumont Circle, Baton Rouge, Louisiana 70809, was found near Red Bluff Canyon, approximately two miles northwest of Morgantown in Marion County, Mississippi. Tire tracks establish that the vehicle veered off Highway 587 into a ravine and exploded upon impact. A seat-belted male was found in the driver's seat. The body was severely burned. Spouse has been notified. Baton Rouge PD will coordinate investigation with Mississippi State Police and local law enforcement.*

The report brought closure to the search for Marshall. But it didn't explain why his vehicle veered off the roadway or why an *electric* car exploded.

A National Highway Traffic Safety Administration report Crowder found on the internet answered one of her questions. It had concluded: "Almost all electric cars use lithium-ion (Li-ion) batteries that have a tendency to catch fire and occasionally explode." The report documented several instances of explosive fires that resulted from severe impact crashes.

Crowder looked up Marshall's 2018 Prius. It was a hybrid model—it had both a battery and a gas tank. It made sense. The battery probably caught fire and exploded when the vehicle crashed in the ravine. The eleven-gallon gas tank blew up afterward.

Crowder leaned back in her chair. She was convinced that it was Marshall who had called her. But what made him change his mind about meeting with her? He must have believed that it was *safer* for him to leave Louisiana.

But where was he going and … why?

Chapter 17

Finch sat in silence on the sofa in his office, sifting through a half dozen five-by-seven-inch color photographs. Christine was smiling in most of them. When she wasn't, she had that seductive look in her eye that Finch had found disarming the first time they'd met—at an art show of aspiring young artists at her mother's New York studio. Christine's paintings were among those exhibited. Finch had passed the studio with a female companion the day before. Since his young paramour was an art lover, he figured that a painting would be sufficient compensation for their month-long romantic tryst—mostly spent fornicating at her studio apartment in Soho. What the young woman didn't know was that it would also be her farewell present.

Finch bored easily. It had been that way with most of the women he'd slept with. He couldn't remember a relationship that lasted more than a few months. When the sex was no longer interesting, he left for greener pastures and a new cow to milk.

He liked them young and experienced. The more experienced the better. He wasn't about to waste time mentoring a new sex partner. When the bedspread was pulled down and the lights were dimmed, he expected a roller-coaster ride—one that reminded him of the paid-for sex from professionals he had for so long enjoyed. No proclamations of love. No expectations. No strings. No hassles.

His partners often mistook his aggressive lovemaking for passion. But his connection to them was purely carnal. He frowned on talking during sex except to invoke the name of God or his one and only son just before or after his orgasms. Whether she climaxed or not was her problem to deal with on her own afterward.

Tender caresses and soft, moist kisses during his many romps had been few and far between. Finch didn't drink alcohol, use drugs, or smoke. So there was little to do after the ride was over other than to shower, dress and say, "I'll be in touch," on his way out the door.

The photos of Christine brought back the memory of the moment he'd first seen her. She appeared that day at the art show while he was looking at a painting titled *A Child's Reverie*. It depicted a rainbow arching over a young girl with golden hair and emerald eyes who sat on a bench in a garden smelling a rose. She had an intensely meditative look on her face.

The first words Christine spoke came a second after Finch caught the scent of her perfume. He was like a fish being baited before he was hooked.

"What do you think of it?" she asked.

He turned and there she stood beside him wearing a green minidress that matched the color of her eyes and nail polish. Tall and slender but well-endowed where it counted, her porcelain complexion required little in the way of cosmetics, and her naturally wavy, brilliant-blonde hair rested gently on her shoulders. She reminded him of the high school freshman cheerleader he'd seduced after the senior prom in the back seat of his parents' Chevy Nova. A certain degree of physicality was needed that evening to convince his young date to submit to his urges. She wouldn't be the last girl … or woman … to submit that way to his yearnings.

"I just might buy it," Finch replied. "A gift for someone I know who appreciates art and who will very shortly be going away." He held out his hand. "Jared," he said, introducing himself.

She reached out and squeezed his hand firm and long enough to suggest she'd be receptive to more familiarity. "Christine," she said. "I'd buy it, but I already have too many of her paintings hanging on my walls."

Finch had taken a quick look for the artist's signature, *C. Benchley* inscribed at the bottom. The ruse uncovered, he played along. "Something tells me that the artist is a beautiful young woman who painted herself as a child. A very talented woman with a lust for life. Someone who enjoys new, exciting, and pleasurable things. Someone I'd very much like to meet and get to know."

Finch could bullshit with the best of them. He too was an artist—a con artist—quite capable of flattering a female to lure her into bed. Women found his rugged good looks, keen dry wit, and extraordinary wealth intoxicating. He knew instantly that he would wine and dine the young beauty until he got what he wanted. What he didn't know then was that she'd gladly let him … until she got what she wanted—a whirlwind romance that led to the altar.

For Finch, owning the cow meant one thing—only he could milk it.

He'd seen enough. He had his proof. He returned the photos to the envelope and gave them back to the colonel.

"I want to know what they talk about," Finch said.

"I'll make sure it happens," the colonel replied obediently.

Finch tapped his fingers on an arm of the sofa. "What about

that *other* matter?"

The colonel sat in his usual chair across from Finch. He leaned forward and gave the only answer a commander in chief ever wanted to hear. "It's been taken care of."

~

It was seven in the evening. The sweat dripped down Crowder's forehead like raindrops off the eaves of a roof. The headband she'd worn had done little to soak up the perspiration after three two-minute rounds on the bag. The real downpour came during the final three one-minute speed rounds. With only her neatly trimmed eyebrows to ebb the flow, her body fluid drained into her eyes, stinging them shut. She squinted the last thirty seconds when she ended her workout with a barrage of jabs, punches, and kicks to the bag's mid-section.

A tall, fit-looking, African American man in a black suit, white shirt and lime-green tie stood with his back against a wall watching her. Crowder noticed him as soon as he came into the gym. Boyishly handsome, he appeared to be in his forties, and his tailored look showed off a lean, athletic build. She saw it better when he took off his suit jacket and loosened his tie.

She sat on a bench, removed her boxing gloves and headband, and used a towel to wipe the sweat off her face and neck. The man's gaze remained locked on her. Finally, he walked over.

"I hope you didn't think I was a stalker standing over there watching you," he said, breaking into a smile that made him look like actor Sidney Poitier in his prime.

Crowder was used to the warm, humid air inside the gym. The perspiration on the man's face gave off a sheen that glistened in the illumination of the overhead fluorescent lighting. He pulled out a folded handkerchief and dabbed his forehead. The lack of any regional accent and his polished diction suggested to Crowder that he was probably from the East or West Coast, either Philadelphia or San Francisco—and well-educated.

"You sure gave that bag quite a beating," he continued, still blotting the moisture from his face.

Crowder threw her towel over a shoulder. "It's just the Louisiana humidity you're not used to," she said.

"Do you box competitively? I did, years ago, when I was in the army. I'm afraid I wouldn't fare very well against you today if we were to go a few rounds in the ring."

Crowder was suddenly aroused by the thought of physical contact between them—and it wasn't the exchange of blows she was thinking about. Crowder let her mind wander. She had never had an African American lover. Her partner before Steele was African American. Five years on the streets frequently put them in confrontations with some very dangerous people who put little or no value on human life. Her partner intervened to save her hide on more than one occasion. And she, his. Over time, a bond of mutual trust and admiration formed between them. They'd grown accustomed to each other.

It was hard for them to resist taking their relationship to the next level. When it came to him, Crowder didn't care a bit about the department's policy that prohibited sexual relationships between cops. Nor did he. But he was already married to a woman who'd been by his side through the mostly difficult times they'd faced growing up in and out of the ghetto. The reward for their fortitude was a stable home in which they raised a son and daughter who were respectful and considerate—honor roll students who had the chance of achieving their American dreams.

She'd known that her partner's world was perfect, even if he had his doubts.

Crowder refocused. "I competed in some kickboxing and

martial arts competitions when I was in my twenties. I'm not sure I could still go the distance."

"From what I've seen you do to that bag, my wager would be on you."

Crowder couldn't help but smile. The chemistry seemed right—just as it had been when she'd met her first partner. She checked for a ring. This time … none. A possible first hurdle had been cleared.

It had been a while since she'd allowed herself the luxury of a relationship. The last one ended after several months as she'd known it would. He wanted much more in the relationship than she felt she could offer him.

That was months ago. She'd been as chaste as a nun ever since.

But nothing lasts forever. Like relationships. And chastity.

"So what brings you all the way from"—Crowder hesitated just long enough to pick the city he came from—"Philadelphia?"

"Close. Baltimore. I flew in last week."

"Something tells me you didn't come all that way to check out the gym facilities of the NOPD."

"I came to see a homicide detective, Joe Crowder. I was told when I called district headquarters that the detective was working out at the gym." He looked to his left and right at a half dozen men scattered around the gym who were also working out.

Crowder wondered if he really believed the detective he was looking for was a man. Either way, he scored bonus points with her. If he didn't think she was the detective, kudos to him because he was interested in her … as a woman. And, if he did know, his playful banter had broken down the barrier of political correctness between them that could stifle a relationship.

"Close. Right detective, wrong Joe. I'm the detective you came to see." She held out her hand to shake his. "Jo Crowder—without the e."

They laughed, each with a twinkle in their eyes.

The friendly expression on his face turned serious when he said, "I'm Alex Hill, special agent with the organized crime unit of the FBI. We need to talk."

Chapter 18

Benny's Sports Bar was as good a place as any to have their talk. Crowder showered at the gym while he waited in his government-issued, black Chevrolet Tahoe, engine running, air conditioner on. She primped the best she could. But the best was some extra deodorant, a dab of hair gel, and two swipes of lip gloss. Her nails were a mess. She hadn't had a professional manicure since her last relationship ended months ago. Same for a pedicure.

Maybe it was time to schedule a visit to the salon. Bridget Helmsley could probably recommend a good one.

Hill followed Crowder's pickup truck to the bar. Crowder found a spot that could accommodate both vehicles, and he pulled in behind her. They met on the sidewalk. He'd shed the tie and jacket. The upper two buttons of his shirt were open, his sleeves rolled up.

Off duty now, Crowder left her badge and gun in the locked glove compartment of her pickup.

Hill walked beside her and opened the door for her when they arrived at Benny's. Crowder didn't expect it. It was tacitly understood in law enforcement that such gender-generated shows of respect were neither expected nor welcomed.

But Crowder wasn't complaining … not tonight.

It was a weekday. The crowd was light. They sat in the booth farthest from the bar.

"I asked for the meeting, so our dinner and drinks are compliments of the FBI," Hill said when they sat down.

"Tax dollars well spent," she quipped.

The waitress came right over for a drink order. He ordered a double whiskey. Normally she ordered a beer after a workout. Tonight she'd show a little class and order the house Chardonnay.

When the waitress walked away and they were alone, Hill said, "Brian McManus. He worked for us."

Crowder's ears perked. "I suppose you know he overdosed on heroin."

"Things aren't always as they appear to be," he said, pausing for a moment.

Crowder knew it was to allow his words to sink in.

"I recruited him," he continued. "I knew from the background check we did on him that he was clean."

Crowder was never comfortable with how the case had been closed out. But she'd signed off on it being an accidental drug overdose. She'd be embarrassed, and more than just a little pissed off at herself, if Hill was saying it was otherwise.

"His prints were all over the drug evidence found at his apartment and in his desk at work," she said, trying not to sound too defensive. "I can share the file with the FBI if we go through channels."

"I know what your file will tell me. I heard the facts from Beverly McManus who I met with last week. You were very thorough in your investigation—and honest with her about what it uncovered. It's just that you didn't know what I know."

Crowder felt relief that Hill didn't think she bungled

the investigation. But what didn't she know? She needed to come clean with him about her doubts if she was to gain his confidence. "I never really believed he used drugs; I just couldn't prove it."

Crowder summarized the evidence for Hill and shared her suspicions—the ones she hadn't conveyed to Beverly McManus—that the injection of a double dose of heroin from an oversized syringe by a left-handed person delivered with pinpoint precision into a vein in his left forearm made no sense.

"What did you think of Hanratty?" Hill asked.

Crowder had told the sister about her meeting with Hanratty. So it didn't surprise her that Hill knew about him. "Ex-military. Runs the place like he's secret service protecting the president."

The waitress came with the drinks. When she left, Hill explained. "Twenty-plus years of military service, mostly as a member of the Special Forces. Commendations. Medals. Retired a full colonel." He paused to take a slow sip of his drink, then continued. "After that, he was off the grid for five years. No residential address. No known employments. Had his pension money deposited in CDs with the Armed Forces Bank. Never made a withdrawal—not once. His bank statements were sent to his married sister's address in Providence, Rhode Island. Returned to earth eight years ago when he was hired by Heartland Insurance."

"Private contractor for overseas clients," Crowder speculated. "Lots of former combat-tested military types play soldiers of fortune when they get out. They do it for any number of reasons—the excitement, the money, the inability to adjust to the boredom of civilian life."

"I'm thinking more like—CIA. But they claim they never heard of him."

Crowder's brow wrinkled. "And you believe them?"

"Of course not," he chuckled.

"Covert operations?"

"The kind nobody ever finds out about."

"So what was McManus doing for the FBI?" Crowder asked.

"Three months ago, one of our field offices in Alabama got a call from a lab technician who worked at a research facility near Hanson, about an hour drive from Mobile. He said experiments were going on there. Animal blood was being used to make a serum. They injected the serum in the animals and waited for them to die."

"Did he know why they were doing that?"

"No. He reported it because he believed the animals were being subjected to inhumane treatment."

"What has that got to do with McManus? He worked for Heartland Insurance."

"It has everything to do with him and the company he worked for. Like McManus, a week after I had the informant working undercover for us at the research facility, he was found dead in his apartment."

"How did he die?"

"Suicide. He hung himself … according to Hanson's sheriff and the local coroner."

"What's that got to do with Heartland Insurance?"

"We traced back to when the research facility came into being. It was purchased by a shell company doing business as Kratos Research Laboratory. But the money came from a single source—Jared Finch."

"Finch, as in Finch Tower?"

"The founder and CEO of Heartland Insurance," Hill replied. "Turns out the facility is being run by a German doctor by the name of Maximilian Litchman, who killed some people a while back with some kind of cholesterol agent he developed and used in unsafe clinical trials."

"So?"

"He just happens to also be the director of medical services for Heartland Insurance."

Putting two and two together, Crowder said, "You're thinking that the suicide was staged by the same people who staged McManus's accidental overdose?"

"I recruited McManus. He agreed to dig for information about the link between Kratos and Heartland Insurance—see what connected the two companies. I was very careful. He was to write down what he learned after he left work and mail the information to me at a post office box. He was to contact me directly only if he thought he was in danger."

"Did he ever call?"

"He texted me the evening he overdosed. He was scared. I texted him back when and where we were to meet. My plan for him was that he'd quit his job and I'd put him in our witness protection program until it was safe for him to come out." Hill paused and looked down into his empty glass. "He didn't show. I found out why when it was reported in the newspaper that he died from an overdose."

"His phone must have been tapped," Crowder suggested.

"I feared it might and gave him a burner phone to use in case of an emergency. In his haste, he used his cell phone instead. His decision to use it proved fatal."

"So should both cases be reopened and treated as homicides?" Crowder asked, figuring Hill wanted the meeting to partner up with local law enforcement in the McManus case.

"No. Let whoever is responsible for those deaths believe they've gotten away with it—at least for now."

"And in the meantime?"

"How would a homicide detective from New Orleans like to partner up with an FBI agent from Baltimore and take a trip to Hanson, Alabama?"

Chapter 19

Mobile was a two-and-a-half-hour drive from New Orleans. It was a pleasant drive on coastal roads that took them through the quaint town of Fairhope and along the lovely Alabama white-sand beaches of Gulf Shores and Orange Beach.

The driver of the car with the California plates wore khaki cargo pants, a white t-shirt with *Forever Green* printed inside a shamrock on the front, and desert boots. An earring dangled from his left ear. His passenger wore a shoulder-length auburn wig with bangs, comfortable Anne Klein oxfords, and an ecru pantsuit a shade darker than her cotton blouse. An Indian beaded necklace hung from her neck. Their camera and travel bags were in the trunk.

"Let's take the causeway over Lake Pontchartrain," Crowder said. "It's the longest continuous bridge over water in the world, and it will add only a few minutes to our drive."

Hill exited when the sign appeared, and the two made their way to Mobile.

"Do you like Mobile?" she asked.

"I haven't had much time to see it. I was told it's much like New Orleans. Similar history and culture."

"It's even older than New Orleans. Mardi Gras originated there—in 1703." Time to cut through the small talk and get to the point. "Do you know anyone who comes from the rural southwestern part of Alabama?"

"Can't say that I've had the pleasure."

"Maybe I should do most of the talking when we get to Hanson, then. I'm more familiar with the kind of people who live there."

Hill laughed. "What … y'all think a carpetbagger from the Northeast can't pull this off?"

"The polished diction is the giveaway. You'll fit in—in Mobile. But where we're going is a good half century behind the times."

"I-z-a be a good boy. I promise, Miss Scarlet," he joked.

Crowder had her doubts. The backwater town of Hanson was named after a confederate slave owner. The roughly ten thousand residents who lived in the area were overwhelmingly White. The double-wides outnumbered the two-story homes two to one. Some of the last lynchings occurred there. Crosses still occasionally burned in the fields. The most popular bar in town was named Tar and Feather. The town had yet to see a woman or someone of color run for elected office.

Diversity was as popular as a hurricane off the Gulf.

"Your captain told my boss you've worked undercover before. What was the experience like?"

"I was excited about doing it," Crowder said.

"I've never heard anyone who was excited about doing undercover work."

"I got to act—play a streetwalker. Someone ten years younger. I was flattered I could still pass as a teenager. We had a serial killer to catch. I was the bait. He'd selected his victims from four of the seven known locations where hookers gathered. He had three remaining spots to choose the next ones. He liked them young and, being the gentleman he was, preferred blondes."

"How did it go down?"

"I got calluses on my feet walking in five-inch stilettos every night for two weeks. I had to move from one street to another every hour so the other girls wouldn't get suspicious when I kept turning down one John after the other."

"How did you know who you were looking for?"

"One of the hookers saw the last victim, a teenager, get into a white van. Before she got in, the man wanted to see some form of identification first. The young blonde showed him a fake license that a lot of the underage girls carried. You know, to prove they were of legal age. I just waited for someone who fit the profile."

"And?"

"The creep stopped. I knew it was him even before he asked for my ID."

"What gave him away other than the white van?"

"The faint smell of bleach."

"Bleach," Hill said inquisitively.

"He had a nasty habit of removing his victims' breasts before slitting their throats and dumping their bodies in an alley. With that much blood, he'd have no choice but to clean his van."

"How was the collar made?"

"I got in and was wired, of course. I baited him into describing the kind of girls he liked. He said he liked them young, blonde, and with a little fight in them. He made the mistake of bragging that the girls he'd had sex with were always *stunned* afterward that he was able to give them the thrill of their lives."

"So you're putting all this together as he's about to make you his next victim?"

"Saying the girls were 'stunned' told me how he subdued

them after he had his sexual desires gratified. What he didn't know was that I had a taser tucked under the back of my bra strap. When we stopped in the parking lot behind a vacant warehouse on the outskirts of the city, I said to him, 'While I undo my bra, you show me what you have to offer.'" Crowder paused a moment as if reflecting on a pleasant memory. "Have you ever been tased in the testicles?"

"Never had the displeasure." Hill said, wincing as if in pain.

"He hadn't either … until that night. But every time I saw him in the courtroom afterward, he kept his hands on his lap protecting his package."

Hill shook his head and laughed heartily.

They spent the remainder of the trip to Hanson going over their plan again. Hill's informant—a young man named Jason Crockett—had a girlfriend, Belinda Pitts, whose brother Sam had worked with Jason at Kratos. Jason met Belinda one evening at the bungalow she shared with her brother. A relationship developed, and it was Belinda who'd found Jason's dead body at the mobile home he rented—he'd strangled himself with a clothesline. He had wrapped one end of it around his neck and the other end to the shower head. All that was left for him to do was kick his feet away and fall back. The weight of his body tightened the noose around his neck. At least that's what the sheriff and local coroner had concluded.

The plan was for them to pose as reporters on assignment for a piece of investigative journalism on the unpredictability of suicides. The series of articles was to begin with the suicide of Jason Crockett—a bright, well-educated young man with a good-paying job, a girlfriend, and no history of mental illness or depression who, for no apparent reason, decided one day to kill himself.

Crowder had her reservations about Hill's plan. It was

a "stick a pin in a sleeping lion and see what happens" plan. "What happens when the girl refuses to talk, or says she doesn't know anything?" Crowder asked.

"We'll talk to her brother. He might know what was going on there and the connection between Kratos and Heartland Insurance."

"And if he doesn't give us what *you* want?"

"We go to Plan B."

Crowder didn't want to hear Plan B again. It worried her too much when she heard it the first time.

Chapter 20

"Jared is going off the deep end," Goldman said. The sound of him snorting a line of cocaine momentarily muted the soft orchestral music playing in the background. He passed Christine Finch the glass tray with a line remaining. A porcelain tube lay beside it. "Here, have another."

They lay naked in bed at the high-end condo Goldman leased, the sheet pulled up just enough for them to be decent.

They met at Goldman's place whenever Finch was out of town; otherwise, the Hotel LeBlanc in Slidell served for their rendezvous. Goldman had the company's driver on his personal payroll. His primary responsibility was to contact Goldman whenever Finch had landed his helicopter and called for the company limo to take him home.

Goldman had to be careful. Finch would exercise the nuclear option if he ever found out he'd been screwing his wife for the past year.

Christine's unpredictable behavior concerned Goldman. She'd stopped in unannounced that day to enjoy some afternoon delight—uninhibited sex and a few lines of blow. She even brought the cocaine. Her hairdresser was the middleman in the transactions. Goldman had his own connections.

"The problem with Jared is … Jared," Christine said. She ran her index finger under her nose to remove the residue of white powder. "He's maniacal when it comes to making money. He cut short our European honeymoon so that he could come back and close on a business deal. I don't know what I would've done if you hadn't been there to save my sanity."

Goldman laughed. "His loss. My gain."

"I'm an afterthought to him," she groused. "He lost interest when I ran out of new ways to gratify his urges." She reached under the sheet and felt Goldman's penis. It had not yet softened. "You aren't bored with me. Are you, Marty?" she whined seductively. "I even hinted that I'd be all right with him having a lover."

Goldman arched his back. The smile left his face. He felt his dick go limp in Christine's hand. "You've got to be careful what you say to him. If he ever found out about us, I'd hate to think what he might do to you."

Christine wasn't the only one he was worried about.

"I want to be with you, Marty," she pouted. "I'll divorce him. That way, we can be together."

"Never mention divorcing him—ever. I know Jared better than anyone. To divorce him is to say he failed at something. Jared doesn't fail at anything. He will never let you walk away—not because he loves you but because he considers you his property. I still can't believe that he made you sign a prenup that gives you nothing if you divorce him and a fraction of what he's worth if he divorces you … unless the marriage produces a male heir."

"I know, he's so … medieval."

Goldman lived in fear that Christine would slip up. Say or do something that would make Finch suspicious and find out about them. Finch seldom got mad, but he always got even.

Still, his enchantress bewitched Goldman. She was beguiling, for sure, and dangerous to be around when Finch was also present. But he didn't care—his addiction to her was too strong. He needed her too much to ever give her up. He'd risk everything for her.

Yet he felt a sense of impending doom. And it wasn't only because of Christine's whimsical attitude about the importance of secrecy in all matters relating to them. Heartland Insurance was like a house of cards. If you kept adding more and more cards, the foundation would eventually weaken and collapse. Finch's company was founded on lies and deceit. Its activities were fraudulent and unlawful. Its business model was one of insatiable greed.

"He's too greedy for his own damn good," Goldman said. "It isn't enough that our revenues will increase now that we're making lifetime payments every eighteen months instead of every twelve months. He still wants to change the algorithm for selection of people with life expectancies under two years. It unnecessarily exposes the company to federal and state investigations of our business practices."

"I still don't understand what this algorithm is all about."

"It's best you don't know. And never say anything to Jared about it. He'd know you learned of it from me." Goldman let out a sigh. "I've decided to get out before everything falls apart."

Christine turned her head to look directly at Goldman. "I thought that Jared made you and the others swear an oath that no one gets an exit visa until *he* decides when enough is enough."

"That's just it. For Jared, enough will never be enough. The feds are nosing around looking for some reason to investigate us because of some breaches in security we've had to take care of."

"Why are you afraid of an investigation?"

"Heartland Insurance doesn't report all of its income. The company's books and tax filings have been fraudulent from day one."

"What happens to what's not reported?"

"It ends up in an offshore account."

"Who is the account holder?" she probed.

"A dummy corporation. Jared doles out some of it to us once a year, but the bulk of it stays in the account until he decides to close up shop."

"Who are *us*?"

"Me, Gray, Max, and the colonel."

Christine inched closer to Goldman. "How much is your share?"

"Jared gets half. We split the other half equally."

"Jared must have an exit plan. He's not going to continue to play a game he knows he will eventually lose."

"He does have a plan," Goldman explained. "When it appears the roof will fall in on us, we funnel as much money from the company as we can to the offshore account. We cash out the bulk of our personal assets and put the money in our personal offshore accounts. We book a golf weekend at a resort in Tallahassee. Jared takes us in his helicopter. He lands near Gulfport and lets us out. He flies off, circles around, puts it on autopilot heading out to the Gulf, and then parachutes back to us. Our bodies are never found, only the wreckage from the helicopter. We go on to where our offshore accounts are located. Jared splits up the rest of the money and wires us our shares."

"Why not wait until you can leave together?"

"I don't trust Jared. It wouldn't surprise me if he has another plan—one that doesn't include the rest of us."

Christine sighed. "Or me."

Goldman turned and looked at Christine. "I have my own

plan—a plan for us." She nudged closer. He instinctively put his arm around her, and she slid down and rested her head on his chest. "What I have to tell you … never are we to discuss any of it over the phone. From today forward, you have to assume that Jared will be suspicious of your behavior as he will be of mine."

Christine's eyes widened. "So, Marty, what's *our* plan?"

~

They sat in their usual places in Finch's office. A recorder lay on the table between them.

The colonel pressed the stop button.

Finch leaned forward in his chair and asked, "Where were they when you recorded this?"

"His place. I got lucky. I had it bugged the day before."

"What room were they in when you recorded them?"

"The bedroom."

"Is this the entire recording?"

"No. Only what they said about you while they were in his bedroom."

"I want to hear the entire recording from beginning to end," Finch said matter-of-factly. He sat back in his chair.

The colonel started the recording over—this time from the beginning—then poured himself a glass of bourbon. Finch viewed reliance on alcohol and drugs as crutches. Signs of weakness. But he tolerated the colonel's one shortcoming—the tradeoff for having his undivided loyalty.

The colonel's last swallow of his third glass of bourbon coincided with the end of the recording. Usually, when he was with Finch, he limited himself to two drinks, but this time was different. The colonel knew that things were falling apart. "So how do you want this handled?" he asked.

"I have a plan of my own," Finch said. "One that kills two birds with one stone."

The colonel leaned forward in his chair, looked into his empty glass, and listened as Finch revealed his plan.

Chapter 21

Belinda Pitts answered Crowder's knock on the screen door.

The two-bedroom rental her brother Sam leased was a weathered, asphalt-shingled bungalow on a back road a mile from town. The young woman was unremarkable in appearance in all ways but one—her abundant, uncontrollable, curly strawberry-blonde hair. Her freckled face and fair complexion revealed an Irish heritage, but she spoke with a lazy local drawl.

Crowder handled the introductions. When she told the woman why they were there, a skeptical stare replaced her uneasy smile.

"What paper you with?" she asked while standing in the doorway with the screen door only half-opened.

"Associated Press. We're on special assignment for the San Francisco Chronicle," Crowder lied, showing her a fake employee badge. Hill did the same.

"Belinda, we were hoping you could help us understand what happened to Jason. From all outward appearances, he seemed to be a well-adjusted young man. His suicide is one of several we are investigating—all young men and women with no history of mental health problems who suddenly decided to end their lives. There may have been some subtle warning signs these individuals shared in common that can help us identify those who are at risk. Will you help us to—"

Belinda interrupted Crowder mid-sentence. "Jason didn't commit suicide," she blurted. "We had plans—him and me. We were going to quit our jobs and move somewhere else. He had a friend who was going to help him relocate."

Crowder knew that friend was standing beside her.

"Can we talk about it inside?" Crowder asked, sensing that Belinda had things she wanted to say.

"I don't want my name in the newspaper again … are we clear?"

"Of course," Crowder promised. "We often rely on anonymous sources. We can't be forced to reveal them."

When they were all seated in the common area room, Hill nodded in the direction of two suitcases and several boxes on the floor. "Planning a trip?" he asked.

"My brother Sam and me, we're moving as soon as he gets himself a car."

"Are you moving because of what happened to Jason?" Crowder asked.

"You swear you won't print none of what I tell you."

"No one will ever know what you tell us," Crowder assured her. "I brought a recorder, but it stays in my bag during our interview."

Belinda shot a suspicious look at Hill. "And my camera stays in the carrying case," he promised without being asked. Hill removed the strap from his shoulder and put the case on the floor beside him.

Crowder had told Hill it was better a White woman did the questioning. She got right to the point. "Why do you believe Jason's death wasn't a suicide?" she asked, hoping she sounded more like a journalist than a cop.

"Because *they* fired my brother from his job last week and then tried to kill him."

"Who are 'they,' Belinda?"

"Kratos."

"The research facility here in Hanson where Jason worked?"

"Yeah. The one that's protected by armed guards. Me and Sam moved here from Mobile last year. He was offered a good-paying job at Kratos. He worked in the lab like Jason."

"Why was your brother fired?"

"They thought he knew too much."

"About Jason's death?"

"About what goes on at Kratos."

"And what goes on there?"

"They experiment on animals," Belinda explained. "They inject them with something and wait for them to die."

"Did Jason or Sam tell you that?"

"Jason told Sam and me the night before he died."

Crowder asked, "Did Jason know why they were doing the experiments?"

"He had his suspicions. He overheard the director of the lab talking to some rich guy who flies to the lab in his helicopter."

"What did he overhear them talking about?"

"The director was explaining how this serum made clots in healthy blood."

"You mean in the animals who were injected with it?"

"Yeah, how they died, because of the clots."

Crowder and Hill exchanged inquisitive looks. She felt she could read Hill's mind. Perhaps Litchman was continuing his research—still searching for a breakthrough discovery. He couldn't test it on humans, so he was using animals. "What else did he hear them say?"

"Nothing else," Belinda replied. "They saw him eavesdropping and told him to call it a day. Security sent him home. He was dead the next morning."

"The news reported that you found Jason."

"It was horrible what they did to him." Belinda began to choke up, but fought back the tears. "And what they tried to do to my brother."

"And what was that?"

"Someone ran him off the road. He crashed. His car was totaled. He suffered internal injuries and a concussion. He was lucky he wasn't killed."

"Did the police investigate?"

"They took a blood sample from him at the hospital. The deputy sheriff said it came back over the limit and charged him with drunk driving."

"Had he been drinking?" Crowder asked.

"One beer after work. I know—I served him. I'm one of the bartenders at the bar in town. He wasn't drunk."

"You feel it's unsafe for you and your brother to stay here?"

"Unsafe? We're out of here as soon as Sam gets his insurance money and buys another car."

Crowder paused long enough in her questioning to signal to Hill that she believed the information well was about to go dry. Then she asked, "What's the connection between Kratos and the town?"

"Kratos has the sheriff's office in its pocket and a bunch of locals on its payroll—they clean the lab and dispose of dead things."

"Dead things?"

"The animals that die there. They burn the bodies."

"How did you learn that?"

"The regulars at the bar tell me things. When they get to

drinking, they brag about how much money Kratos pays them to work there … and to keep a lid on what goes on there. You want some advice? If I was you"—she paused to glance at Hill—"and him, for sure, I'd stop nosing around and get the hell out of Hanson."

Crowder saw a sparkle in Hill's eyes that worried her.

He had decided to go to Plan B.

Chapter 22

The sign above the front door warned, "Locals—Welcome. Strangers—Beware."

The Tar and Feather was an old wood barn with a wrap-around porch that creaked when walked on or the wind blew hard. Inside, peanut shells and dried-up chew littered scuffed floorboards. An empty bandstand and small dance floor occupied the rear of a large open space. A handmade sign on an easel announced the weekend's entertainment: Hillbilly Heaven—Friday and Saturday Nite. A jukebox and dartboard had designated spots opposite the bar. Tables for four occupied the mid-section. The air had an underlying scent of salt and sweat.

Black-and-white photos of scenes in and around Hanson hung crookedly on the walls. Others showed people—White people—holding hunting rifles and bows. Some stood beside animals they'd hunted and killed. A typical townie bar in an atypical town.

Hill parked their vehicle with the phony California plates in the lot behind the bar. He turned to face Crowder. "It's my turn to ask the questions."

Plan B was Hill's way of forcing the issue. He wanted Kratos to know they were in town investigating Jason Crockett's death. "What better way of smoking out vermin than to light a fire where they nest," he'd told Crowder when he decided to offer them up as bait.

Normally, Crowder would be up for the challenge, but it was one thing for a White female reporter to stick her nose into White people's business—quite another for a Black dude ostensibly from the West Coast to do it among a bunch of deep-south rural rednecks.

It was after seven when they entered. The locals already perched in their usual spots. Hill and Crowder took seats on stools at the bar. A sign on a wall read *Every Hour is Happy Hour —Beer – four bucks*. To blend, they ordered beer from the tap.

Hill, the only Black man, and Crowder, his well-groomed White companion, were the zebras in the room.

The mirror on the wall behind the bar reflected the patrons' eyes —steely, critical glares meant to intimidate. A table of four good-old-boy types had their stares fixed on Hill.

"Is it always this crowded on a weeknight?" Hill asked the woman behind the bar.

The bartender, in her early thirties with bleached-blonde hair and exposed black roots, gave Hill a suspicious look. "Can be," she replied, an edginess in her voice.

Crowder had hoped the bartender would be a man. A Black man talking at length to a White woman he didn't know might be perceived as impudent … or worse. She thought she'd intervene and take the attention off Hill. She knew the game plan.

"So I suppose you get a lot of business from people who work at Kratos," Crowder said, taking a sip of her beer.

"Who wants to know?" the bartender asked.

Her confrontational attitude didn't surprise Crowder. She'd be cooperative and answer her question. "We're here to do a story on Jason Crockett, the young man who committed suicide a couple of weeks ago. He worked at Kratos. We thought he might have come in here. Did you know him?"

"Yeah. He came in a lot. His girlfriend works here."

"Oh!" Crowder said, feigning surprise by the revelation. "So Belinda Pitts works here? I saw it reported that she found him. How is she handling his death?"

"She's missed some days here. I've had to take her shifts. I see her on weekends when we both work behind the bar."

"And?"

"And what?"

"How is she holding up?"

"I'd say not too good. They'd been planning to leave town and get a place together is what she told me."

Crowder leaned into Hill when the woman moved away to service other customers. "It's better I handle this," she whispered.

Hill smiled. "You're doing great. Keep digging."

The bartender returned and stood close to Crowder. She was open to more small talk.

"Did Jason have any issues he was dealing with that bothered him enough to want to commit suicide?" Crowder asked bluntly.

"He acted pretty normal to me, but for all I know he could have been a serial killer. You just can't tell about people."

"What about at work? Did he have any problems at Kratos?"

"Look. A lot of people around here work there—maintaining the grounds, cleaning the cages, disposing of trash. They're told not to discuss what goes on there."

"Why all the secrecy? I hear they have an electrified fence around the place and a militia guarding it."

"Hey! I've already said too much. They don't like it when people want information about what goes on there."

"Who are *they*?"

Crowder didn't need her to answer. One of the townsmen, a giant of a man with thick tattooed arms and an untrimmed beard, came over to the bar and stood beside Crowder.

"These people bothering you, Jessie?" he asked.

"Just making conversation is all, Patch," Jessie replied.

Crowder could smell the alcohol and scent of chewing tobacco on Patch's breath as he leaned into her to speak. "So what brings you and … your boy … to Hanson?" he asked, turning his shaved head and a pair of bloodshot eyes in Hill's direction.

"Newspaper reporters looking into the death of that young man who worked at Kratos—the one that hung himself a couple of weeks back."

"People kill themselves all the time," Patch said. "What's so special about this guy?"

"He had no reason to commit suicide." Crowder replied. When she turned to look directly at Patch, she got another whiff of good-old-country-boy halitosis. "Did you know him—Jason Crockett?" she asked, trying her best not to gag.

"Well enough to know he didn't fit in here," he replied sharply. The townie shot a glance at Hill. "Just like you and your boy don't fit in here."

Hill had enough of the redneck's attitude. "What … you don't have newspapers in Hanson?" he snickered. "I'm sure at least some of you can read."

"Listen smart-ass, we don't need no newspaper tellin' us things we already know."

"What do you already know?" Hill prodded.

"That when people don't fit in here, bad things seem to happen to them."

Hill laughed loudly—Crowder thought on purpose to piss off Patch and see how he'd react.

Patch's face contorted. "I think it's about time for you and your bitch to say 'bye, bye' to this bar and this here town and head back to sunny California."

"What makes you think I'm from California," Hill said, shaking his head and still laughing. "Does my suntan give me away?"

Crowder figured the guy at the motel where they were staying put the word out that they were in town.

"Yeah, and the faggot earring you're wearing," Patch hissed.

Hill's behavior unnerved Crowder. She did the math. Patch had three of his buddies back at the table. Four against two. She didn't like the odds. The place had probably had its fair share of barroom brawls. Was Hill itching for another one?

"But she hasn't finished her drink," Hill said, looking at the half-full mug of beer on the bar in front of Crowder.

Patch reached over in front of Crowder, picked up the mug, and spilled what remained of the beer on the bar. "Now she's finished."

Some of the beer splashed on Crowder's clothes.

Hill jumped off his stool. "I still have some left in my mug I've not finished," he barked. "You care to finish mine too?"

Crowder slid off her stool and stepped in front of Patch as the big man moved toward Hill. "Let's settle down," she said, gently pushing on Patch's chest with both hands. "No harm done. We'll be on our way now." Crowder backpedaled into Hill to bring some separation between them.

Hill stood still-framed, glaring at Patch. Tensions eased only slightly when Hill pulled out a money clip, removed a ten, and left it on the bar.

"What's the matter, sissy boy, you going to let your girlfriend do your talkin'?" The redneck's grin showed off a set of crooked, yellow-stained choppers. He brushed his shoulder against Hill's as he passed by.

Crowder had a sudden bad feeling about things. She looked at the table where Patch had been sitting with his buddies. It was now empty. Patch walked past the stage and left through a rear door.

On the way out the front door, Crowder said, "You know we probably haven't seen the last of him … or his friends."

"Don't worry," Hill said. "It's all going according to Plan B."

"I hope you know what you're doing."

"Patch is doing what he's getting paid to do. I just want to see how far he'll go."

They walked to the parking lot behind the bar. A pickup truck was blocking their car. Standing in front of it were Patch and his three companions. When Crowder and Hill were about twenty feet from their car, the three comrades fanned out to form a semi-circle behind them.

One of the rednecks dangled a chain from his hand. Two swayed back and forth with their fists clenched ready to pounce. While his confederates took their places, Patch rested his bulky frame against the side of his pickup truck, his oversized arms folded against a massive chest, a toothpick sticking out his mouth.

Hill stopped about six feet from Patch. A quick look over each shoulder located his comrades. He took a deep breath and let it out slowly. "Really?" he said with an exasperated sigh.

Crowder, who had stopped well behind Hill, could picture him rolling his eyes in mock disgust. She hoped Hill's boxing skills hadn't diminished. It looked like he would need them.

"Friend, can I ask you to move your truck?"

"Askin' ain't gettin' boy," Patch said defiantly, flicking his toothpick at Hill. "You got a smart-ass mouth, nigger."

A bad sign. He used the N-word. Even members of hate groups had largely abandoned openly using racial epithets. They relied on non-verbal communication instead—a refusal to share a sidewalk, an abrupt brush of the shoulder passing through a doorway, a hateful glare. They didn't denounce people of color as inferior, they boasted about the superiority of whiteness instead.

Same ugly result.

Crowder sensed that Hill was not about to step down. She moved back as if fearful of being caught up in the melee that was about to happen. But she had another purpose in mind. The guy with the chain was now closest to her. He was the one who posed the greatest threat to Hill. If she had to, she'd take care of him. Hill would have to deal with the other two after he neutralized Patch—assuming that he was able to handle the giant, who was several inches taller than Hill and outweighed him by seventy or eighty pounds.

"Look, man. I don't want to cause any trouble. If I've offended you, I apologize. Now will you move your truck?"

"Sure. I'll move it," Patch said. He got in, started the engine, put it in reverse, and slammed the trailer hitch on the back of his truck into the front of the car. Patch pulled up, cut the engine and was out of the cab in a matter of seconds. He planted himself about ten feet from Hill.

Hill stood his ground.

"Let's see what you got, boy," Patch snickered as he raised his tightly clenched fists.

Crowder caught Hill turning his head slightly to his right and left just enough for him to bring into focus the one holding the chain and the one on his left.

Patch shuffled forward a couple of steps, fists raised, a smirk on his face.

"Okay, fat man," Hill said, flexing the fingers of his extended hands in a gesture of engagement. "If it's a licking you're after, I'm just the nigger to give it to you."

Patch stopped swaying back and forth and stood erect as if surprised by the boldness of Hill's words.

Crowder understood Hill's ploy. Piss off the redneck so that he comes at Hill with a wild first punch. Nine times out of ten it will miss when directed at a trained boxer.

Patch shuffled forward, pulling back his right hand, ready to unload. When he was within arm's reach, he lunged forward—his fist on a straight-line trajectory to Hill's face. Hill sidestepped to his left and parried Patch's extended forearm with his left hand, deflecting the punch.

The big man's momentum caused him to lose his balance. He fell forward to the ground. Unable to brace himself for the fall, his face struck the gravel hard.

Hill turned and moved to where Patch had been. He now had a panoramic view of the four combatants. His odds of surviving the night had considerably improved.

Crowder had an adrenaline rush from seeing Hill toying with the bully. She knew now that Hill's agility hadn't diminished one bit—but what about his boxing skills?

She'd soon find out.

Patch got up and turned to face Hill, hands once again balled up in fists. This time he moved toward Hill, cautiously and more deliberately. He inched closer and closer until a jab from Hill's right hand caught Patch squarely on the cheek. His head snapped back. Another jab delivered to the nose caused a similar reaction. The final strike was a brain-rattling, left-hand punch to the jaw.

Patch stumbled back, arms flailing, and fell on his backside. Blood flowed from his nostrils and trickled out his mouth.

Crowder learned two things from the one-sided bout. Hill was an experienced boxer—and he was left-handed, a distinct advantage when confronting opponents who were right-handed. More so when the opponent was unaware of his foe's dominant side.

Patch lifted his bulky frame upright. He stood there, spitting blood from his mouth and wiping it from his face with the collar of his shirt. This time, before approaching Hill in the contest, he reached his right hand into a rear pocket and pulled out a switchblade knife. A thumb press to the handle released a five-inch blade. He waved it side to side, occasionally stabbing the air as if he was sticking it in Hill.

Crowder watched with tense eyes. She kept Patch's confederates in her peripheral vision—they shuffled their feet but remained in place.

The guy with the chain spoke out. "Cut him, Patch. Slice him up real good. But save some dark meat for me." He rattled his chain for emphasis.

He was the one Crowder would need to take out.

Hill moved clockwise, then counterclockwise, as Patch lunged at him, slashing and poking with the knife, but hitting only air. Hill's sudden directional changes confused the big man. His frustration led him to point the knife at Hill's face with his arm fully extended.

Crowder knew what would happen next. Her training, and Hill's, included disarming an attacker holding a knife in an outstretched hand. In the blink of an eye, Hill quickstepped forward and used the palms of his hands to simultaneously strike Patch's hand and wrist from opposite directions. The hand bent, the fingers opened, and the knife flew from his hand.

It landed next to Crowder.

One of Patch's allies moved quickly toward the knife. Before he was halfway there, Crowder kicked it with her shoe. It came to rest under the pickup truck and out of reach. The man stopped dead in his tracks and glared at Crowder.

Out of desperation, Patch rushed forward and caught Hill by surprise. He wrapped his thick arms around Hill's chest in a wrestler's hold, picked him up, and drove him backward into the door of the pickup truck. It knocked the breath out of Hill. The Brobdingnagian had him in a bear hug and was squeezing the life out of him. Hill grimaced in pain and gasped for air.

The tide had turned in Patch's favor. Crowder felt a sudden rush of anxiety. The chain rattler moved up a few steps as if preparing to pounce on Hill whenever his breathless body collapsed to the ground. Hill had to do something … and fast.

Crowder stood there helpless. Her mind screamed at Hill as to what he should do. Then she heard herself cry out, "Hill, use your fucking head."

Patch stood three or four inches taller than Hill. He was in the perfect position. Hill slammed his forehead into the bridge of the giant's nose. The head butt shattered the big man's nasal bones and stunned him. His hold on Hill loosened and created just enough separation between them for Hill to deliver the final strike.

It was another martial arts technique Crowder knew well. The pain from a properly delivered eye gouge was like a jolt of electricity that went directly into the brain and temporarily blinded the attacker.

Hill's thumbs shot out like darts into Patch's eyes. He shrieked in pain, released his hold on Hill, and covered his eyes with his hands. Hill finished him off with a quick kick to the testicles.

Goliath collapsed to the ground howling and shaking like a wounded animal. He rolled over on his side and curled up into a fetal position with his hands between his legs.

The guy with the chain moved quickly toward Hill. As he passed by, Crowder stuck out her foot and tripped him. He fell hard to the ground. Before he came to his senses, Hill was standing in front of him, the heel of a shoe pressed firmly on his wrist. The hand released its grip on the chain. Hill reached down and picked it up. When the man looked up, Hill delivered a foot stomp to his face and knocked him out.

Hill turned to confront the two men who remained. He rattled the chain as their comrade had done. "Okay, White boys, who's next?"

The two men looked at each other. They didn't need to verbalize their plan of action. They turned and hightailed it out of there.

Hill surveyed the concave dent in the front of the car. The damage was minimal. The car could be driven.

They got in and drove away, leaving two men on the ground—one still shrieking in pain, the other still out cold.

Chapter 23

They drove into the parking lot of Lucille's Diner in the heart of Hanson. It was after eight, and the place was busy with customers—mostly men wearing the same blue work shirts with Kratos embroidered above the pocket. Identification badges dangled from chains around their necks.

They found an empty booth and took a seat.

"And I thought it would be safe to eat here," Hill said, muffling a laugh.

"No place is safe for us in Hanson," Crowder said in a low voice. Three Kratos employees sat in the booth behind her.

A waitress came over with two glasses of water and laminated menus—the yellow tint suggested the selections and prices hadn't changed in a while.

"Shift change?" Crowder asked the waitress.

"A number of the boys eat here when they get off from work," she replied. "The special's meatloaf and mashed potatoes. You interested?"

Hill spoke up. "No. We need to be somewhere soon. Can we get takeout?"

"Sure, but you'll have to give up the booth," the server

warned. "We've got people waiting."

Hill and Crowder turned their heads to survey their surroundings and the front door. There were two empty booths. No one was waiting.

More Hanson hospitality.

"No problem," Hill said. "We'll stop at a convenience store on our way out of town."

"You do that," she said curtly, then placed the glasses of water back on the tray and gathered up the menus.

When they reached the car, Hill said, "I want to go out to Kratos and take a look around."

"Sure." Crowder laughed. "All you'll need is a Kratos work shirt, an identification badge, and a pigmentation change."

"I've got a drone in the trunk. If we can find a place near enough to the lab, we can send it in. At three hundred feet at night, it won't be seen."

They arrived at Kratos around nine o'clock. The front gate was well lit and well guarded. They passed by without stopping, followed the road around the back of the facility where it bordered the river, found a clearing about fifty yards from the perimeter fence, and pulled over.

Crowder stood watch as Hill went to the trunk and opened a case just large enough to store the drone and the receiver that would display what the drone's camera recorded. Five minutes later the drone was airborne.

Hill operated the controls with ease. "The key is to be high enough not to be seen and low enough to record things clearly."

The drone flew into Kratos airspace and circled the property along a ten-foot-high perimeter fence. The electrified enclosure surrounded the facility even in the rear, where the property bordered the river. There, where a dock jutted out from the bank, two large gates secured access to the property. A couple of guards with holstered handguns and rifles slung over their shoulders stood sentry, and a boat approached and moored at the dock. Hill used the time to fly the drone over the facility to the front gate. The lights on the ground illuminated an empty helipad.

"If Litchman is intending to conduct clinical trials on humans," Hill said, "he'd need FDA approval and the cooperation of a medical facility—a hospital or clinic—with a dedicated staff to administer the injections and record the results."

"Unless he's planning on doing it without FDA approval," Crowder said, "and has some clandestine way of recruiting participants and following them to see what happens."

Hill sent the probe back to the dock. By then two men on the boat had removed the tarps covering its cargo—cages stacked on two pallets. A man on the dock operated a crane and winch assembly and unloaded the pallets from the boat. Another man drove a forklift and moved the cages inside the facility. Hill flew lower and zoomed in on one of the cages. The screen of the receiver displayed fingers—animal fingers protruding through the wire. Standing beside Hill, Crowder could see the images too. "The experimental animals," she remarked. "See if you can find the name of the boat or its registration number."

Hill positioned the probe above the boat, then moved it along the sides and stern. Nothing appeared. But when he focused the camera on the bow, the name *Cajun Rose* appeared and below it, the registration number LA L848 AX.

Crowder pulled out a ballpoint pen and wrote the number across her wrist. "Kratos is using a fishing boat registered in Louisiana to transport the animals," she said. "We'll be able to identify the owner when we get back."

Hill flew the drone to a position where it could follow the forklift's path. It passed by a shed-sized concrete structure with a steel door on the front. Two pipes protruded a couple of feet from the roof. "The crematorium," he said.

A guard appeared with a rifle in his hands, one with a scope on it—the kind of weapon snipers used. He raised it and pointed it directly at the drone.

A gunshot rang out from within the compound, breaking the quiet of the evening. A moment later, the screen went blank. He'd destroyed the drone.

"They'll be looking for us." Hill said. "Let's get out of here, and I mean now."

A siren blared. Lights beamed out from poles on the fence.

They ran to the car and drove away on the road back to town.

Only a few cars passed them on the three-mile drive back to Hanson—all coming in the opposite direction. None appeared behind them until they entered town. Hill pulled into a convenience store where they purchased some sandwiches, snacks, and a six-pack of cold beer, then they headed back to the Sunset Motel where they'd checked in earlier in the day. The c's in the neon vacancy sign were still out. The ten rooms it offered were more than enough lodging to accommodate Hanson's tourism needs. The guy in the office who checked them in looked like Patch—only half his size. He'd gawked at Hill as if he had two heads and spelled out the rules. "No plastic. No checks. No noise. No ice. No vending machine," and, "No cash—no room."

They'd gotten two rooms and were the only ones staying there.

Hill was circumspect approaching the motel on their return. The "No Va an y" sign was lit, even though no vehicles parked in front of the rooms. The lights in the office were off.

As they passed by, Crowder said: "There's a truck parked in the shadows alongside the office. Some kind of tow truck. I couldn't see if anyone was in it."

"I'm not liking what I'm seeing," Hill said.

"I say we head back tonight," Crowder suggested. "It wasn't like I was looking forward to staying at the Bates Motel and seeing the office guy dressed in drag coming at me with a knife."

Hill sped up. The road was a mostly unlit, rural two-lane road that snaked its way through woodlands for twenty miles until it reached the state highway that led back to Mobile. The speed limit was forty miles per hour, and it chanced fate to go faster around the many curves with only headlights illuminating the way.

Not yet a mile from the motel, Crowder noticed Hill tense up, then adjust the rearview mirror. She looked at the passenger-side mirror and saw them. Headlights.

Without saying a word, Hill drove faster. The headlights behind them grew brighter as the vehicle got closer, close enough for Crowder to identify it. "It's the wrecker that was parked at the motel," she said, looking over her shoulder for a better view.

"Whoever's in it was lying in wait for us to return," Hill said. He looked at Crowder just long enough to say, "The pilot has put on the fasten-seatbelt sign. We may soon be experiencing some turbulence."

Chapter 24

Crowder watched the speedometer move from forty-five to fifty … then to fifty-five. She tightened her seat belt.

The truck kept pace even through curves that caused them to sway in their seats. When the road straightened, Hill sped up to sixty. It didn't matter—the wrecker, going seventy, still smashed into the rear of the car. Crowder's upper body compressed the taut shoulder strap of her seat belt so hard she gasped.

The car veered in and out of the lane.

Hill regained control.

Crowder turned around for a better look at the truck, now only a car length behind and armed with a front-end bullbar that had just been used as a battering ram. That close, it looked the size of a tank.

Crowder saw the sudden burst of speed just before the second impact—a crushing blow into the trunk that propelled the car forward like a shot from a canon. Their heads slammed against the headrests, then snapped forward. The car veered off the road, sideswiping trees and trampling the brush. Hill slowed down, regained control, and navigated back to the road.

The truck backed off, but only momentarily. When it

again tailgated the car, Crowder saw in her side mirror a person leaning his upper body out of the passenger's window—arms outstretched and hands holding a shotgun. A few seconds later, a shot rang out and the rear window shattered, showering Crowder and Hill with pellets of glass.

"Fuck this," Crowder yelled. She unbuckled her seatbelt and reached under the seat for her Smith & Wesson, which was tucked away in its holster just waiting for an opportunity to assist her in the task at hand. "You drive. I'll try to blow out a tire or the headlights."

She quickly unholstered her weapon and slid over the console into the rear seat. The truck had backed off a few car lengths, but approached again. The man with the gun reappeared, but before he got a shot off, Crowder fired, blowing out a headlight and putting a bullet into the middle of the windshield.

The sudden counteroffensive must have surprised them, because the person holding the shotgun fell back into his seat, and the driver braked so abruptly that the truck started to skid, tires squealing.

Hill had good control of the car and sped up to put distance between them and their pursuers. "You okay?" he asked.

Crowder noticed Hill's concerned eyes looking at her in the rear view mirror. "I'm fine," she replied. "Can't say the same for whoever might've been sitting in the front seat."

"Let's see if they back off now they know we have a weapon," Hill said.

Crowder turned and looked through the windowless opening. "Don't count on it. I see a headlight closing in on us. I'll stay here for now." She buckled her seatbelt.

A minute later, the truck was again on top of them. This time it moved into the opposite lane and roared ahead until it came alongside the car. Crowder opened her window. The man with the shotgun reappeared through his window, the barrels aimed at the car's front tire. Enough of his head was visible for Crowder to identify the gunman as Patch.

Crowder gripped her pistol in both hands to steady her aim and directed it at the hands that held the shotgun.

Two shots sounded, one after the other. The shotgun blast blew out the car's left front tire. The bullet from Crowder's pistol struck enough of the barrel of Patch's shotgun to cause him to drop it on the roadway.

They were going close to seventy when the tire exploded. The car shook violently. Crowder's gun jarred loose from her hand and fell to the asphalt. The vehicle veered to the right off the road into the dense brush. Hill and Crowder bounced up and down and side to side like puppets on strings as they barreled forward on the uneven terrain. The thick leafy foliage opened into a clearing. The beams of the headlights focused on what Hill saw ahead—the stone façade of a rock formation.

Crowder saw it too.

Hill gripped the steering wheel and slammed on the brakes.

The last words Crowder heard before the car fishtailed and crashed sideways into the stone wall was Hill shouting, "Brace for impact."

Crowder's body whiplashed sideways. Her intestines twisted. Bile formed in her throat. Disoriented and dizzy, she felt she might vomit. She slumped to her left against the door.

The car engine stalled.

All was quiet.

When her head cleared, she saw Hill's body slouched in his seat. He gripped his left shoulder with his right hand. Because the car struck sideways, the front airbags didn't deploy. The seatbelts were all that kept them from flying out of their seats.

"Hill, are you all right?" Crowder asked when her

nausea subsided.

"I've felt better." He groaned as he spoke. "I'm having trouble moving my left arm. I think I've separated my shoulder."

"Don't move. Let me come to you."

Crowder unbuckled her seatbelt. As she reached for the door handle, she heard the revving of an engine, and then the wrecker's single headlight appeared out of the dark. It moved through the brush like a combine harvesting a field of cornstalks, and it didn't stop or slow down when it got to the clearing.

"Move away from the door," Crowder yelled. "We're going to be rammed."

Hill unbuckled his seatbelt with his one good hand and slid into the passenger seat. His back came to rest against the passenger door.

Crowder did the same, and they sat there staring out the side window as the bullbars plowed into the steel strut that separated the front seat from the back seat. The strut bent inward pulling the front and back doors with it.

Crowder's body shook like a rag doll in the hands of an unruly child.

The truck shifted into a lower gear. The engine revved, and the wrecker crept forward crushing more of the metal frame against the stone wall, and tilting the car up on its side. The roof bent inward, leaving space inside the vehicle at a minimum. The collapsing metal was about to crush them.

The truck shifted into reverse and slowly backed away, leaving the car teetering, then it dropped to the ground with a thud. The truck idled in place. The illumination of a single headlight didn't allow Crowder to see what Patch and the driver were doing, but she could hear what they said.

"Git that stretch of rope," Patch said to the other man. "I'll git the can of gasoline."

Hill must have heard him too. "What the fuck?" he cursed. "They're going to blow up the car."

"That you in there I hear, boy," Patch said. "I told you bad things happen to people who don't fit in here."

"Patch, listen to me. We are law enforcement officers. I'm an FBI agent, and the woman is a homicide detective with the New Orleans PD. We know Kratos is paying you to do this, and so do our superiors. Don't take the fall for them."

"Boy, there won't be nothin' left of you but ashes, and not enough of this vehicle of yours to know what happened."

"They cops, Patch," the other man said nervously. "Maybe we should git the hell outta here."

"You leave now, and you be a dead man like them. They know who we is, you stupid bastard. Now git me that rope—then git in the truck, back away … and wait for me."

The man did as ordered. Crowder heard the car's gas tank cover pop open and the gas cap unscrew. The sound of the gas can opening came next—Patch was that close to her. Through the glassless rear window, she saw Patch pour gasoline on a piece of rope and insert it into the gas tank.

When Hill had pleaded with Patch, he'd also reached into the glove compartment for his pistol. "Crowder, take my gun," he whispered. "You have a better angle. Shoot the bastard before he lights us up."

Hill dangled the gun over the seat with his one good hand. Crowder grabbed it and moved up on her knees to get a better view of Patch. He held the gas can in one hand and a lighter in the other.

Suddenly, the smell of gasoline had a lethal scent.

Crowder took aim. Her mind screamed, *act now. Shoot him.*

She fired a shot into Patch's shoulder, and his hands instinctively went to the bullet wound. The gasoline can dropped from one hand and the lighter from the other. A plume of fire erupted from the spilled gasoline and engulfed Patch in flames. He ran like a wounded wild animal, arms flailing, smacking his hands against his trousers and shirt to put out the flames.

Crowder, peering through the fire and smoke, saw Patch fall to the ground and roll over.

His comrade must have had enough. He made a U-turn and drove away.

Hill and Crowder sat up and looked out the glassless rear opening. The trunk was ablaze, the fire spreading there when the gas can exploded. Exiting that way was too risky.

"Hill," Crowder said, "put your head down." She pointed the gun at the windshield and got off three shots in quick succession, blasting holes across the windshield that produced a series of cracks. Hill acted as Crowder knew he would. He arched his back against the front passenger seat and kicked out the window.

"Crowder—out now," Hill shouted. He reached over the seat and grabbed her by the arm.

She slithered across the console and pulled herself through the opening to the hood, then turned around and reached into the front seat with her right hand while gripping the rooftop with her left. With only one good hand, Hill might not be able to pull himself through.

"Give me your hand," she yelled.

A sudden flash of fire consumed the rear seat. The fire was spreading—fast.

"She's going to blow," Hill hollered. "Jump—jump now."

"Fuck you, Hill. Grab my hand," Crowder yelled back, gasping in the intense heat from the gasoline fire.

Anything combustible, like the upholstered seats and carpets, made fuel for the fire. Crowder felt like her flesh was melting. Air was suddenly absent. Her body was shutting down. She tried to inhale but couldn't—like she held her breath against her will. She felt intensely alone … and helpless.

Hill was inside an inferno. If she was struggling, what was he feeling?

She took one long gulp of the burning oxygen and cried out, "Hill, I'm not leaving without you."

She felt a hand grip her hand. She tightened her grasp and pulled hard until Hill was through the opening. He collapsed face down on the hood, coughing and groaning. Crowder rolled over him and fell to the ground. She got up on her knees, grabbed Hill's belt and pulled him off the hood.

Hill landed on Crowder and knocked her onto her back. She lay there exhausted—her reserve of energy spent. Hill must have had an adrenaline rush because a couple of blinks of her eyes later, he stood over her, his good arm and hand extended.

Their roles now reversed, he said, "Grab hold of my arm."

She instinctively clutched it, and in one quick movement, he pulled her limp body up and over his good shoulder. Then he made a dash for it, the toes of his boots scraping the ground as he put distance between them and the burning vehicle.

Ten steps into it, the car exploded into a fireball.

A blast of heat enveloped them, but only momentarily. Hill stumbled to his knees and laid Crowder on the ground, then lay next to her, both of them on their backs. They coughed and wheezed as they gulped in fresher air.

Crowder looked to her left—at Hill. His head was turned toward her. Their eyes narrowed their focus onto the face of the other. She moved her hand closer to his until they touched. Hill cupped her hand in his. Crowder felt no need to speak. Nor did Hill. Their actions had spoken louder than words. Crowder had pulled him from the car and from what would have been his funeral pyre. But it was Hill's dash to safety with her on his back that had saved her from being blown up in the explosion.

They uncoupled their hands and sat up. The acrid scent of gasoline and burnt rubber permeated the air. Crowder pulled off her wig, and they sat in silent awe, watching the fire rage.

"Well, I guess your Plan B worked," Crowder said, putting an end to the hush.

"Oh," Hill said, rubbing his aching shoulder. "How's that?"

"We now know how far Kratos will go to keep their secrets safe."

Crowder had no idea how wrong she was.

Chapter 25

Sirens blared from a distance. The sheriff and a deputy arrived in separate vehicles. A firetruck and ambulance completed the caravan to the scene.

"That's some response time," Crowder said, standing next to Patch while Hill was on his knees giving him mouth-to-mouth resuscitation. "The driver must have called it in. He saw what happened to his buddy."

They'd found Patch lying there not breathing, his trouser bottoms still smoldering. Hill had felt for a pulse and, unsure that he had one, decided to do the assistive breathing part of CPR.

Patch coughed. Though alive and conscious, he was paralyzed by pain and fear.

Crowder had seen third-degree burns before. Victims of arson. She was familiar with the protocols that would be followed at the scene—airway checked, oxygen given, IV started for hydration and sedation, loose clothing cut off, and immediate transport to the nearest hospital with a burn unit. He had multiple burn sites—on the arms, hands, legs and chest. Patch was looking ahead to a lengthy hospitalization and multiple skin grafts.

Hanson law enforcement stayed back by their vehicles, allowing the EMTs to work on Patch. When they approached, Crowder briefed the first responders on Patch's gunshot wound. She'd checked for an exit wound and, finding none, knew the bullet was still lodged in his shoulder. The burns were obvious and needed no explanation. She thought it best to say nothing else about the incident.

A paramedic took Hill and Crowder's vital signs, which were stable. Hill allowed her to snap his shoulder back in place and put his arm in a sling. Both declined further treatment and hospital evaluations.

The sheriff came over after talking to the EMTs who'd attended to Patch's injuries.

"Ambulance people tell me you claim to be law officers," the sheriff said gruffly. "You got the credentials to prove it?"

The question came from Buford Jackson, Jr., Hanson's elected sheriff. Junior's next term would best his father's six four-year terms. Hill had warned Crowder that their paths might cross when he briefed her on the mission. The bull-necked, pot-bellied lawman's question was directed to Hill, and spoken with a southern drawl as thick as overcooked grits.

"Sure, sheriff," Hill replied. "They're in the duffle bags in the trunk of our car." Hill turned his head in the direction of a black hunk of smoldering metal that had once been a motor vehicle.

Crowder liked the sarcasm but knew it wouldn't impress the sheriff.

"Boy, right now I have only your say about that," he shot back.

Jackson's language and attitude were familiar to Crowder. She spoke up, hoping to defuse the situation, as she'd done with Patch in the bar. "Sheriff, this is Special Agent Alex Hill of the

FBI. I'm Lieutenant Jo Crowder, a homicide detective with the New Orleans PD. Our superiors will confirm that when you call them."

"Sure will, little lady," Jackson said condescendingly. "As soon as I git both of you back to town and process you through the system. My information is that you are newspaper people who engaged in some road rage, lost control of your car, crashed it into that wall of rock over there"—he paused long enough to nod in the direction of the crash site—"and then shot one of our citizens who was going to your assistance when the fire broke out."

Hill and Crowder exchanged eye-rolls. Jackson meant business. He'd harass them for as long as he could get away with it and hope to learn facts about their investigation—information that he could provide to his friends at Kratos.

Hill was fed up with Jackson's bullying, and his attitude. "Listen, Sheriff, you can avoid a whole lot of grief for yourself if you would just call the FBI's field office in Mobile. They'll verify who we are, and that we were in Hanson on official business."

"Official business?" Jackson said, feigning surprise. "You come to Hanson pretending to be someone you ain't. You beat up a couple of guys in the parking lot of a bar. And then you shoot one of them afterward." The sheriff glared at Hill. "Boy, that's more like *monkey* business."

Crowder knew the emphasis was purposeful and hoped that Hill's fuse wasn't too short.

Hill stared down the sheriff but controlled his temper. "One call, Sheriff. That's all it will take. We would have made it, but our cell phones were in the console of the car."

"You'll git that one call—compliments of the municipality—after you two are printed, photographed and booked on suspicion of assault with a deadly weapon."

Crowder knew to keep her mouth shut until help arrived. But she wanted to be sure the sheriff was cautioned on the need to preserve evidence if the matter proceeded to more than a pissing contest between him and Hill. Before she could speak up, Hill took the lead.

"If you look tomorrow when there's daylight, you might find a shotgun somewhere down the road. The burned guy—a man called Patch—his prints will be all over it. He used it to shoot at us. His accomplice used his tow truck to run us off the road. Patch got caught up in the fire he was setting while we were pinned in our vehicle."

"You are some kind of storyteller, boy," Jackson said mockingly. "I didn't see no shotgun on the road on my way here, and there ain't enough left of that vehicle to prove anything you sayin' is true."

"You'd be surprised how good FBI forensic investigators are, Sheriff," Hill warned. "May I assume you'll preserve the car and collect what you find on the ground near it, which is evidence in the attempted murder of two law enforcement officers who were in Hanson on official business?"

"You can assume any damn thing you want. Right now, the only ones facing charges are you and the woman."

"Are you placing us under arrest?" Hill asked.

"Let's say you are being detained while under suspicion of assault. I don't know who did the drivin' and who did the shootin'. But unless one of you did both and fesses up to it, you both are spending the night in jail until a decision can be made on formal charges tomorrow."

Crowder wanted to clarify who did the shooting and why. "Sheriff, I—" she said, but stopped when she saw Hill put up his hand for her to keep quiet. She'd take her direction from Hill.

"We'll need to cuff you while you're being transported—

standard procedure."

The sheriff pulled out a pair of handcuffs from his belt and cuffed Hill, causing him to wince in pain. The deputy followed his boss's lead and put handcuffs on Crowder.

They were transported in separate vehicles. From that moment on, Crowder knew they'd have no contact with each other, or the civilized world, unless and until, someone came to their rescue.

~

"All rise," the deputy sheriff, who doubled as the bailiff, blared. "Court's in session, the Honorable Bifford Jackson presiding."

Magistrate Jackson insisted on the formal introduction, even though the small courtroom had only one entrance and a gallery of folding chairs for no more than twelve. The room was conveniently located on the second floor of an unassuming brick building that also housed the sheriff's office and jail.

It was ten in the morning. The time set for the reading of formal charges against Hill and Crowder for assault with a deadly weapon and conspiracy to commit mayhem.

On one side, Buddy Kendricks, the town's solicitor, sat beside Sheriff Jackson at the prosecutor's table. On the other side, Rita Morales sat beside Hill and Crowder. Behind them, three men and two women in business suits sat stone-faced in the gallery.

Hill, his arm no longer in a sling, turned to Crowder and whispered, "The magistrate is the sheriff's brother. The town's lawyer is his nephew." Hill paused to chuckle. "The Jacksons have had their fun. Now it's our turn."

Crowder didn't have long to wait to find out what Hill meant.

The magistrate—an older, heavier, sterner-looking version

of his brother— surveyed the courtroom. Below bushy, unruly brows, a pair of steely dark eyes looked out over horn-rimmed reading glasses that rested on the tip of his nose. They came to set on the petite Latino woman with the mountain of curly black hair who sat beside Hill.

"Miss, are you appearing as counselor for the defendant?" he asked stiffly.

Morales stood. Barely five feet tall, she looked more like a high school cheerleader than a federal prosecutor. Morales had interviewed Crowder in her holding cell that morning. Crowder knew looks could be deceiving.

"And speak up, Miss," the magistrate barked even before she said a word—his way of establishing an intimidating presence in his courtroom.

"Rita Morales, Assistant United States Attorney for the southern district of Alabama, on behalf of both defendants," she said, her voice powerful and confident.

"Who and why are all those people seated behind you in my courtroom? This ain't no trial. And what's a federal prosecutor doing representing defendants in a state criminal case?"

"Magistrate, let me answer your questions in the order asked."

Crowder had heard Kendricks tell Morales before the hearing started that Jackson wanted to be referred to as "Your Honor" and "Judge," not "Magistrate."

Point—Morales.

"The gentleman seated immediately behind me is a United States Marshal, here to serve a writ of habeas corpus and search warrant on Sheriff Jackson. He will then take FBI Special Agent Alex Hill and Detective Lieutenant Jo Crowder of the New Orleans Police Department into federal custody."

The marshal stood, walked over to the sheriff, and handed him the papers. When the sheriff took hold of them, the marshal uttered two words, "Duly served."

Morales continued, "The man and woman seated beside the marshal are forensic investigators. They are here to investigate the scene, gather evidence, and take possession of the vehicles involved in an incident last night, when two men attempted to murder two law enforcement officers who were in Hanson on official business of the Federal Bureau of Investigation.

"And the man and woman seated behind them are agents from the FBI's field office in Mobile. They are here to make sure that what I've just told you … happens.

"Finally, I'm here to advise you that from this moment on, Sheriff Jackson and this court have no authority or jurisdiction over Agent Hill and Detective Crowder, and that any interference from the sheriff or this court will require you to appear in federal district court in Mobile and show cause why you should not be held in contempt of court."

There was a hush in the courtroom. All eyes were on Morales. Kendricks and the sheriff sat there slack-jawed, their faces portraits of incredulity.

The cheerleader had just kicked some redneck bully ass.

"Let me see those papers," the magistrate bellowed. "If you think you can come into my courtroom and order me around, you'll be sadly disappointed."

Kendricks walked over and handed him the papers.

"By what authority can the federal government interfere with the state's right to prosecute these defendants for crimes committed in Hanson against its citizens," Jackson mumbled, as he scanned the writ looking for answers. "We just might fight you over this," he blustered.

Morales spoke up. "Sir, under the immunity granted by the United States Constitution, the state of Alabama and the town of Hanson have no legal right to charge agents and authorized representatives of the federal government with crimes committed while performing their official duties. In fact, the sheriff's detention of the defendants has been a violation of their constitutional rights, that gives rise to a civil action for damages against the sheriff and the town of Hanson. I strongly encourage the sheriff and this court to not interfere further in this matter unless the sheriff and this town have the resources to pay legal fees and damages awarded in a federal civil rights action." Morales paused a moment to let her words sink in. "Now, if there's nothing further, *Magistrate* Jackson, may we be excused?"

Crowder looked over at Kendricks and the sheriff who were talking to each other at the same time, both shaking their heads in disbelief.

The sheriff and town of Hanson didn't have the financial resources to fight the federal government. If a civil action was filed, the town would go bankrupt defending the case and paying the judgment. Buford, Jr., wouldn't break his father's record, and brother Biff's distinguished career as a jurist in Podunk, Alabama would come to an end.

The magistrate was red-faced mad.

The town's attorney stood to address the court. "You Honor, after discussing the matter with Sheriff Jackson, the town of Hanson would like to drop all charges against the defendants."

Bifford Jackson took a long, deep breath and said the only two words left to say to end the debacle: "Case dismissed."

Chapter 26

After the charges were dismissed, Hill and Crowder gave formal statements to Morales about what happened in Hanson, and briefed the forensic investigators on the evidence they'd find there. Hill returned to the field office in Mobile to begin formal investigations of Kratos, Max Litchman, and the *Cajun Rose*. Crowder was to remain on standby.

When she returned to district headquarters, she found a note from the desk sergeant taped to her chair: *Call Sara Marshall.*

Marshall's widow was home when Crowder called. "I found Bob's desk calendar while I was going through his papers yesterday," she said. "On the day after he went missing, there's a notation, NOPD, at 2 p.m. I remembered what you told me about a meeting you had with someone that day who wouldn't give his name."

Crowder nodded. "That was the time. So it had to have been your husband."

"I believe that too. But there's more I need to tell you."

Crowder moved up in her chair.

"Just below the entry are some letters and numbers that make no sense to me but might to you. I can send them to you."

Crowder provided the homicide division's fax number, and the page from Marshall's calendar arrived fifteen minutes later. She placed it on her desk. It looked like shorthand notes or a cryptogram. The entry at 2 p.m. read:

NOPD
CM |L| OH |L| NH |L|
DI = |CCC|

The letters and symbols made no sense to Crowder. Her brain shouted, "Think logically." Marshall wanted to see her to discuss what three dead people had in common. NOPD were the department's initials and where they were to meet. The initials just below had to be the three dead people he wanted to discuss. What was DI on the line below? Possibly a fourth victim. But who?

The symbol beside the initials—what did it mean? It was the same for all three victims. A symbol for death perhaps.

She searched the internet and found many symbols for death—skull and crossbones, a vulture, a jackal, the chrysanthemum flower, the grim reaper—but no symbols that looked like what Marshall had drawn.

Steele came over to Crowder's desk with two coffees. "Cap told me you nearly ended up in a heap of scrap metal," he joked.

Crowder chuckled. "All in a day's work."

"How did you like partnering up with the feds?"

"Hill's a risk-taker, for sure. High risk, high reward."

"Don't let him put you in the line of fire, Jo," Steele cautioned.

"I trust his instincts, Sid. And it helps that he has the FBI, Homeland Security, the NSA, US Marshals, and federal prosecutors on his team."

"Still, if these locals were being paid to take out two

reporters investigating an apparent suicide, whoever paid them won't stop just because those reporters happen to have been undercover cops."

Crowder knew Steele was speaking from personal experience. He'd worked undercover in narcotics and had had two attempts on his life after his cover was blown.

Steele sat in the chair in front of Crowder's desk and took a sip of coffee. "What are you working on?"

"A cryptogram of sorts." She turned the calendar page upside down and pushed it in front of Steele. "If I told you that the initials below the acronym are the initials for Moss, Hartman and Helmsley, what do you make of the symbol next to their initials?"

Steele studied the letters and symbols. "No idea. But it's the same for each. So maybe it's the symbol for death."

"Been down that road—a dead end. And the symbol changes with the fourth set of initials which makes me believe it refers to something other than death. I need to consult with an expert."

"What kind of expert?"

"A symbologist."

Steele laughed. "Where's Robert Langdon when you need him?" The reference was to a fictional character—a Harvard Professor of Symbology.

"No. They exist, Sid. We have a symbologist here in Louisiana. I consulted him in the Thrasher case—my first serial-rape-murder case."

"Stanley Thrasher. I remember the case. The guy they called Thrasher the Slasher."

Crowder nodded. "Three victims before he was caught. All attractive women in their twenties. He had the nasty habit of snipping off their fingertips and toes and scalping them after he'd raped them."

"So where did the symbols come into play?"

"He used lipstick to paint two smiley faces on their stomachs. Not sure of the significance, I consulted with a professor at LSU who was a symbologist. He suggested the sameness of the faces could be interpreted as twins and a reference to the zodiac sign, Gemini.

"I looked up the name, Gemini, in the directory. There were several businesses by that name. One was a salon. I pieced the rest together after that. The killer took the same body parts as mementos. But why those particular body parts? Because they included fingernails, toenails, and hair—all things that women take care of at a salon.

"Once I knew what the killer wanted, it was logical that he may have selected his victims at a salon—perhaps one or more of the salons where he'd worked, maybe he had the women as clients. Sure enough, Thrasher had worked at Gemini Hair Salon where the first victim was a client. He used the symbol of his first kill after that, even though he changed salons for each of the next two victims. Once we'd traced the women to their salons, I could identify the killer as the only person to have worked at all three of them. He was working at a fourth salon, and looking for another victim, when we made the arrest. A search of his apartment uncovered the memorabilia—a bag full of fingertips, toes, and scalps in the crisper drawer of his refrigerator."

Steele grimaced. "Is there anything you want me to do?"

"One thing. DI are initials I haven't yet identified. If it's a fourth victim, the death may show up in the obituaries. Check Louisiana deaths—last six months, people in their sixties and seventies with the initials DI."

After Steele walked away, Crowder phoned the professor, who agreed to look at the symbols. She scanned the calendar page and sent it to him.

Her phone rang five minutes later. She had her answer—the symbols were roman numerals for the numbers five million and thirty million. She called Philip Maron to ask why his partner was investigating the three deaths. She then called Steele to say that it was unnecessary to check the Louisiana obituaries.

Her next three calls were to the next of kin of Cletus Moss and Olivia Hartman, and to Nathan Helmsley's daughter from his first marriage.

Chapter 27

Finch sat at his desk looking at his desktop computer screen. The desk was an elegant version of the ones in the inner circle's offices. Another feature they had in common was that they were intended to be paperless.

Finch was careful. Paper trails led to arrests, convictions, and jail sentences. Computer memories could be easily erased. No need for time-consuming paper shredding.

Finch trusted no one. Only his and the four computers of the inner circle contained the files that told the story of Finch's corrupt enterprise. If necessary, they could be permanently deleted.

He looked up from his computer screen. The desk served as a barrier whenever Finch rebuked subordinates—including members of the inner circle. "What went wrong in Hanson?" he asked.

"Our operatives lacked the necessary skills," the colonel replied. "I take full responsibility. The next time, I'll use *my* people."

"The next time," Finch said in an emotionless monotone. He paused to allow an icy glare to reveal his displeasure. "There may not be a next time ... This FBI agent and homicide detective persist. Did they learn anything?"

"The drone they sent in was shot down before anything of value could be recorded, and the recorder was destroyed when their car caught fire and exploded. To be safe we should mothball the *Cajun Rose* and have the crew take a vacation for a while."

Finch looked back at the computer screen. "We have six, maybe seven months' worth of serum. We shut down the *Cajun Rose* for two weeks—no more than that."

The colonel had his marching orders. He got up and left without another word.

~

Hill sat in the chair in front of Crowder's desk. He could have called from his field office in Mobile, where he'd been temporarily assigned, but he wanted the face-to-face.

Crowder suspected that he wanted a late afternoon meeting so he could ease into asking her out for dinner. At least she hoped that was his plan.

"The *Cajun Rose* is registered to Gulf Fisheries, a limited liability company," Hill said. "The incorporator and registered agent are a law firm in Shreveport. The boat is rented out for fishing excursions in the Gulf."

"When it's not being used to supply Kratos with animals to experiment on," Crowder added sarcastically. "The surveillance?"

"We tried. The boat's usually moored at a marina in Mobile. But it set out the day before we got there. Hasn't been seen since."

"The boat operator?"

"We're watching his apartment in Mobile. So far, no activity."

"Is Kratos conducting clinical trials?"

"None that are authorized by the FDA."

"Do you have enough for a warrant to search the lab?"

"Not even close. The best we can do is investigate the facility's illegal experimentation on non-human primates. If the fingers we saw outside the cages were those of chimpanzees, we will have them on violations of the Animal Welfare Act."

"The Animal Welfare Act?"

"It requires research facilities to follow certain protocols. The problem here is that Kratos never obtained a license from the US Department of Agriculture to conduct experiments on animals. Probably because chimpanzees are now an endangered species. They knew they'd never get approval. If they'd been licensed, we could have arranged for the USDA to do an unannounced inspection. It might have revealed the purpose of their experiments."

Crowder frowned. "So, because they're unlicensed, we need a search warrant, and that requires us to show probable cause that a crime has been committed."

Hill nodded. "Right now we have insufficient facts that experimentation on chimps is occurring. Jason Crockett only overheard people at Kratos talking about experiments. He didn't see them being conducted."

"And Belinda Pitts and her brother Sam heard about it from Crockett, which make their statements double hearsay," Crowder said, sensing Hill's frustration.

"So unless we can intercept the *Cajun Rose* delivering primates to Kratos, we have no basis for an arrest, or for a warrant to search the lab."

Crowder looked at the clock on the wall. It was after five, and he hadn't suggested they meet for dinner. She needed to give him a push. "There's something I wanted to discuss with you that has nothing to do with Kratos but everything to do with Heartland Insurance."

"What?"

"Well, it's complicated. It's getting late. You probably want to get back to Mobile."

Hill cleared his throat. "I thought I'd have dinner in New Orleans. Any suggestions?"

Crowder had to laugh. Fine dining in New Orleans wasn't her specialty. Diners and sports bars were her areas of expertise. "What do you have a hankering for?" she asked.

An impish grin appeared on his face. "Well to be perfectly honest, anything … and anywhere … that has us dining together this evening."

Crowder felt as playfully mischievous as Hill. "That sounds an awful lot like a date, Hill."

"Well … not to put too fine a point on it, but … yes."

"Well, in that case, I know the perfect place."

Chapter 28

They sat across from each other at the dining-room table in Crowder's home in Holly Grove, a rising, rehabbed neighborhood in the 17th Ward. The one-story, two-bedroom, two-bath, white-clapboard home sat on a corner. Crowder liked the house and the neighborhood.

She'd bought the house at auction for $165,000, plus the $4,000 of delinquent property taxes, and replaced the kitchen appliances, refinished the floors, and painted the ceilings and walls. Shrubs and a new front door added some curbside appeal. The house was a bargain in a neighborhood where the average home of similar size sold for $200,000.

Crowder's neighbors were mostly first-time homeowners—singles and a lot of young couples—and a contingent of seniors who'd weathered the aftermath of Katrina. Tradesmen, city workers, public school teachers, hospital employees, and cops called the place home. The heavy police presence in recent years had led to a fifty-percent reduction in violent crime and a diminished need for regular police patrols in the neighborhood.

Hill showed up at seven as planned, with takeout from Claude's Creole Shack on the waterfront, a fifth of Chivas Regal seventeen-year-old blended scotch whiskey, and a bottle of 2013 Rhys Vineyards Chardonnay.

Crowder learned two things about Hill from his selection of beverages—he liked good liquor and expensive wines. Crowder hid her half-empty container of cheap box wine in the cabinet below the sink in case Hill decided to venture into her refrigerator.

Hill looked sporty in his canary-yellow polo shirt, khaki pants, and polished cordovan loafers. She got a better look at his sculpted physique when he unbuttoned and removed his perfectly sized lime-green sports jacket.

Crowder's mind buzzed with speculation. Hill must have brought a change of clothes in anticipation of his date with her. He probably had an overnight bag in his car. Was he expecting to stay the night—perhaps sleep in the spare bedroom?

The nerve. How brazen of him to think she'd let him sleep over—she, naked in her bed; he, naked in his bed. Only a wall and willpower separating them.

The chutzpah. Did he think he would charm her out of the lace panties she'd put on after she showered, deodorized, gargled, gelled her hair, glossed her lips in scarlet red, and spritzed with just enough body cologne in all the right places.

The unmitigated gall. Was she supposed to swoon when he snuck up behind her in the kitchen and put his arms around her and whispered something sweet in her ear? Did he expect her to lead him by the hand to her bedroom where she'd do a quick striptease: first, the white stretch camisole, then her only pushup bra, and finally the black leather pants she'd saved for the most special occasions.

And then he'd expect her to fuck his brains out.

How totally presumptuous.

How completely shameful.

How utterly delightful.

Crowder refocused. Her libido, having momentarily roared, eventually ebbed. Then the two of them worked like a newly-married couple—each performing a meaningful function. Crowder handled the food preparation, Hill the beverages.

They made easy conversation over dinner, talking about their lives growing up—Hill, the only son of a father who was a career mailman for the United States Postal Service, and a mother who raised him and two younger sisters while doing hair and manicures from a makeshift salon in the basement of their row home in South Baltimore.

Hill went to college on an athletic scholarship, and then law school, funding his education with student loans and a variety of jobs—always sending money home to his family. He'd married his high school sweetheart—losing her and their young sons in a six-vehicle pileup on the interstate during a blinding summer thunderstorm.

Crowder reminisced about her life growing up in the small town of Breaux Bridge, the oldest child of a father who was a career cop and afterward the twice-elected sheriff of St. Martin Parish, and a mother who was a stay-at-home parent until she died from injuries in a car crash when Crowder was a teenager. Afterward, Crowder spent her time playing surrogate mother to her four younger brothers. She played a "ton of sports," learned martial arts, kickboxing and judo and, like Hill, competed as a boxer.

Crowder saw the similarities. Both of them had shouldered adult responsibilities at an early age, worked hard their entire lives, dedicated their careers to public service, and experienced the sadness of losing loved ones.

She felt a closeness to Hill—a special kinship. Their lives had suddenly become intertwined. Was it fate or just dumb luck that brought Hill to New Orleans? Either way, Crowder was happy for the chance of feeling close to someone again … or maybe for the first time in her life.

When dinner was over and they'd narrated their biographies, Crowder's mind redirected to work. She'd felt uncomfortable calling Hill by his last name when he arrived for dinner. He must have sensed her reticence because, to Crowder's surprise, he began calling her "Jo," as if he'd known her all his life. She called him "Alex" at her very next opportunity.

The change in salutations brought a familiarity to the relationship that pleased Crowder, and she sensed it pleased him too.

"Alex, there's been three deaths in the last two months in or near New Orleans—a homicide and two accidental deaths—all involving people in their late sixties. All were my cases. Recently, a man contacted me about the deaths."

She summarized the facts. How Marshall had contacted her. How she'd learned from his partner that he was working for three life insurance companies to investigate claims for the proceeds of five-million-dollar double indemnity life insurance policies. How she'd contacted the families and learned that the beneficiaries of the policies weren't relatives of the insureds.

"So what does the connection mean other than that there are three beneficiaries out there who'll be receiving an incredible amount of non-taxable money?" Hill asked.

"In each case, the people who died had sold their policy because they needed money," Crowder explained. "Moss, capital to fund his farm operations; Hartman, money to maintain a lavish lifestyle; and Helmsley, cash to pay off gambling debts."

"So?" Hill prodded.

"Alex, all three policies were bought by Heartland Insurance in the last two years. It was then that the double indemnity endorsements were added to the policies. It's the sole beneficiary of claims that will pay a total of thirty million dollars." Crowder paused a moment to reflect, then verbalized what she was thinking. "What are the chances of the same company buying three five-million-dollar, double indemnity life insurance policies in the last two years and having the insureds die within two months of each other?"

Hill answered the rhetorical question. "About the same chances as someone winning the Louisiana lottery three times in the same year."

~

A half hour later, the table was cleared, and the plates were in the sink. Hill had moved about the kitchen like an experienced restaurant worker. Crowder would've been content to leave the dishes in the sink for her to deal with later. But Hill was insistent that she dry while he washed.

She wondered how the evening would end as they cleaned up in silence.

"I don't want to overstay my welcome, Jo," Hill said as he wiped the kitchen counter dry with a dish cloth. "But if you'll join me in a nightcap, I'd like to say some things to you."

Crowder suddenly felt warm. She felt an uptick in her heartbeat and wondered if she was blushing. She hated feeling like this. It made her vulnerable. She worried that she might do something she seldom did—think with her heart rather than her head.

She liked Hill—a lot. He was brash and bold, upfront and honest. Not the type of person who'd ever bullshit her. But what did he want to say to her? His words were as cryptic as Marshall's calendar entry.

"Sure, Alex," she said, suddenly dry-mouthed.

"Is the living room all right with you?" Hill asked, refilling Crowder's glass.

"Of course," she replied demurely.

He poured himself another drink and followed her from the kitchen.

The living room had a new sofa and two matching chairs that Crowder had picked up at a secondhand store. She passed by the chairs and sat on one end of the sofa. How would Hill react? Would he sit in one of the chairs or on the sofa with her?

He chose the sofa, sat on the other end, and fixed his gaze on her.

Crowder suddenly felt like she wasn't the one in control, which was out of character for her. She was the dominant one in relationships with men. The alpha female. If she intended to be intimate with a man, she'd be flirtatious and forward to a fault. The men lacked control, not her. And she'd always had her way with the men she was sexually attracted to—they'd end up in bed with her in due course without having to be cuffed to the bedposts … unless they wanted to be.

Hill was different. He was so much in control that she felt like a weak-in-the-knees schoolgirl who'd been asked to the prom by the most popular boy in the school.

Crowder wanted to regain control. "So what do you want to say to me, Alex." She hoped her tone of voice wasn't too meek, too timid.

"I want to tell you something about me that I've only told to one other person."

Crowder put her glass on the table and looked into Hill's eyes as he spoke.

"When Sasha, my wife, and my sons were killed in the car accident, I had a very bad time of it. I blamed myself. I was supposed to pick up our boys from school. Something came up at work ... something, in retrospect, unimportant. I asked Sasha to leave her job. She worked as a reporter for the Baltimore Sun. She was where she was that day because of me.

"I was a very angry man for a long time. I was intolerant of others, critical of their shortcomings—or at least of what I perceived as weaknesses on their part. I lobbied for the most dangerous assignments and dragged other agents with me, often putting them unnecessarily in harm's way."

"You were just doing your job," Crowder said empathetically.

"No. I was reckless, and my behavior had tragic consequences. I was working undercover. I'd infiltrated a Miami drug operation that was working for the Cortez cartel. Breaking protocol, and acting on my own, I stole some Cortez drug money and planted it at the home of a local businessman who did the laundering for the cartel. I wanted to scare him into ratting out the cartel. I didn't realize the person was an informant working for us.

"He was found the next day in the trunk of his car—his hands and feet cut off, his eyes gouged out, his tongue gone. The sting operations went south. A total bust. And I'd caused a man to be tortured to death."

"You didn't know he was working for the FBI," Crowder said supportively.

"I didn't know for a reason," Hill said in an uneasy tone of voice. "Protocol was for informants to be known to field agents on a need-to-know basis. I didn't need to know—it was that simple."

"So who else knows about what happened?"

"My supervisor. He told me to keep it to myself. He saved me from being booted out of the agency. But I've had to live with that mistake ever since it happened."

"Why tell me, Alex?"

"I wanted you to know that I acted recklessly in Hanson. I could've gotten you killed—almost did get you killed. As it turned out, you saved my life when you shot the redneck and pulled me from the car."

"And you saved my life, by carrying me away from the car before it exploded. Alex … that's what partners do—they protect each other no matter the consequences." She wondered if she was being unduly idealistic and naïve. O'Malley and Steele thought Hill had acted recklessly in Hanson—had put their lives in jeopardy. For a while, so had she.

Hill had revealed to her the demons that tormented him. It was his way of telling her that he hadn't yet recovered from the emotional trauma of the death of his wife and sons, or the psychological injury he suffered when his actions caused someone to suffer an ignominious death.

Crowder wanted to be with Hill that night, and she sensed he wanted to be with her. But it was too soon for him to get close to another person—more so when he felt responsible for that person's safety. Perhaps someday he'd bury his sorrow and grief with the bodies of those who had died on his watch. Perhaps then he could once again trust another person—not only with his life … but also with his heart.

Chapter 29

Hill and Crowder sat in a conference room at the FBI's field office in Mobile. They were there to review the findings of the FBI's investigations into the deaths of Cletus Moss, Olivia Hartman, and Nathan Helmsley.

Crowder was certain that Robert Marshall was murdered because he was investigating Heartland Insurance's connection to the three deaths. She'd retrieved the garage security camera recordings of the last day Marshall worked. The camera didn't capture him walking to his car. According to building security, the lens had been intentionally redirected. The cameras did show his Prius leave the garage. A hand reached out to insert a keycard. It showed the sleeve of the suit jacket Marshall had worn that day and the watch his wife had given him as a gift on their twenty-fifth wedding anniversary. Crowder was skeptical. She reviewed the recordings for the entire week. A white van entered the garage just after Marshall's Prius on three days of the week he went missing, and left shortly after he went home after work.

Hill agreed to open federal investigations into the deaths of the three victims. The FBI had the resources to do more thorough investigations. He headed a team of field agents who interviewed family members and persons of interest. CSI technicians went to Moss's farmhouse and Hartman's mansion to look for evidence the intruders might have left behind that had been overlooked by the NOPD. Helmsley's car was inspected by a forensic team. They did simulations and reconstructions of the three incidents.

On the table in front of Hill were the three FBI files of the investigations.

"I'll take them one by one in the order in which they died," Hill said. "Forensics came up with nothing when they went to Moss's farmhouse. It was too late to do additional impressions of the footprints in the ground. But after studying the impressions your evidence technician took, we were able to determine that the intruder was five feet eight / five feet nine inches tall and weighed between 135 and 140 pounds. The person could be a woman.

"We analyzed the particles of grass and mulch found inside the house beneath the window. The grass had microscopic evidence of soil on the ends, indicating that the blades were pulled from the ground. The pieces of mulch were too large to have embedded in the soles of the shoes the intruder was wearing. We concluded the evidence was put there by the intruder to make it look like an everyday break-in.

"Our ballistic team determined that the bullets removed from the wood paneling came from a Sig Sauer P226—a handgun used by Special Forces.

"We reconstructed the angle of Moss's hand with the trajectory of the bullet from his Colt revolver. The shot wasn't made from a standing position. If he'd been standing, the bullet would've gone into the ceiling."

Crowder frowned. "So he had to be kneeling or lying on the floor when he got the shot off."

"Yes, he would've been lying on the floor."

"Which is impossible," Crowder deduced. "He was shot while standing and a dead man by the time he hit the floor."

"Right. And the partial palm print on the gun suggests that Moss's grip on the handle wasn't firm enough for him to have fired the shot."

"But there were powder burns on his hand," Crowder said, thinking out loud about what her forensics people had found. "Moss had the gun in his hand when it was fired," she continued, then paused a moment, "unless the gun was placed in his hand and fired into the wall while he lay dead on the floor."

Hill nodded. "The absence of powder burns on the back of his hand means that someone held Moss's finger over the trigger when the gun was fired. The scene was staged by one or more professionals—to make it look like a single intruder broke into the house and had no choice but to shoot Moss. That way, they excluded the possibility that paid assassins came that night with only one purpose—to kill Moss."

"It bothered me that two shots were so precisely made milliseconds apart," Crowder added. "Each wound was nearly instantly fatal. Those shots were fired by an expert marksman."

Hill put down his copy of the report. "Yes. That was the last of our findings."

Crowder's first impression of felony murder—an unintended homicide committed during a robbery—was the hurried conclusion the assassins wanted the police to reach. Once the focus was on whether the incident was staged, the investigation took on an entirely different perspective.

Before her meeting with Hill, Crowder had reconsidered the Hartman accident as if it was a staged murder. "Before you go over your findings on Hartman," she said, "let me give you my impressions after I reviewed my file a second time. Knowing that she was probably murdered, a slip and fall became a push and fall from the top of the staircase."

Hill put down the FBI's report on Olivia Hartman. "What did you conclude after a second look?"

"The toxicology report suddenly became proof of murder. I reviewed it again with the medical examiner, who agrees with me. Hartman was taking ten milligrams of Ambien at bedtime. That's twice the recommended dosage for women her age. The half-life of the drug found in her blood made it unlikely she'd be awake and out of bed at the time of her death."

"Precisely what our forensic toxicologist concluded," Hill confirmed.

Crowder finished with an observation. "I thought it odd that there were no tea stains on Hartman's robe if she dropped the tray when she fell down the stairs."

A smile of satisfaction lit Hill's face. "Our reconstruction of Hartman dropping the tray as she fell down the steps had the tea set pieces scattered much differently. The absence of tea stains on her robe meant that she was either pushed down the stairs before the tray was dropped, or she was flung over the tea-set debris afterward."

"What did your forensic pathologist conclude was the cause of death?" Crowder asked.

"That she died from a broken neck, but not the kind you see from a tumble down steps. Those fractures are usually lower in the cervical spine, not high up like they were in Hartman's spine."

"She was alive after the fall," Crowder deduced. "Someone snapped her neck and tore the spinal cord."

"A technique some Special Forces units are trained to perform," Hill said.

He handed Crowder a copy of the FBI's findings on Nathan Helmsley's accident. "I know you disagreed with the finding of accidental death—and you were right, of course. Our simulation of the accident, using a man of nearly Helmsley's height and weight, showed that it was impossible for him to exit through the side window or the sunroof. The car was driven into the river upstream from where his dead body had been placed."

Crowder reached the same conclusion as Hill. "All three were murdered by assassins—probably former members of our Special Forces."

"Hanratty spent most of his military career as a member of the Delta Force," Hill reminded Crowder. "He'd know how to recruit them."

Crowder sighed. "You know what this means, Alex."

"I know what this means," Hill said. "Heartland Insurance is in the business of committing premeditated murders for profit."

Chapter 30

Goldman spoke into his cell phone from the main parlor of Finch's home. "Jared, I'm worried about Christine."

The colonel stood beside him. The phone was on speaker so Hanratty could listen in.

"Why are you worried, Martin?" Finch said from his luxury suite at the historic Hay-Adams Hotel overlooking Lafayette Square with a view of the White House. "Is she in some kind of trouble?"

Goldman understood Finch's first impression. Christine's recurrent misdeeds proved that she hadn't learned from history and was doomed to repeat the mistakes of her past. Goldman had resolved a number of disputes with shop owners and police—her penchant for shoplifting, speeding, and substance abuse had required his intervention.

"She didn't show up at the gallery tonight," Goldman continued. "Her works were being exhibited. She was supposed to give a welcoming speech. When she didn't return my calls and text messages, I went to the house. She wasn't there. Her car was gone."

"When did you last have contact with her?"

"About three this afternoon. I called her to see if she wanted me to pick her up. She told me she'd drive herself and meet me there. And you, Jared?"

"This morning around eight, just before I left the house for the airport for my flight here. I had dinner with the senator and his cronies this evening, and got back to my room an hour ago."

"Jared, it's almost ten. We haven't heard from her for seven hours. Maybe we should get the police involved?"

"Colonel, what do you think?" Finch asked.

Hanratty moved closer to Goldman. "The police won't get actively involved until she's been gone the night. I'll call the ERs and check with the NOPD and state police. See if she's been in an accident … or has been detained for something."

Detained for something. The words resounded in Goldman's mind. The colonel viewed Christine as Finch's most significant liability. He openly referred to her as "Jared's problem child." Finch's wife detested the colonel. She'd complained to Goldman that he was always checking up on her and snooping around. That was another good reason for Goldman to bolt from the inner circle sooner than later. It was only a matter of time before the colonel discovered her infidelity—and his involvement.

"I'll check the security recordings and see when she left the house," Hanratty proposed. "If there's anything suspicious, I'll call you right away, and you can decide what you want to do."

"Good. We have a plan. Martin, you wait at the house for the colonel to check the … wait, hold on. Christine just texted me."

An eerie moment of silence followed—like everyone was frozen in place and holding their breath.

Goldman's anxious voice cut through the quiet. "Jared, is Christine all right? What did she text you?"

Seconds felt like minutes. The only sound Goldman heard was his breathing into his cell phone.

"The message isn't from Christine," Finch replied calmly.

"I don't understand," Goldman said, perplexed. "It's from *her* phone, isn't it?"

"Colonel, I think we'll have to get the police involved sooner rather than later," Finch said.

"Jared, what does the message say?" Goldman demanded.

"I'll read it, Martin, just as it's written—*We have your wife. Instructions will follow.*"

~

"So this ex-military guy who works for Heartland Insurance called the mayor, who called the superintendent, who called me—which is why I called you." O'Malley sat behind his desk, shirt sleeves rolled up to the elbows, top button undone, tie loosened, and muscly forearms folded across a robust chest. An interior lineman on his high school football team, O'Malley's squat but sturdy frame supported two hundred thirty pounds—his weight when he played football. He'd lost twenty-five pounds four years ago after he suffered his second heart attack in three years.

"Finch's wife's been taken," he continued. "Her abductors want ten million dollars. Otherwise, she's coming home to him in pieces."

Crowder stood with her hands gripping the back of the chair in front of O'Malley's desk. "Why the honor?" she asked, knowing that her escapades with Hill in Hanson must have gotten back to Finch and the colonel.

"He wants our best detective and, at least for now, you are our best detective. Steele's your backup if you need him. But I want you to keep a low profile."

"Just curious. Did the colonel suggest me?"

"In a word—yes. You must have made an impression on him when you visited Heartland Insurance."

"Did it occur to you that his intention might be to set me up to fail."

"Then don't fail. Finch is prepared to pay the ransom. All you need to do is nursemaid him until his wife is returned." O'Malley put his hands on his desk and took a long, deep breath. "I thought you'd be jumping up and down at the opportunity to get up front and personal with Finch. After all, his company is the target of a federal investigation."

Crowder released her grip on the chair and stood erect. "Unless he feels that if something goes wrong, he'll have me to blame. You know, compromise my investigation of his company's involvement in the deaths of three people who had something in common."

"What three people?"

"Cletus Moss, Olivia Hartman and Nathan Helmsley."

"What did they have in common that involved Finch's company?"

"They all had double indemnity life insurance policies that named Heartland Insurance the sole beneficiary."

Crowder spent the next five minutes summarizing the FBI reports on the three deaths. She paused a moment and stared into her boss's face, trying to read his mind from his facial expression—always hard to do when you're looking into the face of a bulldog. She ended with, "Thirty million dollars is a hell of a motive."

O'Malley sat poker face for a moment, then said, "You're saying that Heartland Insurance is bumping off people for their insurance money. But all that you have are a possible motive and a lot of unproven theories. Is there any evidence linking Finch or anyone at his company to any of the deaths?"

"Not yet. It's complicated. The killings were done by professionals—military types, probably trained in black ops. The colonel, Finch's right-hand man, would know how to recruit them."

"All speculation on your part," O'Malley said dismissively. "For now, we have the wife of a prominent businessman who's been kidnapped. Your job is to make sure she gets back to Finch unharmed. He was in Washington, DC, when she was abducted. He took a red-eye back last night and is waiting for you. The colonel wants you to come alone in your personal vehicle in case someone is watching the house. Enter through the rear gate. An empty garage will be left open. Park in it."

"And Moss, Hartman, and Helmsley?"

"Two accidental deaths and a murder case that's gone cold," O'Malley replied curtly. "If Hill feels otherwise, let him make a federal case out of it."

"I'd like to have the medical examiner hold up issuing certified death certificates in the three cases. It will delay the payment of the insurance proceeds. I want to turn up the heat on the frying pan."

"They're still your cases. You do what you need to do—*after* you get Finch's wife home safely."

"I'm on it," Crowder assured her boss.

"One more thing."

"What?"

"You almost got yourself killed in Hanson. Don't be the one who jumps from the frying pan into the fire."

Chapter 31

Crowder drove to Finch's home in her four-year-old pickup truck with forty-five thousand hard miles on it. She bought the truck new. Same make and model as the one she'd traded in. It was as jet-black as her hair—cut in a short pixie bob for as long as she could remember. Crowder didn't much like change. Particularly things that had worked well for her in the past.

She needed the reliable all-terrain vehicle because she frequently spent her vacation days traveling to nearly inaccessible recesses of the national parks of Utah, Wyoming, and Colorado, where she camped under the steep, sheer rock faces she'd come to climb. Crowder liked the solitude of the campouts as much as the challenges she faced ascending walls of granite. It was the one activity where the only rules were ones she created, and the only limitations were ones she imposed. If breaking rules or exceeding limitations caused her to fall to her death, she would only have herself to blame.

She liked controlling her destiny.

She'd thought about taking a few days off after the fiasco in Hanson. A rock climb might have cleared her head of her near-fatal adventure with Hill. Without the help of the other, both would be dead—blown to pieces and burned to ash. So much was left to chance. If one of them had been knocked senseless when their car crashed, neither would've been saved. Plan B would've ended with honor-guard funerals at the government's expense.

The misadventure weighed on Crowder's mind even as Finch's mansion came into view. She hadn't told Hill that their nemesis had invited her into his life. She had no reason to. Not yet. Unless there were interstate connections, the FBI didn't have primary jurisdiction in an adult kidnapping case. They had to play a supportive role.

Finch's Victorian mansion sat on a three-acre, meticulously landscaped parcel of land. Built in 1873, the fenced and gated residence was the third-oldest private home in the Garden District of New Orleans, one of the most iconic neighborhoods in the country. A Who's Who list of actors, artists, writers, jazz musicians, rappers, and entrepreneurs lived there with two things in common—they were wealthy, and they valued their privacy.

Crowder entered through a gate at the rear of the property and parked in an open garage as instructed.

The colonel met her. "I just got back. No one's watching the house—at least not yet. But we can't be too careful."

"I took a turn through the neighborhood too," Crowder said. "I saw nothing suspicious."

Crowder followed Hanratty into the house through a door on the terrace. Finch and Goldman sat on a sofa in the main parlor. Finch introduced himself but remained seated, while Goldman stood and introduced himself as Finch's close friend. No handshakes. Standard police protocol that Crowder knew everyone in the room understood.

The colonel left the room.

Finch waved his hand in the direction of two empty chairs across from him. An ornate marble-top coffee table lay in between. Crowder sat in the one directly across from Finch and did a quick study of him as he explained what they knew of his wife's abduction the day before. A confident, self-assured man, she deduced. Someone used to being in charge. A person quite capable of handling any crisis in his personal life and business affairs dispassionately. Someone not easily unnerved. A man who was calm and deliberate in the actions he took.

The colonel returned to the room and sat in the chair next to Crowder.

Finch reached across the table and handed Crowder a sheet of paper. "These are the text messages from my wife's phone that I received last night. I had them printed for you."

Crowder read them in chronological order.

Christine Finch
9:52 p.m.
We have your wife. Instructions will follow.
Jared Finch
9:54 p.m.
Is she all right?
Christine Finch
9:55 p.m.
For now. No more texts from you. No calls. Only respond to my texts with a yes or no. Understood?
Jared Finch
9:55 p.m.
Yes.
Christine Finch
9:57 p.m.
Your wife is being held in Louisiana. You are to send an emissary who will confirm that your wife has not been harmed. You will be instructed on how to find them after ten million dollars is

wired to an offshore account. Emissary will bring with him all necessary information to make an online wire transfer of the funds from your personal account to the offshore account tomorrow at 2 p.m. Emissary is to come alone. No cell phones, weapons, wires or tracking devices. No police. Violations of instructions will result in the execution of wife and emissary. Further instructions to follow. Understood?
Jared Finch
9:58 p.m.
Yes.

Crowder looked up at Finch when she finished. She glanced at an antique grandfather's clock. "Mr. Finch, it's eleven-thirty. Is it your intention to pay the ransom?"

"Of course," Finch replied. "I'll do everything in my power to secure my wife's release."

"Can you get that much money today by two this afternoon?"

"It's already in my account."

"Did you try tracking your wife's cell phone using the GPS locator?" Crowder asked.

Hanratty spoke up. "It's been turned off."

Crowder pulled out a pen from an inside pocket of her blazer and put it on the table next to the printout of the text messages. "I need your wife's cell phone number. I want to have the calls triangulated by her service provider. It may help us locate the phone … and her."

Finch wrote down the information on the printout.

"Do you have an emissary?" Crowder asked.

Goldman answered for Finch. "It's been decided. I'm going. Christine will be frightened. She knows me and will trust me when I tell her that Jared has everything worked out."

"You could be walking into a trap," Crowder warned. "Once

the wire transfer goes through, nothing prevents them from doing away with the only evidence there is against them … and killing both of you."

Goldman was emphatic. "Jared and I are willing to take that chance."

Finch leaned forward in his chair. "I'd do it myself, of course. But they've instructed me to send an emissary with my banking information so that they can do the wire transfer themselves."

Crowder's eyes widened. "I could be the emissary," she proposed. "They may see a woman as less threatening to them. If something went wrong, I'd have a better chance of protecting your wife."

Crowder knew the risks in kidnapping cases. Even when ransoms were paid, it was a crapshoot whether the hostage would be returned alive and unharmed. The notorious kidnapping of Charles Lindbergh's twenty-month-old son from the nursery of their New Jersey home ended tragically when, after the ransom was paid in full, the child's corpse was discovered by the side of a nearby road.

Goldman shifted forward in his chair, gripped the arms with his hands, and glared at Crowder. "You're likely to get Christine and yourself killed," he said angrily. "The kidnappers will suspect you're law enforcement. Why would Jared Finch send a woman as his emissary and put her in harm's way. I'm the best chance Christine has of returning unharmed."

"Martin's quite right," Finch concurred. "The subterfuge is likely to be uncovered, putting Christine at risk."

Crowder understood their concerns. If they suspected the emissary was a cop, they might believe there was a plan in place to apprehend them. The fear of never seeing a penny of the ransom money could easily lead them to commit a double homicide.

Still, she needed to warn Goldman of the risks of confronting kidnappers who were bold enough to pull off a ten-million-dollar robbery. "Sir, if you show up and Christine's abductors haven't disguised their identities, you will be walking into a trap. I'm quite certain of that. And after they use you to get the ransom, you … and Mrs. Finch … will be expendable."

"I don't care," Goldman protested. "There are no alternatives that make sense. We have to hope they will be wearing disguises, are true to their word, and release us after the wire transfer is made."

Crowder's eyes redirected to Finch. "It's your call who you want to send. But allow me to tail Goldman. I'll be in my pickup truck. I know how to remain inconspicuous."

"Well then, we have a plan. Martin will go as my emissary. I've provided him with the account information he's been instructed to bring. You will follow him in your vehicle. But I warn you. Do nothing to apprehend anyone until Christine is safely in your custody."

The ping on Finch's cell phone that lay on the table signaled the receipt of an incoming text message. Crowder followed Finch's hands and eyes as he accessed and read it. Before Finch said anything, he used his thumbs to respond with a three-letter word.

Crowder knew the word was "Yes."

Chapter 32

The text message from Christine Finch's cell phone read: *Taxi will arrive at noon to pick up emissary. Do you understand?*

The clock chimed at the quarter hour.

Finch looked at Goldman. "The taxi will be here in fifteen minutes. Are you ready?"

"I'm ready," he replied confidently.

"Aren't you forgetting something, Martin?"

"What, Jared?"

"Your cell phone. Remember the instructions we were given. Leave it with the colonel."

The colonel reached out his hand with a resolute look on his face.

Goldman hesitated a moment before he reached into a side pocket of his jacket for his phone and gave it to Hanratty.

Crowder understood Goldman's reluctance to part with his phone. It was his only way to call for help. But she sensed his hesitation was more an unwillingness to give it to the colonel than leave it behind.

Goldman might be having second thoughts. "Without a cell phone, you'll be on your own with no means of communication,"

Crowder cautioned.

Her warning did nothing to shake Goldman's resolve to be the one who rescued Finch's wife.

Finch was content to let him.

Goldman stood. "I'll wait for the taxi by a window in front of the house."

Crowder got up from her chair, approached Goldman and said, "One thing I want you to do when the taxi gets to its destination."

"What's that?"

"Pay with a credit card. It will leave a paper trail to the taxi and who called for it."

"Good luck, Martin," Crowder heard Finch say as she followed Goldman out of the parlor to go to her vehicle.

She found Finch's words eerily ominous. Finch's emissary was on his way to confront kidnappers who had too much to lose to leave witnesses behind.

Goldman would need more than luck.

A lot more.

~

The clock chimed twelve. The colonel closed the double doors to the parlor. Finch remained seated and watched Hanratty speed dial someone on his cell phone.

"They just left," he said to the person he'd called.

~

Crowder followed the taxi into the city. The traffic was lighter than she expected, until they reached the French Quarter. There, it was usually bumper-to-bumper midday during the week, and today was no different. She stayed two cars back.

Where was Goldman being taken?

The dispatcher must've been told the destination beforehand—*unless the driver was in on it.* Crowder used a ballpoint pen to write the license number of the taxi on the back of her hand. She couldn't see the driver's face, and it was too risky to pull up alongside the taxi for a look. "Keep a low profile," O'Malley had warned her. If the kidnappers knew a cop was tailing Finch's emissary, the infraction could have deadly consequences. If it ended badly, Crowder would be the one left holding an empty bag.

The taxi proceeded down Bourbon Street into the heart of the jazz capital of the world. Perpetually abuzz with street musicians, vendors, and pickpockets, the mania began late morning and really never ended. Every day, locals and tourists poured into the clubs, bars, and strip joints that littered both sides of Bourbon Street. The party atmosphere and binge drinking kept the police busy arresting the drunk and disorderly. The end result? The French Quarter was the most heavily policed district in the city.

Could Christine Finch be hidden there?

It would've been a bold move for the kidnappers to hide her in plain sight. The abductors would blend with the crowds that walked the streets daily. An errant scream by their captive—even a gunshot—might go unnoticed. A woman's wailing could be smothered by the cacophony of sounds that engulfed the airspace of the French Quarter.

Still, a crowded city would be a difficult place from which to escape if something went wrong.

Crowder's mind conjured a more likely scenario. Goldman was on his way to meet someone—perhaps one of the kidnappers. If it was one of Christine's abductors, he'd be in a disguise so it would be difficult for Goldman to identify him later. That person would take him to his final destination, most likely a house in the rural outskirts of the city where neighbors were few and far away. If the kidnappers weren't also in disguises and allowed Christine Finch and Goldman to see their faces, it would seal their fate—neither one would be coming home alive.

Crowder believed that the kidnappers were clever and lucky. So far, at least. It was a good idea to abduct Christine while Finch was away on a trip. But to have taken her during the daylight hours while she was driving her car through the city meant they were lucky not to be seen. It made more sense to kidnap her from her bed while she slept and leave under the cover of darkness. But they'd need to disarm the security cameras and alarm system at Finch's home—a skill they may not have possessed.

They knew to disable the GPS locator on Christine's cell phone, and were clever in using it to text, not call Finch. No voice identification. No handwriting or fingerprints on ransom notes. Using Christine's cell phone to communicate with Finch, and her unexplained absence, proved they had his wife.

It was smart to have the ransom money wired to an offshore account. There was no limit on the amount of money that could be wired out of the country. No in-person exchange of the captive for the money like in the movies. No traceable currency. It allowed them to demand ten million dollars. That amount of cash would be difficult to move out of the country.

Kudos to them for wanting to make the transfer remotely using online banking. No chance of a screwup on Finch's end. The transaction could be made using Christine's cell phone, leaving no trail to another mobile device. And by the time law enforcement was able to locate and legally freeze transactions from the offshore account, the money will have been withdrawn and the account closed.

One thing Crowder found perplexing.

Why have Finch send an emissary?

If Finch demanded proof that his wife was alive and unharmed, all that they had to do was remove the duct tape from her mouth and have her speak into her phone. Once the ransom was paid, the kidnappers could have released their captive somewhere in a wooded area with her cell phone. Enabling the GPS locator on her phone would lead the police to her. And the kidnappers could have had Finch send the account information in a text message or email to Christine's cell phone instead of involving an intermediary. One less body to dispose of if their intention was to leave no evidence—or witnesses—behind.

No matter how Crowder looked at it, it didn't make sense to send an emissary.

The taxi proceeded down Bourbon Street until the Saint Louis Cathedral, one of New Orleans's most notable landmarks, came into view. Its triple steeples looked down on Jackson Square, where the bronze statue of Confederate General Andrew Jackson stood guard.

As they approached the square, the taxi stopped at a red light at Orleans Avenue. When the light turned green, the taxi turned left, but the car behind it didn't move. A moment later, Crowder honked her horn. The vehicle had stalled. Its driver, a woman, cranked the engine several times but couldn't restart it. A car behind Crowder prevented her from backing up—she was sandwiched between the two vehicles.

Each second that passed put the taxi farther from her and closer to its destination. The man in the vehicle behind Crowder went to the woman's aid. He asked her to pop the hood. She did as requested, and then got out of her car to watch what he was doing.

Crowder left her truck, hurried to the corner, and looked down Orleans Avenue. The taxi was already a block away.

The man appeared to be adjusting the battery cables of the woman's car when Crowder walked back to her truck. She heard the man tell the woman to get into her car and start the engine. Crowder stopped only long enough to tell the woman she was a police officer and needed her to drive away immediately. When the engine roared to a start, the man closed the hood and the car drove on.

By the time Crowder turned onto Orleans Avenue, the taxi was no longer in sight, and traffic in front of her slowed her passage through the intersections. She looked down every one of them, but the taxi was gone.

So was her only chance of finding where Finch's wife was held captive.

Chapter 33

Goldman had looked out the rear window every few minutes when the taxi entered the French Quarter. When they'd left Finch's home, he asked the driver how best to lose the pickup truck that was following them. The French Quarter deep in traffic at midday was his answer.

The taxi proceeded from inner city to the interstate, exiting just outside city limits. Two miles later, the driver pulled into a strip mall—a graveyard of businesses that couldn't handle recessions and competition. The survivors—half of the ten stores—were representative of the kind of businesses that thrived no matter what—a laundromat, nail salon, barbershop, pizza parlor, and Dollar Store. Marginal profits meant faded signs and peeling paint—only the graffiti was freshly spray-painted.

The driver dropped Goldman off in the middle of the off-street parking area in front of the stores. He paid the thirty-eight-dollar fare with a hundred-dollar bill and told the driver to keep the change and his mouth shut. The driver smiled and drove off.

Goldman looked to his right and left. No one was milling about. Several cars and a pizza-delivery vehicle occupied a few of the parking places that lined the storefronts. A late-model Lincoln sedan was parked in a space at an end of the complex. It looked out of place in front of the boarded-up storefront window of a vacant building. Goldman pulled an electronic key from his pocket as he walked toward it. One squeeze and the doors unlocked.

Ten minutes later, Goldman was driving northeast into the heart of bayou country.

As he proceeded deeper and deeper into the seclusion of Louisiana's marshland and swamps, Goldman had only one thought on his mind—getting to Christine Finch as soon as possible.

His mind recapped the day's events. He had to shake Crowder. Her decision to follow him was reckless. He was surprised that Finch allowed the detective to follow the taxi. The instructions in the text message were clear. *No police.* Crowder had broken the rules.

She'd jeopardized the plan, and he couldn't allow that to happen. It was too dangerous. For Christine … and for him.

Finch didn't send the colonel to rescue his wife, even though he was the logical choice—a military man trained to subdue and, if necessary, kill combatants with his bare hands. Goldman knew why Finch chose him instead—he was expendable.

So was Christine.

Finch had never loved Christine. Not like Goldman loved her. He would sacrifice everything—even his life—for her. But to Finch, Christine was nothing more than a trophy wife. Another possession—like his Lamborghini, his stately mansion, and his helicopter.

The colonel wasn't sent because he was … indispensable. Finch's right arm. The quarterback on a team Finch owned, managed, and coached. Finch called the plays, the colonel executed them. Finch needed to keep his *executioner* close.

The colonel, more than any other member of the inner circle, had the highest security clearance. He shared Finch's deepest, darkest, dirtiest secrets. And most of all, he knew how to fix things—and solve problems. Like Brian McManus, Jason Crockett, and Robert Marshall.

Finch was the colonel's commander in chief. He had his undivided loyalty. The colonel had never questioned Finch's orders—not once. Goldman believed he never would.

He also felt that Heartland was a ship adrift and taking on water. It was only a matter of time before the Internal Revenue Service audited the company. Unaccounted for were millions of dollars of life insurance proceeds of people who had died much earlier than expected—hidden in offshore accounts. Indictments for tax evasion and bank fraud were inevitable.

It would get worse.

Heartland's connection to Kratos would uncover the algorithm and the malignant business practices of a company founded on greed that was evil at its core. If necessary, the colonel was willing to go down with a sinking ship.

Goldman was not.

~

The fishing cabin sat on a lot that bordered a slow-moving tributary of Lake Pontchartrain, an hour drive from New Orleans in a secluded area of a bayou, with the nearest habitable shelter more than a mile away. The unpaved road snaked its way through a forest of bald cypress trees covered by thick Spanish moss that hung like hair from their limbs. The dense vegetation and dark, murky waters made it the perfect habitat for alligators, turtles, egrets, pelicans, venomous snakes, and more than a hundred species of inedible fish. A place for humans to visit, not live in.

A perfect place to hold a kidnap victim captive.

Goldman turned the rental car into a driveway defined by tire tracks etched into dirt. It curved enough to nearly keep the cabin invisible from the road. He lowered the windows when he approached, but heard no voices, no sign of people, only the chatter of indigenous wildlife and the uneven sputter of a generator behind the cabin. The musky, acrid smell of stagnant swamp water and diesel fuel hung heavy in the breezeless, humid air. Goldman coughed and cleared his throat.

The windows on either side of the windowless prefabricated front door had the shades pulled down. He drove past and parked alongside the cabin behind another vehicle. Goldman got out and peered through a side window into a single room in the front of the cabin and a small kitchen in the back, both unoccupied. A bathroom and bedroom bookended the kitchen, both with doors open. Weathered throw rugs covered walkways between hand-me-down furniture in what served as the principal living area.

He proceeded around back to the bedroom window that looked out to the water behind the cabin. Two carry-on bags rested on the floor in a corner of the room. A body lay still on a double bed—a woman dressed in a khaki pantsuit with wavy golden locks spread evenly over her shoulders.

Goldman entered the cabin through the unlocked kitchen door and walked softly into the bedroom. At the edge of the bed, he leaned over—slowly, so as not to abruptly wake the sleeping beauty from a deep and restful slumber—and inhaled the sweet smell of a familiar perfume. He looked into her face as he'd done many times before—always with undying love in his heart and insatiable lust in his thoughts. He bent over and kissed Christine

Finch on the lips.

His lover's eyelids rose like window shades pulled up. Her shamrock-pastel eyes locked on Goldman's face, and a smile came to her face … and to his.

"We did it," were the last words Goldman heard Christine Finch say before a bullet blew a hole the size of a quarter in the back of his head.

Chapter 34

"I was given assurances that you were the NOPD's best detective," Finch scoffed. "Yet here we are, my wife is still missing, and I've paid a king's ransom to her abductors."

Crowder stood in the center of the parlor at Finch's home being scolded like a child who'd come home from school with poor grades on her report card. She'd spent an hour trying to locate the taxi and had spoken to the dispatcher at the taxi company office. When she'd finished, she headed over to see Finch.

The housekeeper had brought Crowder into the room where Finch and Hanratty sat on the sofa. No one stood when she entered or offered her a seat.

It wasn't a social visit.

It had been a half hour since the wire transfer went through. Still no word from Goldman or Finch's wife.

"Bad luck. No one could have foreseen what happened," Crowder explained.

Finch glared at her from dark, unblinking eyes.

"Normally, I'd have had my partner involved," she admitted. "We'd occasionally change positions behind the vehicle we're tailing. He might have been able to follow Goldman's taxi when I got stuck in traffic."

Finch jumped on the admission. "So you disregarded police protocols."

Crowder pushed back. "Your instructions were for me to come alone," she reminded him. .

"Detective Crowder, if Christine is harmed in any way..." Finch didn't finish the threat. He shook his head to signal his disgust instead. "I did my part. I wired the money. You told me you were my wife's best chance if something went wrong. Something went wrong, and you weren't there to protect her."

Things had played out as she worried they might—something unexpected happened and he blamed her for it. But Crowder thought she'd jog Finch's memory. "I told you I was your wife's best chance *if* you had agreed that I should go instead of Goldman," she reminded him. "I would've convinced her abductors that I was one of your personal assistants and had insisted on being your emissary. Once I was among them, I could have assessed the situation and acted as the circumstances required."

She shifted gears. "Sir, our goal should be on finding your wife and Goldman. I've been to the taxi company. The call came from Christine's cell phone. The dispatcher couldn't remember if it was a man or a woman. Goldman was driven to a rundown strip mall a couple miles from the city. Some of the businesses are closed and shuttered. It's possible that your wife and Goldman are being kept in one of them. I sent my partner and backup to check the buildings and talk to persons who work at the stores that are still open."

Crowder's cell phone rang. She took the call. It was Steele. When the call concluded, she gave Finch the bad news. "The vacant buildings are unoccupied. No one saw anything suspicious today or yesterday."

"So why haven't they released them?" Finch snickered. "They've gotten what they wanted."

Crowder's mind sifted through the possibilities. As always, she put herself in the minds of the criminals she pursued. "They may have them bound and gagged," she suggested.

"So leave them for dead," Finch said scornfully.

"No—force them to sit tight for a few hours. Give their captors a head start to the closest airport—probably New Orleans International or Baton Rouge Metropolitan. They would've already booked their flights. They'd have taken Christine's cell phone with them. They may be planning to text you her location when they're safely on board the plane."

"You don't know that," Finch snarled. "What we do know is that Christine isn't with me right now because of your incompetence."

Finch was probably right. She'd have found a place to park her truck. She'd have approached on foot, gotten the plate numbers of any vehicles, and called them and her location in to Steele. She would have waited until the abductors left or, if she heard screams for help or gunfire, crashed the scene gun in hand.

Too late for a do-over.

The grim reality was that the kidnappers may never have intended to hold up their end of the bargain. She'd soon find out.

~

The text message from Christine's cell phone came with a ping on Finch's cell phone. In the quiet that blanketed the room, it resounded like the peal of a clock tower bell.

Finch opened the message and laid his phone on the table so that Hanratty and Crowder could read it too.

Christine Finch

2:45 p.m.

Emissary was a no-show. Say goodbye to your wife.

Finch tapped the video link just below the message, and then tapped a second time to enlarge the screen as the video began.

It showed Christine Finch seated on a kitchen chair—her ankles and forearms secured to it with duct tape. A piece of tape covered her mouth. Her face was bruised and swollen. The gaze of a pair of bulging, terrified eyes was fixed on the person filming her. The camera moved closer and closer to Christine until all that was visible was her face. She squealed and sobbed. Tears streamed down her cheeks.

An outstretched arm appeared on the screen. The finger and thumb of a gloved hand reached out and gripped an end of the tape that covered Christine's mouth. A quick yank removed it.

It was like the volume button had been turned up full blast on a high-end speaker. "I don't want to die, Jared. I don't want to die," Christine Finch pleaded.

The hand returned.

This time it held a Glock pistol.

Chapter 35

"What went wrong?" O'Malley asked.

Before answering, Crowder reflected on the events of the day. When Christine Finch's head snapped back from a gunshot at point-blank range, Crowder's head had recoiled slightly too. Finch had shown no empathetic response—at least none she could see. The same was true of the colonel. All three remained speechless for a moment.

Finch had spoken first. "That heartless bastard," he said.

Crowder knew he wasn't referring to the person who had just murdered his wife.

She sat in the chair in front of O'Malley's desk. She'd be there for a while. "Finch's best friend and lawyer went as his emissary," she explained. "He was supposed to confirm that Finch's wife was unharmed, and to be with her when she was released. Goldman had other ideas. Ten million dollars was too much money to turn over to someone else. He knew that the traffic in the French Quarter was his best way of losing me. As it turned out, he had some luck too."

"How did Finch take it?"

"Taken completely by surprise. They were friends and

business associates. Goldman was best man at Finch's wedding. But he put the pieces together pretty quickly. Goldman had begged to be his emissary. Finch had wanted to send the colonel—because of his military background and training."

"This Goldman's a piece of work. He had to know he was writing Christine Finch's obituary. How was the ransom paid?"

"A wire transfer. Goldman must have had a rental car waiting for him where the taxi dropped him off. He probably had a mobile device in the car. Using the information Finch gave him to give to the kidnappers, Goldman accessed Finch's online account at two this afternoon and wired the funds to himself. Finch thought the kidnappers had made the wire transfer until they texted him that Goldman was a no-show."

"What's being done to find Goldman?"

"APBs to all state and local police departments here and in neighboring states. I called Hill. The FBI has alerted TSA at all international airports within five hundred miles of New Orleans."

"Where's the money?"

"For now, sitting in a bank in Panama City. Heartland Insurance is a corrupt enterprise. Goldman was the company's CFO and general counsel. He'd know how to set up an offshore account with another identity."

"Can we get to the money before he does?"

"Unlikely. Hill told me Panama was probably chosen because its privacy laws make it a criminal offense to disclose account holder information. It's a favorite place for the cartels to launder money. We'll need court orders here and in Panama, and that will take weeks. By then Goldman will have found a way out of the country—perhaps by chartering a boat—and the money will be gone."

"So how did you leave it with Finch?"

"He said he'd take care of Goldman. He'll go private for

sure. Maybe even have the colonel take care of it personally. Finch isn't the kind of man you double-cross."

O'Malley asked, "Will he cooperate with us and the FBI, now that they're involved?"

"Don't count on it," Crowder replied. "He wants our only involvement to be finding his wife's body."

"And how will you do that?"

"I'm having Christine Finch's cellular service provider triangulate the cell towers that transmitted the messages. That will put us within a three-quarter-mile radius of the phone when the messages were sent."

"That's a wide berth."

"Maybe not. She was probably being held in some isolated area. Whoever shot her didn't use a silencer. There may not be that many places to check."

"What about her vehicle?"

"We have an APB out for it. It's unlikely they'd be traveling in it. I'm having Sid contact Porsche. If there was an anti-theft tracking device installed in her car, we might be able to locate it and find her."

O'Malley's phone rang. "Hill's here," he said, after taking the call from the desk sergeant. "He says it's important."

"Are we finished?" Crowder asked.

"For now. But don't let Hill interfere with your investigation of Christine Finch's murder. Your first priority is finding her body."

Crowder got up to leave. "Don't worry. I'm a woman—I can multitask."

"So can men. I called Sessions. He'll put a hold on the death certificates of Moss, Hartman, and Helmsley like you asked. But keep your nose out of Finch's personal life—at least until he's had time to bury his wife."

Crowder muffled a laugh but didn't hide the grin on her face when she left O'Malley's office. He understood her. He'd always had her back.

So far, at least.

Hill—why the face-to-face? Maybe he had a change of mind about building on a relationship. This time she'd let him decide whether their meeting would be all business.

~

"We found the *Cajun Rose*." Hill sat across from Crowder in one of the conference rooms at district headquarters, his briefcase opened on the table. He reached for several photos and handed them to her.

"The boat operator stopped back at his apartment in Mobile just long enough to pack a duffle bag," he explained. "The taxi he came in waited and took him to a small marina near Fairhope. He met someone there, probably a crew member. They went straight to the *Cajun Rose* and spent the night on the boat."

The photos showed the boat operator and the *Cajun Rose* at various points in Hill's narrative. Further proof that the FBI had incredible resources—not only agents on the ground, but also weaponry, modes of transportation, surveillance equipment, forensics, and a lengthy list of independent consultants. The sting operation Hill had planned would cast a tight net around the *Cajun Rose*.

"What makes you think his next trip will be to Kratos?" Crowder asked.

"We intercepted a radio call to the boat from a wildlife preserve in Biloxi that a 'shipment' was ready for pickup tonight. The preserve used to be a zoo, but the state revoked its license because of animal neglect ten years ago. The preserve borders an inlet off the Gulf."

"What's the plan?"

"We'll have agents in Biloxi and Hanson prepared to make arrests at both locations."

"So how do Kratos's animal rights violations get us closer to finding out its connection to Heartland Insurance?" Crowder asked.

"The arrests at Kratos won't be made until some of the animals are taken inside the facility. That way we'll be authorized to go into the facility and get them. Otherwise, we'd have to wait until we have a search warrant."

Crowder understood Hill's authority when making arrests and conducting searches. It was the same for the NOPD and the FBI, and there were limitations. "Even if you're allowed to go inside the facility, you're limited to looking for the animals that were brought to Kratos. You aren't authorized to go into Litchman's office or places where the serum might be stored."

"That's why I want you to accompany me when we go to Kratos tonight. I have a copter ready to fly us to Fairhope where our boats are waiting. We'll make the arrests together."

It suddenly became clear to Crowder. Hill was using the animal rights violations as a means to an end. The nighttime sting operation would get him on the property. While the other agents were busy arresting people and confiscating the animals, he intended to slip into the facility and snoop around.

She probed further. "Why have me tag along?"

"I need you to make sure no one sees me go into the facility, and to warn me if a problem comes up while I'm inside. I'll handle the rest." Hill paused and looked deep into Crowder's eyes. "Jo, can I count on you?"

Count on her? He was asking her to aid and abet him in conducting an illegal search—to violate the Fourth Amendment and their oaths "to support and defend the Constitution of the United States." Maybe the skinny on the FBI playing fast and loose with the privacy rights of American citizens was true. Federal law enforcement, whether it was the FBI, CIA, NSA, or the US Armed Forces, viewed their jobs differently after the 2001 terrorist attacks on the World Trade Center and Pentagon. The gray line between what was lawful and what was unlawful got a lot darker.

Crowder had occasionally overstepped her authority when it came to search warrants. Murderers had killed again while she wasted valuable time finding a judge who would accept her anonymous and confidential sources as credible enough to issue the warrant.

It pissed her off.

She'd wrestled her conscience on more than one occasion when it came to the scope of a warrantless search. Steele had turned a blind eye while she nosed around rooms, rustled through the drawers of desks, and searched clothing items in closets looking for evidence. When she found it, she left it there until she got enough other evidence to obtain a lawful search warrant.

Crowder had watched her former partner do the same thing. Like Steele, she never objected either. It came with the territory. If she waited for a lead to come her way like an unexpected gift on her birthday, too many investigations would grow cold and never be solved. "A search for the truth" was always her justification for bending the rules.

Crowder and Hill knew that Heartland Insurance was an evil enterprise—more so after finding out that Moss, Hartman, and Helmsley were murdered for their insurance proceeds. But their executioners had not yet been identified. And there was no direct evidence that linked Finch or his company to any of those murders, or to the staged deaths of McManus, Crockett, and Marshall.

They strongly suspected that there was a sinister connection between Heartland Insurance and Kratos. But what? Hill wanted proof of the connection and was willing to break the law to get it.

But was Crowder?

Chapter 36

"This is the FBI. Remain where you are! Hands at your side!" The words blared from a bullhorn through the air like blasts of sonic boom.

Two SWAT team boats had come to life a few minutes before. Their twin engines revved as they sped from a hidden cove a hundred yards from the Kratos Research Laboratory. Spotlights illuminated the scene as the catamaran hulls of the boats fishtailed to an idle in front of the dock. Four agents, weapons drawn, jumped from the boat moored to the dock across from the *Cajun Rose*. The other boat came to rest behind the vessel and blocked it in.

The crane operator had already offloaded a pallet of stacked cages of animals, which had then been transported by forklift into the warehouse at the rear of the facility. The boat operator and his mate stood on the deck beside a second pallet waiting on the forklift's return.

Within minutes everyone, including the guard closest to the boats, was in handcuffs and made to sit on the dock, their weapons confiscated. The guard at the warehouse door was detained where he stood.

Hill and Crowder jumped onto the dock accompanied by two agents. All wore lightweight blue Kevlar vests with FBI in bright-yellow lettering stamped on the front—the standard pullovers for agents making arrests during a raid. Hill barked out orders for the *Cajun Rose* to be seized, its crew arrested, and the pallets of cages confiscated. The others would be detained and questioned.

The commotion riled the chimps. They squealed and screeched and rattled their cages.

Hill went over to the guard detained with those on the dock. Sufficient light came from the spotlights to see his nameplate—Carson.

"Carson, is anyone else here?" Hill asked.

After a brief pause, the guard responded. "Only the two guards at the front gate."

Crowder knew Hill wasn't worried about them. As part of the sting operation, agents had arrived by vehicle to detain them. Hill had other reasons for wanting to be sure no one was inside.

Hill stepped in front of the warehousemen. "Where do you take the animals?"

Neither one answered. Hill kicked the boot of the forklift operator. "Speak up," he said. "You don't want us to add an obstruction charge, do you."

"We offload the pallets and bring them into the warehouse," he replied. "Tomorrow, another crew will bring them into the facility."

"Where inside the facility?"

"To a holding area connected to the main lab."

"How many animals are currently there?"

"We don't know," he replied, speaking also for his coworker. "We only work in the warehouse."

Crowder thought Hill's plan might be foiled. The animals

had not been taken inside the facility.

Hill walked back to Carson. "How can we get inside?" he asked.

"You can't," the guard answered defiantly. "The facility is shut down until tomorrow. Our keycards only allow us into the warehouse."

Hill reached down, grabbed the keycard clipped to the guard's belt, and snapped it off. "Well, I suppose you won't be needing this. Crowder, come with me."

They walked over to the other guard, who sat handcuffed on the ground by the warehouse loading platform. His nameplate read Winnington.

"Winnington," Hill said. "Carson says he saw animals inside the facility when he made his rounds. Did you see any when you made yours?"

The guard remained silent at first, as if surprised by what Carson had revealed. Crowder sensed it was because they'd been instructed to be tight-lipped and never allow anyone inside.

"I want to know if what Carson told us is true. It will help us know who is cooperating … and who is hindering an FBI investigation."

The ploy worked.

"I don't know. My walk through isn't until later."

"Do you check the offices?"

"No. Our keycards don't open them.

"Carson says your keycards open the locks."

"Carson is full of shit. There are special keycards for them."

Hill reached down and snapped off the keycard from Winnington's belt.

Crowder smiled her approval. Hill had baited the guards and found a way to get inside the facility.

Hill went over to the two agents who'd accompanied them.

He told them to release the warehousemen and to supervise them while they loaded the animals back on the *Cajun Rose*. After that, everyone was to wait by the boats while he and Crowder searched the warehouse.

~

They gained access to the facility using one of the guard's keycards. Two steel panels opened like elevator doors and closed when they passed through. The lights inside came on automatically.

Crowder had convinced Hill that two people searching meant covering more ground in a shorter amount of time. They put on latex gloves—routine in all searches so the agent's prints weren't confused with others.

The gloves served a different purpose that day—no one could prove they'd been there.

It was time to find out what Kratos and Heartland Insurance were up to.

Chapter 37

They walked side by side down a concrete and cinder-block corridor with windowless metal doors leading into the rooms on each side. Plates on the doors showed that this area of the building supported the facility's physical operations: ELECTRICAL, HVAC, GENERATOR, HAZMAT, TRASH, LAUNDRY, and MAINTENANCE.

They passed by without stopping.

The long corridor came to an end with a door. Hill opened it with the keycard, and they walked through, the lights coming on as before. This corridor, identical in size and construction, angled ninety degrees to the right and ran along the front of the facility.

Signage on plates affixed to the doors showed that this was the area where they did the laboratory research. On one side the rooms were for animals and the four laboratories. On the other side, the rooms were for supplies, surgical, radiology, and phlebotomy. Hill stopped momentarily to look at the sign on the last door—SERUM.

They walked on and discovered that the corridor ended at another set of metal doors that led into a similar corridor that also turned ninety degrees to the right, completing the U-shape design of the building. The offices were located there, a half dozen on each side for the lab technicians, and a phlebotomist, pathologist, and veterinarian. Midway down the corridor, Hill stopped in front of one of the offices.

Crowder knew his journey would end there.

He turned to face her. "Here's where we part ways. I want you to leave the facility and wait for me on the dock. Tell the agents I'm still checking out the warehouse." He handed her one of the guard's keycards to get out.

Crowder knew Hill wanted to protect her. He was careful not to tell her his real intentions. He wanted her outside with the other agents when he broke into Litchman's office and rifled through his desk looking for answers to two questions:

Why was the serum made?

How was Finch using it?

McManus and Crockett were murdered helping Hill answer those questions, and it had almost got Hill and Crowder killed too.

When Crowder got to the end of the corridor and opened the doors, she looked back toward Hill. He stood in front of the same office with something in his hand—something she hadn't seen before but knew he'd need to unlock the door to Litchman's office.

~

Crowder stood in front of the door where they kept the animals and slid the keycard into the slot above the door handle. The lock blinked green. A click confirmed that it had unlocked.

The lights came on when she entered the room. Cages lined two of the walls. Twenty-four cages—all empty. Several tables served as workstations. Cabinets on the walls stored syringes, IV lines, cylindrical tubes, and pint-size plastic bags. Clearly, they drew blood here, and no doubt stored it in the refrigerator humming in a corner. She opened the door to look inside.

The empty refrigerator and cages explained why the *Cajun Rose* had made a visit. It also explained the need for the crematorium. Kratos wasn't a blood bank. It didn't take one pint from the animals. The primates were either bled to death or killed with the serum made from their blood. But why kill animals with their own blood?

The SERUM room drew her like a magnet to metal. The keycard worked like before, and it didn't take long for her to see a cabinet with four boxes. She opened one. It contained vials of clear fluid organized neatly in rows, sixteen vials in a box. The math was easy. Sixty-four vials. On the shelf above sat boxes of syringes and needles packaged individually in paper.

She'd be adding theft to criminal trespass if she left the room with one of the vials in her pocket, so she closed the glass cabinet door. On the glass her mind saw reflections of Brian McManus and Jason Crockett.

Brian's sheet-white face, his lifeless torso lying across the kitchen table, a syringe stuck in his forearm.

Jason's blue-tinted cheeks, bulging eyes and drooping tongue, his body dangling like a puppet on a string from the shower head of his bathtub.

Both men were murdered helping Hill find the connection between Kratos and Heartland Insurance. Their killers would never be brought to justice. The hard evidence proved that McManus was a drug addict who had overdosed on heroin laced with fentanyl, and that Crockett suffered from undiagnosed depression and had committed suicide.

Perfect crimes committed in an imperfect world. A world

where cold-blooded killers had a decisive advantage over law enforcement. They had no laws, rules, or Supreme Court mandates to follow, no moral code to discern right from wrong, and no conscience to understand compassion, feel guilt, and show remorse. A world where cops were expected to play by rules that the criminals they pursued broke with impunity.

Crowder lamented her cold cases. She'd failed the victims. Just as she and Hill had failed McManus and Crockett.

So far, she and Hill had no proof that Heartland Insurance and Kratos were conspirators in a diabolical scheme. Yet within arm's reach might be the proof they needed. Analysis of the serum might reveal its dark purpose.

She opened the door to the cabinet and began to reach in but hesitated to reflect on what her father had told her the day she graduated from the police academy thirteen years ago. "Jo, you are a good person, and you will be a good cop," he'd said when he pinned the badge to her uniform shirt. "There will be times when the badge makes it difficult to know what you should do. When it does, don't let it keep you from doing what you believe is right."

Crowder closed the cabinet door.

And, as Hill had instructed her, she left the facility and waited for him on the dock.

Chapter 38

The shrill ring from her cell phone penetrated her brain like a jolt of electricity. More so because the phone lay on her pillow by her ear and rang at six in the morning.

By the time the boat operator and his mate had been booked and charged, and Hill and Crowder had questioned all detainees, it had been after two in the morning. The dictation of their Form 302 statements came next—the memoranda of FBI agents that memorialized their interview notes. It was nearly five when the helicopter returned Crowder to New Orleans. An FBI agent drove her home.

She'd been dead tired when she collapsed on the bed without undressing and with the phone in her hand. Now she let the call go to voice mail. Without opening her eyes, she put her phone on vibrate. She knew he'd call again. He always did.

The phone vibrated. Unanswered, the call again went to voice mail. This time the caller left a much shorter message. He followed the same routine—like an obsessed stalker. The ping came next. He followed his calls with a text message. So predictable. The same message every time: *Call me as soon as you read this.*

Only one person would call her at six in the morning on her day off, and she always rewarded his persistence. She opened bloodshot eyes, tapped Contacts, and pressed speed dial.

Steele spoke first. "We found Christine Finch."

Crowder sat up and threw her legs over the side of the bed. Suddenly wide awake, she asked, "Where?"

"In her Porsche."

"Where was it found?"

"In a bayou near Flagstaff, an hour from here."

"How did you find her?"

"You were right to have me contact Porsche," Steele replied. "They were able to track the car's location." Steele fell silent.

Crowder sensed he had more to say. "And?"

"We found Goldman too. Dead. In the car."

Crowder's mind shifted into overdrive. Everything suddenly made sense. Things weren't as they appeared to be.

~

Crowder drove her truck to the cabin, picking up Steele on the way. She wanted to see the vehicle before it was hauled away. The bodies of Finch's wife and Goldman were already at the medical examiner's office being autopsied.

The Porsche sat in front of the cabin behind the wrecker that had pulled it out of the water. One of the two state troopers present when they arrived told them that by using the coordinates provided by Porsche, they'd located the vehicle submerged in the water behind the cabin. The two bodies were stuffed in the trunk—a woman shot in the forehead and a man shot in the back of the head. The contents of suitcases in the back seat included passports with their photographs and new identities, and plane tickets to Geneva, Switzerland, on a flight that left the night after Christine Finch's supposed abduction. The cabin was empty when they arrived. There was no indication that anyone had been in it.

After searching the vehicle and looking through the suitcases, Crowder and Steele entered the cabin for a look. Crowder went immediately to the kitchen where she'd seen Christine Finch killed. They found no evidence of blood stains or spatter on the floor.

"There were two chairs at the table in the video of her execution," Crowder said. "They took the one she was bound to when she was shot. The cleanup was done by professionals."

An inspection of other rooms revealed nothing to suggest how Goldman met his end. But when she went into the bedroom and looked around, she said, "He was shot in the bedroom." She stood by the side of the bed. "He was standing or kneeling here at the time."

"What makes you say that?" Steele asked. "Everything looks normal. Nothing's broken or out of place. It's more likely he was shot somewhere outside."

Crowder put the puzzle pieces together and recreated what happened in her mind.

"The shooter was standing behind him in the doorway. He'd have entered through an unlocked door. Goldman had no reason to lock it after he came in. Nobody knew he had Christine Finch waiting for him here while the two of them faked her kidnapping and stole ten million dollars from Finch."

"And where was Christine Finch when Goldman was shot?"

"She was sitting or lying on the bed. Goldman would have blocked her view of the shooter. So she couldn't warn him."

Crowder walked to the foot of the bed. "There's a throw rug on one side of the bed but not the other. Since the end table is on the side where Goldman stood, you'd expect a rug to be there. But there's no rug. And the bed has no sheet, blanket or bedspread. Even the pillows are gone. They stripped the bed and, like the chair, took the bloodstained rug and bedding with them when they cleaned up."

"So who killed them?"

"Probably the same professional assassins who've killed a lot of other people for Jared Finch."

Steele frowned. "Why would Finch want his wife dead?"

"He probably found out she was cheating on him and had planned to leave with Goldman and ten million dollars of his money. What better way to outfox the fox? If Finch knew Goldman's plan beforehand, it was a simple matter of letting it play out. He'd know where the cabin was located. The professionals he hired would know where to find both of them."

"But why would Finch allow Goldman to wire ten million dollars to an offshore account?" Steele asked. "There's proof of the wire transfer."

"Goldman didn't wire the money," Crowder explained. "Finch wired the money to his own offshore account after Goldman was killed to make it look like Goldman had done it. When the ransom wasn't paid, it gave the kidnappers a reason to kill Finch's wife."

Steele's face revealed an "aha" moment. "So Christine Finch texted her husband pretending to be the kidnappers, and Goldman volunteered to be Finch's emissary to get Finch's online banking information to make the wire transfer as if the kidnappers had made it."

Crowder smiled broadly. "Goldman would've written down the text messages beforehand and given Christine the times she should send them. If their plan had worked, their disappearances would've been explained by the kidnappers having killed them and disposed of their bodies."

Steele nodded his understanding, and they walked out the door to Crowder's truck.

"So what evidence proves Finch knew about the affair and hired the people who killed them?" Steele asked.

Crowder had a good reason for not answering her partner's question.

She had no evidence.

Chapter 39

"What I'm hearing so far is more fiction than fact," O'Malley said.

Crowder stood in front of her boss's desk. She'd just summarized the facts that proved that Goldman and Christine Finch had schemed to steal ten million dollars from Jared Finch. But O'Malley wasn't convinced that Finch had found out about the plan and formulated his own plan in response, to funnel his money to an offshore account and have them killed.

"Sure, it's an airtight case against Goldman and Finch's wife. But what evidence links the shooters to Finch, or Hanratty, or anyone else working for Finch?"

"Circumstantial evidence is still admissible in court the last time I checked," Crowder said, not hiding her sarcasm.

The bulldog's face reddened, and it wasn't from embarrassment. "State your best case against Finch and Hanratty," O'Malley demanded.

Crowder did a quick review of the facts in her mind. "The cell phones."

"What about the cell phones?"

"Christine's phone was in the trunk of her car. Forensics

found numerous text messages between her and Goldman. They show a long-standing love affair. Finch had to know about it, and *if* he did, he'd have had a motive to kill both of them."

"That's a big if. He'll deny it. What proof is there he actually knew?"

"Before he left in the taxi, Finch had Goldman give his cell phone to Hanratty, who put it on a table in the room. I took the phone with me later in the day after Christine was killed. I wanted to see who he'd called and texted. It was on the table where Hanratty had placed it. Forensics said everything on it had been permanently deleted. No text messages, emails or voicemails."

O'Malley frowned. "They wouldn't have known his passcode. How would they have gotten into it?"

"The same way we did—with the same spyware technology we use. Hanratty would know how to do it."

"Goldman could have deleted everything," O'Malley countered. "The text message Finch received said *no cell phones.* He probably knew he'd have to leave it with Finch and didn't want him hacking in and finding out about the affair with his wife."

"Not possible."

"Why not?"

"I saw Goldman use his phone to text someone while Finch and I were talking and the colonel was out of the room. He was huddled in a corner, thumbs pounding away like he was beating a drum. It was his last text message to Christine. It was on her phone. It explained Goldman's reluctance to give his phone to Hanratty. That text message had to have been on Goldman's phone."

"Why would they want everything deleted?"

"To keep me from finding out about the affair. Goldman

loved Christine Finch. If I'd known that, I never would've believed that Goldman would steal Finch's money and leave her for dead." Crowder liked the back-and-forth. It was producing results.

O'Malley's tone mellowed. "He tampered with evidence in a double homicide case if his prints are all over that phone."

"I had the phone checked for prints."

"And?"

"The only prints on it were mine. Not even Goldman's prints were on it. Hanratty wiped it clean after he deleted everything in it."

O'Malley scratched his chin as if he'd just thought of something that didn't fit into Crowder's theory. "Wait a minute. If Finch and Hanratty planned to kill them, why would they allow you to tail Goldman. Finch was warned—*no police*. They could've insisted you stay at the house and wait with them. Instead they risked having you follow Goldman to the cabin. Makes no sense."

"Makes perfect sense. I'm not in the house when Finch goes online to wire the money to *his* offshore account, and Hanratty takes care of Goldman's phone and provides his assassins with updates on my location."

"Why your location?"

"Because Hanratty knew the taxi was in the French Quarter. A woman pulls in front of me. Her car stalls. The guy behind me goes to help her. By the time he faked doing something under the hood of her car to fix the problem, the taxi and Goldman were long gone."

"There's only one problem," O'Malley shot back. He hated to lose an argument, particularly with her.

"What's that?" she asked, trying her best to corral a jack-o'-lantern grin.

"If Hanratty's back at Finch's place, how does he know where you are? How does he know where to send his operatives to find you?"

"I wondered the same thing," Crowder replied. She reached into her pocket and pulled out a small square-shaped metal object. "Here … catch." She tossed it across the desk to him.

O'Malley caught it and did a quick study of the object. When he held it an inch from the metal shade on his desktop lamp, it shot from his fingers to the metal. He knew what it was—a magnetic GPS vehicle-tracking device. The department had its own supply of them.

"I found it behind the rear quarter panel of my truck. Hanratty put it there when he left the room while I was with Finch and Goldman. It explains why he wanted me to park my truck in Finch's garage."

"Prints?"

"Only mine. He'd have worn gloves."

Crowder walked over to O'Malley's lamp and retrieved the tracking device. "I'll put it in Sid's car. Let them think they're still tracking me."

O'Malley cracked a smile. She even heard him chuckle as he leaned back in his chair and folded his arms across his chest. "So how do we get enough evidence on Finch and Hanratty to arrest them for premeditated murder?" he asked.

"We turn up the heat."

"How high?"

"Until the pot boils over."

Chapter 40

A padded legal-size envelope postmarked from the United States Post Office in Citronelle, a small town thirty-four miles from Mobile, arrived at the Mobile field office shortly before noon. It had no return address. The name and address on the label had been handprinted in black ink and addressed to Special Agent Alex Hill.

Three days later, Hill and Crowder sat in the United States Attorney's Office in Mobile. Across from them sat Paul Evans and Dr. Gertrude Weiss. Assistant US Attorney Rita Morales sat at the head of the table.

"We got the break we needed," Morales said. "Special Agent Hill received an envelope postmarked from Citronelle. It's the post office closest to Hanson. It contained documents from Heartland Insurance and a small vial of clear liquid. An unsigned handprinted note read, *From Kratos Research Laboratory.* It was probably sent by a Kratos employee who wanted to remain anonymous because of what happened to Jason Crockett.

"The documents were dusted for prints. Only one person's prints were found on them, those of Maximilian Litchman. They matched the ones we obtained from German police authorities.

We finally may have the evidence we need to get Jared Finch and his company for RICO violations."

Crowder was familiar with the Racketeer Influenced and Corrupt Organizations Act, commonly referred to as RICO. Passed in 1970, the legislation aimed to combat organized crime and provide for the prosecution of individuals who engaged in unlawful acts as part of an ongoing criminal enterprise.

Morales looked at Evans. "Mr. Evans is the Vice President of Southeastern Life Insurance Company," she said. "His company issued the life insurance policy to Cletus Moss. I asked him to make sense of the documents we received."

Evans opened the file on the table in front of him, pulled out copies of a document—a chart—and handed them to those seated at the table. "This chart summarizes the actuarial performance of Heartland Insurance for the third quarter of its fiscal year," he began. "It identifies the policies purchased from individuals who died in the three-month period. I'm familiar with these charts. All life insurance companies accumulate this kind of data in some form. On this one, the various columns identify the insured, the face value of the policy, the dates when Heartland Insurance purchased the policy, when the insured died, and the insured's age and cause of death."

"Why do insurance companies keep this information?" Morales asked as if she had Evans on the witness stand.

Crowder sensed that Morales knew the answer but wanted the others around the table to hear Evans explain it.

"Life insurance companies need to know the life expectancy of the people they insure," Evans said. "They use the information to determine the premiums they need to charge their insureds to generate enough revenue to pay claims when they die. They do this by using government-generated statistics that set forth the average life expectancy of people based on their age, gender, and race. Obviously, some people will live longer or die earlier. We have no crystal ball. So we use averages."

"How does the age and state of health of the insured factor in?" Morales asked.

"Generally speaking, the older you are, the higher your insurance premiums will be, because you're closer to the end of your life expectancy. If you have underlying health conditions, like diabetes or cardiovascular disease, you may pay higher premiums because you're more at risk of dying earlier than people without such conditions. Some, like those who have metastatic cancer and other terminal illnesses, may not be insurable at all. That's why life insurance companies assess the insured's state of health before insuring them. Depending on what is disclosed in the insured's application, they may obtain healthcare records and require a medical examination."

Morales asked, "So what does the information in the Heartland Insurance chart tell you?"

"There were twenty-six policies," Evans explained. "This company doesn't identify the insured by name. It uses a *unit number*."

Crowder caught Hill glance over at her. She knew why—the insured was a commodity to Heartland Insurance, and something it bought and made a profit on.

"There were twenty-three one-million-dollar policies. Three others were for five million dollars. There are asterisks over those policies. I checked Cletus Moss's original life insurance application. He's identified on the chart by the last four digits of his social security number. The unit numbers with the other five million dollars policies are Olivia Hartman and Nathan Helmsley. The asterisk means that those three policies also had double indemnity endorsements."

"Is there anything about what's on the chart that's out of the ordinary?" Morales asked.

"Actually, what's on this chart is all extraordinary."

"How so?"

"All twenty-six insureds died much earlier than expected. I'm not talking about a year or two. All of them died ten to twelve years earlier than expected. The chance of that occurring in actuality is about the same chance of being struck by lightning twice in one's lifetime." Evans paused to clear his throat. "But something else bothers me more."

Crowder and Hill stirred in their chairs in anticipation of what Evans was about to reveal.

"All twenty-three insureds with one-million-dollar policies died from a cardiovascular event—either a heart attack or a stroke. None died from cancer, pneumonia, sepsis, or the dozens of other fatal diseases and illnesses that people die from every day. About twenty-five percent of people in the age group on this chart will die from heart attacks or strokes—not one hundred percent. That's an actuarial impossibility. The question I had was why?"

Crowder's gut told her the awful answer before Dr. Weiss opened her mouth.

Morales looked to her left at the person seated next to Evans. The distinguished-looking woman with the silver hair pulled back in a bun wore wire-rimmed glasses. She looked to be in her late fifties or early sixties. "Dr. Weiss is Director of Laboratory Sciences at Hobbs Pharmaceuticals, a renowned German drug manufacturer and research facility that produces serums and therapeutic agents for the treatment of blood disorders, cardiovascular disease, and stroke. She's also on the executive committee of the World Health Organization. Because of her background as a physician and microbiologist, I asked her to analyze the fluid in the vial. She's here to discuss her findings."

Given her cue, Dr. Weiss took over. "It's a serum derived from the blood of lower primates, probably chimpanzees or gibbons because of their close DNA match to humans. Serum is what's left after all white and red blood cells, platelets, and microorganisms are removed. In this case, an artificially engineered protein has been introduced into the serum. About ninety percent of the protein is found in blood thinners that keep blood from producing platelets and the plaque that causes heart attacks and strokes. However, the remaining ten percent of it has the opposite effect and causes the liver and kidney to produce a super hormone that abnormally increases the production of platelets."

Morales asked, "What would happen if the serum was injected in an adult human?"

"It would cause the blood to clot abnormally. Unless the problem was discovered and the process reversed, the person would eventually suffer a cardiovascular event—either a heart attack or stroke."

"Have you ever seen anything that looked like this protein before?"

"Ten years ago," Weiss replied. "When I studied a serum that Max Litchman had used in his clinical trials."

"If the amount of serum in the vial were injected into the blood of a human, how long would it take to cause a heart attack or stroke?"

"If the entire four milliliters were injected—within three years."

Crowder looked at the chart. All twenty-three insureds had died within two and a half years of the date Heartland Insurance bought their policies.

"Dr. Weiss, the company's website and internet advertisements advise applicants that, in addition to requiring at least one million dollars of life insurance, all applicants must submit to routine bloodwork. Could a single dose of the serum be injected when the person's blood is taken?"

All eyes moved to Weiss.

"Yes. A butterfly needle is used for drawing blood and for giving medications. It could easily serve both purposes. The person wouldn't know that before any blood was drawn the four milliliters of serum had been infused into the blood stream. Blood is usually drawn from the median cubital vein which is easily identifiable in the fold of the elbow. That vein's blood flows directly to the heart and from there is pumped through the carotid artery to the brain."

Morales brought the meeting to a close. Crowder didn't need her to verbalize what they were all thinking. Twenty-three people had been given a lethal dose of Litchman's serum.

Crowder left the meeting with a nagging thought on her mind—only God knew how many others there had been.

Chapter 41

"Why didn't we know Crowder was in Mobile with Hill?" Finch asked.

The colonel was in Finch's office briefing him on the raid at Kratos. "Because she didn't drive there. The FBI must have shuttled her back and forth."

"Who was arrested?"

"The captain and the guy he works with. Charged with federal animal rights violations. Released this morning. Their lawyers posted their bail."

"Paper trail?"

"Cash for the lawyers. Cash for the bail."

"Can they be trusted?"

"They know they'll be compensated if they keep their mouths shut and let their lawyers do the talking."

"Did the FBI go inside?"

"Hill and Crowder searched the warehouse. They were there twenty-five minutes and came out with nothing. The facility would've been off-limits."

"Will they be back?"

"They'll be back with a warrant to search the lab for evidence of what we do to the animals."

"Litchman?"

"He'll be arrested if they can find him."

"Will they find him?"

"Not likely. I have him in a suite at the Hyatt under a different name. He'll be eating room service for a while."

"If they search his office, what will they find?"

"According to him, nothing."

"Do you believe him?"

"No. Litchman's old-school German," Hanratty explained. "He has probably documented everything he's done there—and it won't only be on his computer."

Finch shook his head in disgust. "Max is a fool. My instructions were explicit—no paper."

"The virus we've installed on our network system computer wiped out what's harmful on his computers here and at the lab. But I need to go back to the facility and shred what's paper."

"Are they watching it?"

"Our guards patrol every hour. So far, no one's been within sight of the place."

"Let's return to the facility tonight. Warn the guards that we'll arrive around midnight. I'm afraid the lab—and the algorithm—have outlived their usefulness."

Hanratty knew the end was in sight. Without the lab producing the serum, Heartland Insurance would be out of business in a couple of years. The only question was how long it would need to operate to collect on the policies of persons who already had an early date with death.

Finch went on his computer to check the inventory of outstanding policies and remaining vials of serum at Kratos. He'd do the calculations of revenues, and profits, in his head. He'd never think of leaving any money on the table. His company would cease only when he had sucked from it every ounce of blood.

"We have a six-month supply of serum at the lab," Finch announced. "If we can get the serum out to our nurses and into the veins of new units, we can extend the life of the company another two and a half, three years."

It was just the kind of calculated, cold-hearted reaction Hanratty expected from Finch.

~

The rotors of Finch's helicopter whirled like the blades of a circular saw, the chuff-chuff-chuff sound of the blade slap as regular and even as the beat of a human heart. Two high-performance turbine engines purred as the aircraft soared like an eagle through a dark, moonless sky.

No one waited on the helipad at Kratos to greet them when they landed. The guards had been instructed to leave the facility as soon as they touched down.

Finch reached for the empty briefcase on the floor behind his seat. The colonel grabbed the large duffle bag that lay on the seat behind him.

Their master keycards opened all doors. Only Finch and members of the inner circle had them.

The colonel used his card to access the facility. When the doors opened, Finch went directly to the storage room for the remaining vials of serum—four boxes full. He didn't open the boxes and count the vials before putting them in his briefcase.

The colonel busied himself emptying the bag he'd brought. He placed the explosives where they'd have the maximum impact—near structural support beams, the liquid nitrogen tanks, and the cleaning solvents.

The colonel was familiar with all kinds of explosives. He and those he commanded had used them on roadways and bridges, under the gas tanks of vehicles, and in government buildings, hotel rooms, and the occasional mosque. On a few occasions they'd taped them to the back of the heads of hostile combatants to avenge a beheading or punish them because they hadn't cooperated—a time or two, even when they had.

The colonel knew it took a certain type of person to kill without emotion—to put a bullet in the heart and brain of a defenseless old man at point-blank range, to throw an old woman down a flight of stairs and then, with one quick twist of her head, break her neck, and to submerge the head of a fat man deep in debt and keep it there until all air in his lungs was replaced by the swampy water of a Louisiana bayou.

The colonel had followed Finch's orders without question, just as his subordinates had followed his orders without hesitation. He never doubted his assassins' loyalty. They lost their souls the very first time they killed someone for no reason other than that he wanted the person dead. They had no allegiance to any God, country, or noble cause. Colonel James Hanratty knew that he would always have their loyalty. But a question lingered in the colonel's mind. Would Finch always have his?

Chapter 42

Crowder watched herself jump from her truck and run to the intersection. The video from the cameras at the intersection of Bourbon Street and Orleans Avenue in the French Quarter had captured the incident that allowed Goldman to lose her in traffic. The cameras had been installed by the city's Department of Homeland Security more than a decade ago to monitor criminal activity and assist first responders deployed in emergencies. They'd been useful to Crowder in the past and would be again.

She freeze-framed the video twice, each time with the best views of the faces of the man and woman the colonel dispatched to intercept her truck. She figured that the man's sunglasses and ball cap and the woman's platinum-blonde wig were disguises put together in a hurry. She enlarged the frames and printed copies.

Ballistics proved that the 9mm bullets that killed Goldman and Christine Finch came from the same Glock pistol. The same person most likely shot both.

But which one was the shooter?

She reviewed the footage again. This time she stopped it when the two of them stood in the street next to each other. The woman was tall but still a half foot shorter than the man. She remembered the arm of Christine Finch's shooter when it had come into view with the Glock in a gloved hand. The shooter had stood to the right of the person who'd filmed the execution on Christine's cell phone. The angle of the lens aimed down at Christine's face and over the shooter's extended arm. Crowder had her answer. The taller man held the camera. The woman held the gun.

She did a quick review of the facts. The FBI had concluded that the footprints left outside Moss's window could have been made by a woman the approximate height and weight of the one in the photo. Two people were involved in all seven murders—they were too complex for one person to pull off. Most were intricately staged to look like accidental or unintentional deaths, and some involved the extensive cleanup of blood. The meticulous way the assassins worked together meant only one thing—the same pair of assassins murdered all seven.

And she was staring at them on her computer screen.

Crowder had her first good lead. The couple appeared to be in their mid-to-late thirties. They would've served under Hanratty in the Delta Force, been with him when he did covert missions for the CIA—five years of black ops with licenses to kill that further honed their unique skill sets.

It made sense. Finch needed Hanratty because he knew how to recruit trained killers who would take care of the double indemnity policyholders. What better recruits than a man and a woman who'd followed the colonel's orders their entire adult lives.

But she needed evidence that linked them to Hanratty.

The woman was her best chance of finding the connection. How many women had served under the colonel? Had a woman ever been a member of the Delta Force, the most elite fighting unit in the world? Maybe none. Perhaps a few. Possibly only one. It was something that could be checked—but not by the NOPD. She needed help from someone who could cut through the bureaucratic nonsense and bullshit red tape. Crowder knew she couldn't do it.

She picked up the phone and called the only person she knew who could.

~

At one in the morning, a motorcade of FBI vehicles passed through Hanson on its way to Kratos Research Laboratory. No one would be at the facility when the search was conducted. No one to say if areas were searched where law enforcement shouldn't have been. But it didn't matter who was there and would be watching now, because this time Hill had a warrant to search the entire facility and confiscate documents, vials of serum, and computers. This time the evidence would be lawfully seized and admissible in court. The evidence would lead to the arrests of Finch and Litchman, and to the indictment of Heartland Insurance and Kratos Research Laboratory for RICO violations, and murder.

Hill didn't need to involve Crowder in the search. He knew what he was looking for and where to find it. The vials of serum he'd find there would soon be in an FBI laboratory. The serum would be identical to what was in the vial he'd received in the mail—the evidence they needed to prove an ongoing criminal enterprise.

Hill would search Litchman's office and find a file in a drawer of his desk labeled *Algorithm*. He'd open it and find the formula for the blood protein. The active ingredients would all be there. The process for infusing the primate's plasma with various chemicals, additives, antigens, and inhibitors. It would make no sense to Hill. But it would to Dr. Weiss.

Another file would contain a statistical analysis of the effect of the serum on the *unit numbers* who received it when they had their routine bloodwork. Charts and graphs would collect the data showing how the algorithm could predict with uncanny accuracy when fatal clots would form in the lungs, carotid artery, and brain.

It was all there in great detail for medical experts to digest. They would conclude that the manner of death on hundreds of death certificates Heartland Insurance had submitted to life insurance companies to collect insurance proceeds over the years was not "natural causes," but "homicide" instead. The trial exhibits would all be there, organized in folders, compliments of Dr. Maximilian Litchman.

Hill had checked into Litchman's background. His grandfather was a Nazi physician assigned to Auschwitz, who'd been tried for war crimes and died in Landsberg Prison. His grandfather's detailed records of the experiments performed at the camp were among the thousands of documents introduced at the Nuremberg trials.

The Nazis tried their best toward the end of the war to erase all physical trace of their crimes. But they were overwhelmed by what Germans did best—record-keeping. They simply couldn't get rid of all the written and printed evidence of their atrocities. The penchant for documentation, Hill thought, must be an inherited trait. It had proved to be the undoing of the Nazi's criminal enterprise. When Litchman's documents were safely in the hands of the FBI, it would be the undoing of Finch's criminal enterprise as well.

Hill looked at his watch. They'd be there in less than five minutes. They'd gain access to the facility using a guard's keycard. If that didn't work, they'd break the lock, and the locks of every room in the facility, if necessary.

The boom from the blast when the explosives detonated simultaneously was earsplitting. The ground trembled from the aftershock of the explosion, and in the distance, a fireball flashed above the horizon. Hill groaned. He knew before reaching Kratos that the evidence he so badly needed had just been incinerated into ash.

Chapter 43

"They know about the algorithm," Hanratty said, back in Finch's office to deliver the bad news.

"That's not possible," Finch said. "We blew up the lab before they got there. The sheriff made sure the fire department personnel took their time getting to the scene. The roof collapsed just like you said it would. There's nothing left but rubble."

"Before we left Kratos, I pulled the security tapes for the night of the raid. Hill and Crowder used a guard's keycard to enter the facility. Crowder used it to go into the room where we keep the serum."

"Do we know if she took anything?"

"There are no cameras inside the rooms, labs and offices. But she took a vial."

"How can you be so sure?"

"A vial is missing from one of the boxes you brought back from the lab."

Finch didn't act surprised. "Crowder—another dirty cop who'd steal to get evidence," he remarked.

"They must have planned it from the beginning," Hanratty said.

"Why so?"

"Because Hill broke into Litchman's office. He had a device with him that decoded the lock."

"Everything is on his computer," Finch said. "We'd know if his computer was breached, and it wasn't. So why are you worried?"

"I just came from seeing Litchman. I applied sufficient pressure to get him to admit he kept files in the drawers of his desk—everything about the algorithm, how it was engineered, how we use it in the field. He had a printout of the names of the nurses."

"Litchman is a bigger fool than I thought. You'd think he'd learn from the sins of his grandfather."

"How do you want this handled?"

"By you personally," Finch said. "I'll leave the details to you."

The only detail left for the colonel to work out was where in the bayou he'd dump Litchman's body.

~

Crowder was at her desk when her cell phone rang. It was Hill. He'd texted her after the explosion at Kratos to lament his bad luck, and Crowder shared his angst. If the truth ever got out, the evidence they stole would be inadmissible, and any other evidence derived from it would be discarded like poisoned fruit. The case against Finch and his collaborators would evaporate like steam from the press of an iron.

They'd faced a conundrum that night at Kratos. The American system of criminal justice placed undue weight on rules that protected its citizens from unreasonable government intrusions into their private lives and spaces. The problem was that known criminals were given the same protections. They could safely hide evidence of their crimes behind the Fourth Amendment. Can a search ever be unreasonable when it uncovered overwhelming evidence of horrible crimes?

Crowder and Hill had their doubts.

The morning after the raid, they'd confessed their transgressions to each other and hatched the plan to send the evidence anonymously in the mail to Hill. But the plan failed if the ruse was uncovered. What they needed were the files in Litchman's desk that were now ashes buried under tons of concrete and cement.

There would now be increased scrutiny on the evidence mailed to Hill. He'd have to lie under oath about where it came from. Was it too coincidental that Hill received the evidence three days after the raid? Morales might get suspicious. She'd learn that he'd taken the guards' keycards that opened the doors to the facility and to the room where the serum was stored. She'd question the other agents who could not explain why it took Hill and Crowder almost a half hour to search the warehouse. Maybe she'd conclude that the inconvenient truth was that Hill or Crowder, or both, had entered the facility on the night of the raid and had stolen the evidence.

Crowder wondered whether Hill would lie under oath?

Would she?

Hill's call to her did little to ease her anxiety.

"I was able to get a search warrant for Litchman's office at Heartland Insurance," Hill said. "If he has a computer there, we can take it."

"If Finch would blow up Litchman's lab to keep us from getting evidence, what's to stop him from sanitizing Litchman's office and computer?"

"Let him. I want to rattle his chain. Let him know what we know, and that a grand jury is investigating him and his company. That the lot of them will be subpoenaed to testify."

"Has the Fifth Amendment been repealed?" Crowder wisecracked. Her lightheartedness caused a knot to form in her stomach. She might also have to testify and choose between telling the truth, pleading the fifth ... or committing perjury.

"So Morales offers a deal to the weakest link—probably Litchman—in return for his testimony against Finch. He'll squeal like a pig."

At that moment, Crowder felt like the weakest link—the one likely to spill her guts and come clean with the truth. "And if he doesn't?" she asked, trying not to sound too glum.

"We'll talk to every nurse on the distribution list. Someone will testify that the butterfly syringe they jabbed into the veins of the victims contained a clear fluid. They may not have known what it was, but they had to know it wasn't something you inject into someone giving blood for routine lab work."

Hill was relentless and unabashedly unapologetic for his misdeeds. His bold confidence made Crowder feel at ease. She smiled for the first time that day. Hill was right. He'd told her that what they did was "for the greater good." But it put them on a train that had no stops until it reached its final destination. Neither of them knew where the train would take them. Jumping off wasn't an option. Crowder had no choice but to sit back and try like hell to enjoy the ride.

Her faith in Hill bolstered, she said, "I want to come with you when you execute the search warrant. Remind them that the NOPD has partnered with the FBI to take them down. You know, turn up the heat."

"That's one reason I called. I want you there. You're familiar with the place and know Hanratty and Finch. We're on for tomorrow at ten. The offices will be open for business then. We'll shake a couple of tree limbs and see what flies out."

"You said one reason you called was you wanted me there. What's the other reason?"

Crowder had a flashback to the visit he made to her place for dinner. Maybe he had plans for them after the search.

No such luck.

"Is your computer on?"

"It is."

"I had my contact at NSA push some buttons," Hill said. "He told me Hanratty was a hands-on commander in the Delta Force. Because he was given the most difficult assignments, his units were the best trained. He was surprised to see that a woman, and her fraternal twin, were in the Delta Force. I'll send you both files. We just may have the people you're looking for."

Chapter 44

Crowder studied the face of the E7 sergeant with the short milky-white hair. Eighteen years younger but definitely her. A quick scroll through her discharge papers revealed almost nothing about her background, training, deployments, and promotions. Virtually all information was marked *Classified, Secret*, or *Top Secret.*

The photo of her brother of the same rank was the man in sunglasses wearing the ball cap.

Both files gave the same limited information: Elsa Larsson. Liam Larsson. Born July 9, 1986—Stockholm, Sweden. Residence on enlistment: Las Vegas, Nevada. Parents: Deceased. Next of kin: None. Social Security Number: Classified. Forwarding address: Classified. Commanding officer: Colonel James Hanratty, US Army, Delta Force. Date of enlistment: July 9, 2004. The last item caught her eye—Date of separation: August 1, 2009.

Hanratty went offscreen for five years after he left the Delta Force in 2009.

Crowder spent the next hour on the internet accessing multiple search engines looking for the Larsson siblings—no addresses, phone numbers, real estate, or driver's licenses. No Facebook, Twitter or Instagram accounts. No birth records in Sweden with those names and dates of birth. Nothing showed up in the criminal background check or with Interpol. She wondered if the names were phony.

But it all made sense. No parents or next of kin. Probably raised in foster care. They had only each other their entire lives. Enlisted the day they turned eighteen. Probably the youngest soldiers ever to become members of the Delta Force. Hanratty would have trained them. Made them into lethal weapons and been a father figure to them. They were his obedient children.

Hanratty had been the CIA's secret weapon for five years, doing missions so dark the United States government would never admit they were authorized. His offspring had been by his side the entire time, doing what they did best—whatever Hanratty told them to do. When Hanratty became Finch's *caporegime*, his best assassins were part of the package. Nothing would have changed for the Larssons. They still received their orders from the colonel and would obey them without question. When Elsa and Liam Larsson murdered Martin Goldman and Christine Finch, they were following Hanratty's orders.

An idea popped into Crowder's head. Time to roll the dice.

~

The security guard looked up as Hill and Crowder approached his desk in the lobby of Finch Tower. Crowder recognized the jerk as the one who'd given her the hard time—same sunglasses, same smug persona. But this time would be different. Hill and two other FBI agents accompanied her, armed with arrest and search warrants.

Hill wasted no time. "Special Agent Alex Hill of the FBI

and Detective Jo Crowder of the NOPD. We are here with warrants to arrest Maximillian Litchman and search his office at Heartland Insurance. You are to notify James Hanratty, director of security, that he is to come to the lobby."

The guard who stood by the metal detector and body scanner grabbed a pager from his belt and turned his back to Hill.

"Sir, I wouldn't do that," Hill yelled out. "Return the pager to the clip holder on your belt. The guard at the desk will notify Mr. Hanratty of our presence."

The guards obeyed.

Hill spoke forcefully to both guards. "The agents behind me will wait with you in the lobby. You are not to contact Dr. Litchman or inform anyone of our presence."

Crowder liked the preliminary bout. Hill was a fighter who took crap from no one. Whether his bravado would hold up against Hanratty and lead to something important remained to be seen.

~

"Tell him I'll be with them in a few minutes," the colonel said to the guard when he called.

Unfazed, Hanratty called Finch. "They're here. I think it's time for you and Gladstone to make your way to the helipad."

Chapter 45

Hanratty studied the warrants with the care of a demolitions expert defusing an unfamiliar detonator. "Dr. Litchman hasn't been here in quite some time," he said while reading. "He prefers to work from his office at his laboratory. He has no office here."

"He has no office there either," Hill said with purposeful sarcasm. "I suppose you know about the explosion at Kratos."

Hanratty looked up at Crowder, not Hill. "Only from what I saw on the news."

Crowder had never seen a bigger pair of lying eyes. "We thought you might know where he is," she said, staring him down.

"Can't say that I do … when I don't," Hanratty said. He took another look at the search warrant. "The warrant only allows you to search the common areas, the lavatories in the common areas, and Dr. Litchman's office. Since there is no office and no lavatories in the common areas, your search won't take long. The company occupies the top three floors. We'll start on the first of the floors and work our way up." Hanratty turned and walked to the elevators, bypassing security.

Hill asked, "When was the last time you saw Litchman?"

"A month ago," Hanratty replied. "He gave a seminar to

his nurses."

Hill nudged further. "The ones who draw the blood for the lab work?"

Hanratty remained stone-faced. "I have no idea what the nurses do. My job is to provide security."

They entered an elevator that took them to the offices on the first of the three floors.

"We want to talk to Jared Finch while we're here," Hill said. "Can you arrange that for us?"

"He's not in the office," Hanratty replied brusquely.

When they stepped into the lobby of the first floor of the company's offices, the roar of the engine of Finch's helicopter ascending from the roof could be plainly heard.

Crowder saw Hill glance at her and roll his eyes.

Crowder continued the back-and-forth. "Does he have an assistant or secretary who handles scheduling?"

"Mr. Finch has no such people working for him. He does his own scheduling."

Crowder expected as much. When you are in the business of systematically knocking off your clients, the fewer people who know the better.

The common areas on all the floors were the same—hallways with rooms on each side, a keycard lock above the doorknob. The place looked like a hotel. No names on the doors, just numbers.

Not a single person appeared as they passed through. The only noises and murmurs of chatter they heard along the way came from behind locked doors.

They entered the executive suites through a stairwell. The keycard Hanratty used to open the locks was identical in appearance to those of the security guards at Kratos.

"Have you ever been to Hanson or to Kratos?" Crowder asked, biding her time.

"Never," Hanratty replied bluntly.

Crowder thought he'd probably told so many lies in his life that a polygraph would be unable to decipher what was true and false.

The tour ended with no office to search and no one to arrest.

"Is there someplace we can talk?" Hill asked. "You are head of security. I think you have the right to know what we know about Heartland Insurance and Kratos."

Hill was baiting Hanratty—something Crowder had done many times with suspects who thought they were smarter and cleverer than her. If they could get Hanratty to listen, they just might get him to talk—say something they could prove false. Or do something afterward that implicated him or others in wrongdoing.

Crowder had her own reasons for a sit-down with Hanratty. Hill would have to wait to find out what they were.

~

Hanratty sat across from Hill and Crowder at a table in a conference room as sterile as Hanratty's office. It reminded Crowder of the interrogation rooms at district headquarters. Their meeting was probably being recorded. Finch would want to know everything they said, and Hill and Crowder wanted him to.

Hill's opening salvo was to disclose the FBI's analysis of the evidence that had been mailed to him by an anonymous source. "We know that two and a half years ago, Max Litchman's serum ended up in the veins of twenty-three people whose one-million-dollar life insurance policies had been purchased by Heartland Insurance. We know that his serum caused blood clots to abnormally form in all of them. We know that the clots caused all of them to die at least ten years earlier than their life expectancies—a statistical impossibility."

Hill paused a moment to let Hanratty reflect on what he'd said.

Hanratty sat with his hands folded on the table. His face was expressionless, except for the cold, dark stare his eyes couldn't hide.

Hill upped the ante. "We have a distribution list with the last names of nurses. It's only a matter of time before we track them down and they tell us they've been injecting people with Litchman's serum."

Hanratty appeared unmoved—not a facial tic, shoulder twitch, bead of perspiration, or cough to clear his throat.

"The bottom line," Hill concluded. "A grand jury has convened and will indict Jared Finch and Max Litchman on twenty-three counts of murder. This is the time to cut your deal before Heartland Insurance is prosecuted for operating a criminal enterprise the likes of which has never been seen before."

Crowder waited patiently for Hanratty's response. She had the sudden urge to say something sarcastic like, *What, Colonel, the cat got your tongue?*

"So your evidence is what was mailed to you by an anonymous sender?" Hanratty calmly asked.

"So far. But it won't be long before we have a nurse or two lined up to testify."

"A nurse from the distribution list you say was mailed to you?"

Hill answered with a nod.

"Who do you think sent the evidence to you?"

Hill took a deep breath and exhaled as if exasperated. "Someone with a conscience, I'm quite sure of that."

Crowder had a sudden uneasy feeling. Hill got nothing from

Hanratty—not even an expression of concern. She suspected why.

It was Crowder's turn to pounce. She reached into the inside pocket of her blazer for four photos. A forensics technician had pulled them from her computer the day before and converted them into five-inch-by-seven-inch glossy photos. She reached over and placed two of them face up on the table within arm's reach of Hanratty. She wanted to study his reaction when he looked at them.

Crowder understood body language. The surprise of eyes that opened to twice their size, the shock of a jaw that dropped, the worry of a brow that furrowed, the anguish of eyelids that fluttered closed and for a long moment refused to open.

Crowder liked showing photos to persons of interest, particularly crime scene photos—the dead bodies of boys, girls, men, and women who'd been beaten, strangled, smothered, stabbed, or shot. More often than not, she'd get a reaction that told her whether the person of interest was now a suspect.

The photos on the table were not of dead people who'd been murdered but of the persons who had murdered them.

"Do you recognize the persons in these photos?"

Hanratty paused and reached inside his suit jacket for his eyeglasses.

He hadn't needed them when he read the warrants, so he didn't need them now.

He picked up the photos and, holding one in each hand, looked first at the one of a teenage girl who had enlisted in military service eighteen years ago, and then the one of her brother. Hanratty's body language revealed nothing.

He'd have to admit he knew them. A pair that unique was impossible to forget—the only woman and the only twins to have ever served in the Delta Force. And they served under

Hanratty's command.

Hanratty placed the photos on the table and pushed them toward Crowder. He removed his glasses and stared at her. "Of course I recognize the Larssons," he said. "They were under my command between 2001 and 2004. Fine soldiers."

Hanratty had passed his first test.

But Crowder had more to ask. "Colonel, did you keep in touch with them after they left military service?"

"No. As I recall it, they both wanted to relocate to Sweden, where they were born, and live there."

The toll of lies increased with each answer he gave.

"What were their specialties while under your command?"

He answered like she expected. "All information about members of the Delta Force from their training to their participation is classified." He paused and revealed a slight grin. "But you knew that."

"I thought that maybe they joined you in your next endeavor, it being the case that the three of you left the service around the same time?"

"Is that a question or an observation?"

"A question."

"They went their way; I went mine."

"And where was your way?"

"Detective Crowder, I fail to see how answering that question will assist you in any way in the investigation being conducted."

"That's just it, Colonel," she answered with mock respect for his military rank. "It has everything to do with an investigation you are very much a part of."

"And what investigation is that?"

"The murders of Martin Goldman and Christine Finch."

Hill's attempt to unnerve Hanratty had failed. But her gambit with Hanratty was to let him know that he was implicated in a double homicide. She got the reaction she'd hoped for.

"How so? Christine Finch's kidnappers killed her because Martin Goldman made off with the ransom. You were there alongside me to witness her execution on the video clip."

"We found Christine Finch's body in the trunk of her car last week. Goldman's body was underneath it. We held out reporting the deaths until their parents could be notified." A lie. Crowder buried the medical examiner's death notices under a pile of reports so that Finch wouldn't find out his wife and Goldman had been found.

"You think Elsa and Liam Larsson murdered them," Hanratty smirked. "That's preposterous."

"We know they murdered them. There are warrants out for their arrests."

"What makes you think they were in any way involved in their deaths?"

"Murders, Colonel," Crowder stated emphatically.

"But you have no proof they were anywhere near New Orleans when Christine Finch and Goldman were killed," he countered.

Crowder pulled out a second set of photos. She put them on the table and, as before, slid them closer to Hanratty. He didn't put on his eyeglasses this time. He looked at the close-up photos of the Larsson siblings standing on Bourbon Street on the day of the murders and of a wide-angle shot that showed Crowder's car sandwiched between their vehicles.

"We had their plate numbers. They rented the vehicles from the same car-rental company at the airport the day before the murders and returned them the day after. The surveillance cameras in the terminal captured them in line at the counter—one behind the other. There are APBs out for their arrests at every airport, train terminal, bus station, and rat hole in Louisiana and neighboring states. It's just a matter of time before we find them."

"I fail to see where I fit into this?"

"Someone had to tell them where I was when I followed Goldman's taxi from Finch's home. It was you who called them as soon as I left."

"And how could I possibly know where you and the taxi were going?"

Crowder rose from her chair, reached into a pocket of her blazer, and tossed one of the NOPD's tracking devices on the desk.

"Here, keep it. The one you planted in the wheel well of my truck on the day of the murders is in an evidence bag at district headquarters."

Hill spoke for the first time since Crowder took over the interrogation. "You think long and hard about what you want to do. You know how to reach us."

Hill stood to signal an end to the meeting.

They made their way to the guard's station in the lobby. When they entered the public side of the lobby, Hanratty stayed back. He called out to them, "Hill, Crowder."

They stopped and turned.

Hanratty looked at one, then the other, and said, "Let him … or her … who is without sin cast the first stone. John, Chapter 8, Verse 7."

Chapter 46

The company limo waited at the airfield when Finch landed. He received a text message from the colonel as he got out of the vehicle at home: *They know everything. We have a very limited window.*

Finch looked up from his cell phone and turned to speak to Gladstone. "It looks like we'll be making reservations for our golf weekend sooner than we thought."

"One less now that Goldman's gone," Gladstone said.

Finch wanted to say, *Two less now that Litchman's gone too*, but he closed the door instead. For the moment, it was best to keep his comments to himself.

~

The CD arrived in the afternoon mail in a plain envelope. No return address. No accompanying letter. Only the words, "One Week" on the label.

Crowder inserted the disk into her desktop computer. It ran for twenty-two minutes. When it stopped, she called Hill.

They met at Crowder's place.

Hill brought a bottle of wine and a bottle of scotch—even though the first bottle he'd brought and left there was only half-empty. They sat on the ends of her sofa with a drink in their hands. Hill shook his glass so the ice would chill the liquor, then took a long, slow sip.

Crowder did the same with her wine, hoping for an early buzz.

"My CD came an hour after you called," Hill said. "The security cameras were hidden. Some kind of new technology.

"I didn't see any when I looked," Crowder said. "I figured that since all the doors were secured with locks, maybe they saw no need for surveillance in the corridors."

Hill shook his head and laughed. "We proved there's no such thing as a perfect crime." He took another swallow—this time emptying his glass. "So let's assess the damage," he continued. "See what we can and can't control."

Crowder went first. "We can't be sure they won't send the CD to Morales even if we give them a week."

"They believe they're in control," Hill said. "They know the case against Heartland Insurance falls apart if Morales can't use any of our evidence."

"A week. Why so long for them to get out of Dodge? They're a paperless company. They'd know how to get rid of the incriminating stuff on their computers."

"Greed," Hill said. "Finch wants to cash in on the money out there on the streets. There are claims the company has made that are pending and claims of insureds injected with the serum who haven't yet died. He'll need the information on his computer a while longer until he figures out a way to collect on what's out there."

Crowder sensed Hill was right. She reminded him that she'd put a hold on the death certificates of Moss, Hartman, and

Helmsley. "The double indemnity claims I'm sitting on alone are worth thirty million dollars to Heartland Insurance."

Hill got up from the sofa. "Refill?"

Crowder finished what was left in her glass and handed it to him. It was going to be one of those nights when one glass of wine was good, but three were better.

When he returned, Crowder became introspective. "Alex, I hesitated for a while before I took the vial. I asked myself, Is it worth losing my badge over? But Finch and Hanratty were responsible for the murders of eight people." Crowder paused a moment to reflect on who they were. As if she was reading from a list of obituaries in her head, she said their names: "Moss, Hartman, Helmsley, McManus, Crockett, Marshall, Goldman, and Christine Finch." She sighed heavily, then continued, "In my mind, people like Jared Finch, who kill with impunity, will keep on killing. I took the vial because someone had to stop him."

Hill looked at his glass. Mostly ice remained. It was his turn for soul-searching. "When I broke into Litchman's office and found the documents in his desk," he began, "I'd already debated my conscience. I thought about Brian and Jason—two young men with a lifetime of memories to make. Two men I recruited and got killed. When I stole the documents, I did it for them. I didn't want them to have died in vain." Hill looked up from his glass at Crowder. "Jo, I got you into this. I should have had the guts to do it alone."

Crowder felt sorry for Hill. He was haunted by the personal tragedies in his life and angry that he'd been dealt a bad hand. He felt responsible for the deaths of McManus and Crocket as much as he had for the deaths of his wife and sons.

"Alex, what I did, I did on my own. I'm prepared to face the consequences. Law enforcement isn't an exact science. We are not machines. My father told me that it might be necessary someday to choose between 'doing what was legal or doing what was right.' I felt I was doing what was right."

Hill put his glass on the table and moved closer to Crowder. "Jo, I know you're thinking we need to tell Morales the truth before she sees what's on the CD. But to tell her now would halt the investigation and give Finch and Hanratty the chance to destroy evidence. The evidence is on their computers, I'm sure of it. I saw it in the paper files in Litchman's desk that night. Tomorrow, I'll get Morales to issue subpoenas to Finch and Hanratty to testify before the grand jury, and also a search warrant to seize their computers. While they think we're mulling over what we should do, we'll surprise them and grab their computers."

Hill's plan just might give them a way out. If the evidence was on their computers, Morales would have what she'd need for convictions—evidence seized during a lawful search. She'd no longer need the evidence they stole from Kratos.

"By the way, you were terrific today—the way you handled Hanratty," Hill said. "He had us on the security camera footage, so he was unfazed by the evidence I told him we had against Finch and his company. But finding Hanratty's assassins, and then revealing them to him, was brilliant. He knows that he's implicated in the murders of Goldman and Finch's wife and will likely be indicted on a conspiracy charge in a double homicide case."

Crowder felt at ease. Two glasses of wine made her mellow. Three stimulated her libido. There'd been chemistry between them right from the start. After Hanson, she knew she could trust him with her life. But could she trust him with her heart?

Hill moved closer to her on the sofa. She could smell the bold scent of his aftershave. Perhaps the whiskey and wine were removing the remaining barriers between them. Or was it her salacious stare and his lustful smile?

"A nightcap?" Hill asked, reaching out a hand for her glass.

She reached out her hand—the one without the glass. Hill took it in his and gently squeezed it. When he bent his head forward, she did too. They stared deep into each other's eyes, as if to see what lay within each other's hearts.

There was no need for words.

He'd let his heart do the talking.

And she'd let hers do the listening.

Chapter 47

Finch was on his computer when Hanratty barged into his office.

"We should close down operations immediately," the colonel advised. "I'm being followed. The feds make it so obvious. But if they're following me, they're following you."

"I'm not leaving millions on the table," Finch said sharply. "We'll leave tomorrow after close of business as planned. I need today and tomorrow morning to complete arrangements with the lawyers and accountants. I figured out a way to continue the flow of undeclared revenues to the offshore account."

Finch's exit plan called for staging their deaths. Perplexed, Hanratty asked, "How is that possible if you're dead?"

"Unless they find the body, the lawyers I hired tell me that the authorities have to keep open the possibility I'm alive. It will take years before I'm declared dead. They will make sure of it. By then the company will have no revenues and will be dissolved."

"And how's the money going to flow to you?"

"With the powers of attorney I've given the lawyers, they'll receive the revenues and profits and send my share to the offshore account. A hefty twenty-five-percent fee was enough to compromise their ethics ... and what the accountants get comes out of their share."

Hanratty understood Finch's lust for power, but he'd underestimated his boundless greed. By corrupting the lawyers and accountants, he'd found a way to continue to siphon off the fifty percent of revenues that were undeclared. He'd only lose a quarter of it to buy off his collaborators.

Hanratty had renewed hope that his unholy partnership with Finch would continue. In matters of money, Hanratty was very much like Finch. In the CIA, the missions paid well. It was the one government agency that had never been fully audited. When you don't have to account for the money Congress appropriates, you can do whatever you want with it. And Hanratty and his team were paid in non-taxable, untraceable cash.

The services he offered paid much more in the private sector. Finch paid him a salary commensurate to others in the industry. But the real money was in the bonuses he received—bounties on the heads of those with double indemnity policies. Ten percent of the proceeds went to him. That was a lot of money, even after paying half to the Larssons for arranging the *accidental* and *unintentional* deaths.

Hanratty did a quick calculation in his head. The last time he checked, there were at least a dozen double indemnity policies to collect on. Now that Finch had found a way to keep the company's operations going in his absence, he'd want to collect on those policies. Finch needed him to do that.

Heartland Insurance was an ongoing criminal enterprise that could still be prosecuted. But Hanratty wasn't worried. So far, the FBI had no admissible evidence of wrongdoing. The stolen documents and vial of serum were useless to them. The only evidence of wrongdoing that remained was on Finch and Hanratty's computers. Once it was gone, and the remaining vials of serum were destroyed, the government had no proof.

Nothing would stop Finch from posthumously collecting on the remaining policies. When the company had begun buying life insurance policies, the insured was required to pay the premiums and to execute a change of beneficiary form that the company held until the insured died. The FBI could contact every life insurance company in the country, but until the insureds were dead and the proceeds paid out, there would be no way to connect Heartland Insurance to any of them. By then it would be too late to do anything about it; the evidence would be buried with the bodies.

Hanratty's reflections ended when Finch said, "Tomorrow morning, remove what's malignant from our computers, leave only what's benign."

"I'll need total access to our network system computer. Our individual computers won't be operational until I finish."

"How long will you need?"

"Thirty minutes."

"Give everyone a holiday tomorrow. My dealings with the lawyers will be completed tomorrow morning. I'll be logged out of my computer by ten. Do it then. I'll pick you up on the roof at ten-thirty."

"And how do you plan on losing the tail?"

"I don't. Let them see Gray and me in our golf shirts and caps loading our clubs and travel bags into the Eurocopter. It will all fit in when the wreckage is found in the Gulf."

Finch's confidence bolstered Hanratty. He just might be able to pull it off. Finch was right. No money should be left on the table.

~

"I'm not liking what I see in the field," Hill said, when Crowder answered his call.

Crowder knew he'd call her. He'd enjoyed their evening together as much as she did. The text message he'd sent her after he left confirmed it—*Thanks for listening.*

Just where a relationship might go was something Crowder seldom dwelled on—regardless of how much she liked the man—or enjoyed the sex. What she did for a living had always destroyed any chance of a long-lasting relationship, and it probably would again. For now, bringing down Finch and his company should be her first priority, and Hill's. Any meaningful relationship between them would have to wait.

"What don't you like?" Crowder asked when she refocused.

"They're acting like it's business as usual," Hill replied. "Both were in the office today. No one suspicious entered or left where they work or live. They didn't use what time they have left to go to banks or lawyer's offices."

"They know they're being followed. Their plans are being made from behind closed doors."

"You're right, of course. But the clock is ticking. We need what's on their computers, and fast. I want to execute the search warrant tomorrow morning at ten."

Crowder asked, "What about the nurses?"

"We have agents tracking them down who will confiscate any unused serum."

"When will the US Marshal serve the subpoenas?"

"He won't," Hill replied. "We will—right after we serve and execute the search warrant. I want to see the bastards' faces when they realize we have their computers and no intention of playing ball with them."

"So much hangs in the balance tomorrow," Crowder mused. "All the evidence could be right there in their computers."

"Jo."

"What, Alex?"

"About last night..." Hill paused long enough to show he had difficulty putting into words what he wanted to say. Was it to tell her it was a mistake, that it wouldn't work out between them in the long run, or that it was still too early for a relationship?

Crowder had her doubts too, and she spoke before he could say more. "Alex, it's not what happened last night that should concern us, it's what is going to happen tomorrow that should."

When the call ended, Crowder didn't know whether it was disappointment or relief she felt.

Chapter 48

"They're downstairs in the lobby," Hanratty said when Finch answered his call. "I got here a few minutes ago. I can see Hill and Crowder, and a posse of agents, on the monitor in the IT department."

"Were you followed there?" Finch asked.

"I changed taxis twice and lost them."

"Do the guards know you're there?"

"No. I entered through the garage and took the freight elevator up."

"How long will it take you to clean our computers?"

"After I activate the virus, twenty minutes."

"Gray and I are loading up now," Finch said. "Hide in the garage. I'll call you when we approach."

Hanratty was cutting it close. He opened the network system computer and entered a password only he and Finch knew. The data-eating virus needed the full twenty minutes to spread to all the files they wanted permanently destroyed. Stopped earlier, all memory could be restored. It was a fail-safe mechanism that allowed time to reverse a mistake.

He looked at his digital watch—10:10 a.m. He set the timer

for twenty minutes. The tap of a finger on the keyboard activated the virus. The press of a thumb on the side of his watch started the timer.

With nothing left to do but wait, he left the room and headed to the garage.

~

Hill appropriated the guard's keycard and used it to access the penthouse elevator. Two crime scene investigators—one a specialist in opening locks, the other an IT technician who would remove the computers and hard drives—accompanied Hill and Crowder. The five of them and the cart fit easily in the elevator.

The fifth person was Nadav Franks, one of the foremost computer hacking experts in the world. The man looked oddly out of place. Twenty-eight years old, his youthful appearance, casual attire, and broad, toothy grin made him look more like a college freshman pledging a fraternity.

He had impeccable credentials: three years of military service in Unit 8200, the elite intelligence arm of the Israeli Defense Forces, a stint making top dollar as a computer security consultant to Silicon Valley companies, and five years in a federal penitentiary for hacking into the Pentagon … just to see if he could. His sentence was commuted after six months on condition that he became the FBI's cybersecurity expert.

When they exited the elevator, they went immediately to Hanratty's office. It took five minutes for the specialist to decode the lock on the door. It had taken Hill twice as long to decode the lock on Litchman's office door using the same device, which is why he wanted a specialist there. Still, Hill couldn't hide his impatience or his sarcasm. "Anytime today or tomorrow is fine with us," he said to the specialist midway through.

Franks went immediately to the desk and sat in the chair in front of it. He flipped on the computer while the others watched from behind. The date and time appeared on the screen below a picture of a padlock. He plugged in the device he used to override passwords.

Crowder's eyes jumped to the time: 10:17 a.m. The hacker used his thumbs to type in series after series of numbers on his device. Three minutes later the computer unlocked.

"Go to Files," Hill called out. "Let's see what's there."

Franks scrolled to files and tapped his device. A warning immediately flashed on the screen—*Access denied until data removal is complete.*

"What's going on?" Hill asked nervously.

"I'll know in a minute," Franks replied, navigating to other functions on the computer. One after the other, the same warning flashed. "Houston, we have a problem," he wisecracked. "A big problem."

"What kind of problem?"

"A virus is erasing the computer's data. Since no one's here, I must have triggered it when I hacked in. It's an anti-hacking mechanism used by a number of corporations and government agencies. But this one is different."

"Why is it different?"

"It's not just erasing the data; it's permanently destroying it in the cloud."

Crowder frowned. "How much data's been lost?"

"A little more than half," Franks replied. "The timer at the bottom of the screen is recording its progress. It's a little more than ten minutes into a twenty-minute run."

"Can you stop it?" Hill asked impatiently.

"Not from here. I need access to the network system

computer. Where is the IT department?"

Crowder did a quick calculation in her head. It took five minutes to get into Hanratty's office and three or four minutes to hack into his computer. Even if they could find the IT department, they wouldn't have enough time to deactivate the virus.

Hill said they didn't know and mumbled an obscenity.

But Franks remained cucumber-cool, speaking as he navigated his way to Directory. "This should tell us where to find it." He tapped and scrolled down to the floor plan. "We're lucky. Only certain files are being destroyed by the virus. It's leaving everything else alone." He typed *information technology services* in the search engine.

Crowder's gaze shifted to the computer's digital timer as the seconds ticked off. It read 12:01. "We have eight minutes," she announced, inadvertently adding to the tension in the room.

The mounting pressure unfazed Franks.

Hill, less so.

The schematic of the offices two floors below highlighted the location of the room—*central network computer.* Franks spoke calmly. "Room 2803. Two floors down. Left off the elevator. Second door on the right."

Hill turned and dashed out the door. Crowder, the lock specialist, and Franks followed in his footsteps.

~

The colonel stood with his back against a wall in the garage, looking at the timer on his watch. In less than seven minutes, all the incriminating data against Heartland Insurance would be permanently erased: the formula for Litchman's algorithm, the clinical trials he ran on chimps, the actuarial performance of the serum on humans, contact information for the nurses who unwittingly injected the lethal serum thinking it was a preservative for the blood sample, the death certificates and change of beneficiary forms, every dollar of unreported income that ended up in offshore accounts, and every cash payment made to Hanratty to secure the services of Liam and Elsa Larsson, a.k.a. Hawk and Wolf.

Hanratty couldn't believe his good luck. The evidence that proved that Heartland Insurance was in fact *Murder, Incorporated* was about to be released into a cloudless sky, and evaporate into thin air.

Chapter 49

When the doors opened two floors below, they dashed from the elevator. Crowder and Hill stood on each side of the door numbered 2803.

"Open it," Hill shouted.

The lock specialist fiddled with his device as he'd done earlier.

Crowder looked down at her left wrist. It was 10:14 a.m. by her digital watch. Every second was too valuable to waste. "Alex, we're running out of time," she warned, urgency in her tone.

"You're right." Hill tapped the specialist on the shoulder. "Move away from the door."

Everyone backed away, and Hill drew his pistol and pointed the barrel at the lock mechanism. He glanced at Crowder. "Care to join me? The door is steel. I may need your help."

Crowder didn't hesitate. She reached for her handgun and planted herself by his side.

"Fire away," he said.

Each shot twice, the blasts reverberating through the corridor like thunder through a canyon. The door sparked as the lock's metal casing split apart. Hill kicked the door open. Computers of different shapes and sizes filled the room, but

Franks knew immediately where to go. He sat in a chair in front of a computer inconspicuously nestled in a corner of the room.

Hill stood over him. "Work your magic," he said.

Franks plugged in his device and double-thumbed the keypad like he was playing a video action game.

The seconds ticked into minutes.

Three minutes later the computer unlocked. The hacker went directly to Settings, found the icon he wanted and tapped it. The operational numbers of all of the computers at Heartland Insurance came up on the screen. There were dozens of computers, but only two were illuminated in green.

"There are two computers infected with the virus," Franks said, the evenness of his tone showing no urgency.

"Finch and Hanratty's computers," Crowder said, when she saw the initials JF and JH next to a series of numbers.

Hill yelled, "You're wasting time, Franks."

Crowder sensed Hill's agitation was over the tech's nonchalant attitude—like it was a game he was playing and the only harm in timing out was that he'd have to reset and play again.

The timer at the bottom of the screen showed 18:30. A minute and a half to stop the virus. Ninety seconds before the virus destroyed any real chance of bringing down Finch and the evil empire he ruled.

Hill's career hung in the balance. Crowder's too.

The timer ticked to nineteen minutes.

Crowder's heart thumped in her chest. Her mouth went dry. Her stomach knotted.

Hill enhanced her misery when he yelled, "Damn it, Franks. I thought you were the GOAT. Do you know what the fuck you're doing? Can you stop the virus?"

Franks stopped what he was doing, looked over his shoulder at Hill, and gave him his trademark smile. In a calm and confident voice, he said, "Of course I can stop the virus. Isn't that why I'm here?" He turned back to face the computer and tapped a small box illuminated in red in the left corner of the screen. A drop-down appeared with two choices:

Memory Delete.

Memory Restore.

Franks paused only long enough to say: "Agent Hill, as much as I like chatting with you, I have a virus to stop." He scrolled to *Memory Restore* and tapped.

The timer at the bottom of the screen stopped at 19:46.

Hill wasted no time. "Can you access the computers from here?"

"Of course I can," he replied matter-of-factly. Within seconds, he'd gained access.

Hill took over from there. He replaced Franks in the chair, and while Crowder stood looking over his shoulder, he navigated to the files on Finch's computer and scrolled through them quickly, scanning their content. The evidence they needed was there: the algorithm, the lethality of the serum, the nurses' contact information, the double indemnity deaths, the payments to Hanratty, and the banks and account numbers where the inner circle had hidden their ill-gotten gains.

Crowder noticed a file titled CBF that Hill passed over. She knew those initials. "Alex, open the CBF file."

He did as requested.

The file, with its contents separately indexed, contained photos, text messages, and phone conversations of Christine Benchley Finch and Martin Goldman. It was the evidence that proved Finch knew about his wife's affair and Goldman's plan to steal ten million dollars from him.

Hill raised his hand. "Listen. A helicopter. It's Finch." Hill turned his head and looked at Crowder. "How about you and I greet Mr. Finch with a copy of the search warrant and a subpoena?"

"The freight elevator will take us to the roof," Crowder said. "I saw its location on the schematic." She hurried out the door.

Hill followed while speaking into his cell phone. "This is Special Agent Hill, I need the copter—now! The roof of Finch Tower. Hover, until I give you further instructions."

"How long before it gets here?" Crowder asked on the elevator ride to the roof.

"Five minutes—I had it on standby."

The elevator opened into an enclosure that led to the helipad. They quickstepped down the corridor to the door and, through its window, saw Hanratty on the roof, walking to Finch's aircraft.

"Hanratty must have been in the building to activate the virus," Crowder deduced. "Finch is here to pick him up."

Hill pushed open the door and drew his gun. Crowder could see Finch in the pilot's seat. A passenger sat in the seat behind him. "Hanratty—FBI," Hill shouted. "Stop and return to the building—now!"

Hanratty was nearly to the opened door of the aircraft when Hill fired two shots in the air. Crowder, her gun pulled and pointed at the chopper, knew that her role was solely to back up her partner.

It didn't matter.

Hanratty jumped into the co-pilot's seat and slammed the door shut as Finch's helicopter lifted off from the tarmac.

Chapter 50

The FBI's helicopter touched down on the roof of Finch Tower and stayed only long enough for them to board. Crowder sat behind the pilot. Hill took the co-pilot's seat.

"They're headed east," Hill said to the pilot as the aircraft ascended from the helipad. "We lost visual, two, three minutes ago."

"I know," the pilot said. "The agents who tailed Finch to the airfield talked to the ground crew. Finch told them he was on his way to Tallahassee, which is east of New Orleans over the Gulf. Don't worry. We'll catch up."

The helicopter ascended to 10,000 feet and headed east. A few minutes later, a blip appeared on the radar screen. Hill saw it too.

"Stay back when you get a good visual," Hill said.

"If they'd taken the most direct route to Tallahassee, they would've been over the Gulf by now," the pilot said.

"Change of plans," Crowder suggested. "Maybe the business at the airfield was a diversion. He knew he was being tailed. Finch wanted us to believe he was going to Tallahassee."

"You're probably right," Hill said. He turned to the pilot. "Let's get a closer look."

The pilot increased his speed and climbed to 11,000 feet.

Finch's helicopter abruptly veered to the right.

"He's heading southeast," the pilot said. "He should be over the Gulf in a few minutes."

"They just might be going to Tallahassee after all," Hill surmised. "Let's close the—"

Crowder interrupted him mid-sentence. "If they are, there will be two less people arriving."

Hill saw what Crowder saw. Two parachutes opening behind Finch's aircraft. He wasted no time. "Jo, give me the parachute under your seat." He turned to the pilot. "Climb to 12,000 feet in the direction of the chutes. Once I'm out, follow the aircraft. Finch has to be flying it."

The pilot did as instructed.

"I hope you know what you're doing," Crowder cautioned.

"I was an airborne ranger in the army. I know what I'm doing."

Hill was in the parachute in thirty seconds. He reached in his pocket and tossed a tracking device to Crowder. "I brought this in case we needed to separate. It's linked to my cell phone. Use it to find me after Finch is on the ground and in custody."

Before Crowder could say another word, Hill had opened the door and jumped out.

Crowder moved into the co-pilot's seat. "Will he catch up to them?" she asked.

The pilot looked at Crowder. "He wanted to be higher so he could skydive and close the gap before opening his chute. He'll catch up. When they touch ground, he won't be far behind."

"Can you get in radio contact with Finch?"

"If his radio is on the usual civilian frequency, I will. Whether he chooses to respond is up to him."

The helicopter closed rapidly, then descended until it was

alongside Finch's aircraft.

Crowder stared at the pilot's seat.

It was empty.

~

Hill shot through the sky like a missile. He'd found his parachute training in the army exhilarating and had learned to skydive after his discharge. He never imagined he'd need it in his work. But he needed it now.

Two parachutes floated in tandem toward the ground. Hill opened his while he was still above and behind them. While they recovered their parachutes, he'd find a spot with sufficient cover to not be seen from the ground. He had a bead on their location, and he'd track them to wherever they were going. At least that was the plan.

~

"You said there were three on board," the pilot said.

"There were," Crowder replied. "Odd man out. Probably unconscious or dead on the floor of the backseat. We can't waste our time following *a dead man flying.*"

"Funny, very funny … and appropriate," the pilot said, muffling a laugh.

"Let's head back to where the others were going."

The pilot banked into a turn. "I know where they were headed—the woodlands southwest of Gulfport."

Crowder needed to find Hill. He thought Finch was still flying his aircraft. Little did he know that he was tracking two desperate men who would do anything to escape. She didn't want Hill to confront them alone.

Chapter 51

Hill glided into a clearing.

They'd landed in a meadow about a quarter mile from him. He figured that the landing site was predetermined. Someone nearby would be meeting them. On his way down, he'd scoped out the landscape. About half a mile to the west stood a cluster of mobile homes on a two-lane road. A one-story building sat, secluded off an unpaved road, about the same distance to the east. Two vehicles were parked there.

It had to be where they were going.

Hill made a mental map of the geography he'd have to traverse to get there. It was primarily dense woodlands. Good cover. Slow progress.

He stretched out his chute on the grassland to provide a marker for the landing zone when the pilot returned. Once Crowder was on the ground, she'd use the tracking device to find him. His mission was to follow Hanratty to where he was going and keep him there until Crowder arrived with reinforcements.

~

Finch followed Hanratty through the woodlands and brush. Hanratty had rented the ramshackle bungalow a year ago as part of Finch's exit plan. The owner of the dump couldn't believe his good fortune when Elsa Larsson paid him the rent in cash two years in advance. No lease. No questions. No hassles.

The house served a single purpose. It was where the Larssons would meet up with Hanratty and Finch and give them their travel bags, plane tickets, new identity documents, and enough cash to get them to where they were going.

The five-member inner circle was down to two. Goldman had been shot in the head as his reward for having tried to con a master con artist out of his wife and money. Litchman took his last breaths with a plastic bag over his head as his penance for having left a paper trail for Hill to find. Gladstone spent his last moments waiting for his heart to stop from the lethal injection the colonel gave him. Their deaths were preordained; Finch never intended for any of them to share what he'd stashed away.

They arrived at their destination after a twenty-minute hike through the woods. Liam and Elsa Larsson stood outside waiting. The two rentals were parked out front—one for Liam to drive Finch to the Gulfport-Biloxi Airport, the other for Elsa to drive Hanratty to the Jackson Airport. Two Mississippi airports 170 miles apart. Different airports and destinations gave them the best chance of getting out of the country undetected—that's what Finch had told Hanratty.

Finch promised to wire Hanratty the shares of the members of the inner circle the colonel had eliminated. He'd made promises before. Many he'd broken.

~

Hill approached the house from the front. The boxy wood-frame structure was the size of a double-wide trailer, and rested on cinder blocks. Two cars were parked one behind the other about sixty feet from a small, makeshift porch outside the front door. No one appeared to be outside.

Using the larger trees as cover, he worked his way to the rear of the house. He wanted to have a look inside. Get a head count. But the back door was windowless, and the rear windows had shades pulled down too low for him to see inside, so he moved around the side. The front door opened with a click. He froze. A heavy patter of footsteps followed. One person or more? He couldn't tell. He scurried to the back of the house and pulled out his weapon.

The trunks of the sedans opened and closed, one after the other.

More footsteps.

The front door slammed shut.

It was a warm humid day. Hill had seen no wildlife when he'd passed through the woodlands, and the birds he'd encountered flew high above the trees. None rested on the boughs and limbs. It made the place so eerily quiet that he heard twigs break and the crush of leaves under his shoes when he walked. So quiet that he could hear the murmur of people speaking.

He crept to the side of the house for a look inside. Through a window draped with tattered curtains only partially drawn, he saw the colonel standing at a table looking at documents as if he was trying to determine whether they were real or forged. They appeared to be passports, birth certificates, and driver's licenses. New identity documents.

Hill moved to another window. Its shade was only halfway down, giving him a better view inside the room. Finch sat in a chair with a carry-on bag opened on the floor in front of him. A man came into view. He recognized him from the photos

Crowder had shown Hanratty—Liam Larsson. He handed Finch four hardback books.

Finch reached into the bag and pulled out four bill straps of currency. He was close enough to the window for Hill to see that they were two bundles each of dollars and euros, in denominations of one hundred. From their thickness, Hill figured ten thousand dollars or euros in each bundle.

Finch opened the books he'd been given and hid a stack of currency in holes carved out inside each of the books. He placed a heavy-duty rubber band around two books, then around the other two and put the two bundles on a table.

The cash would easily pass through airport security.

Hill had to give Finch credit. His exit plan was well thought out. He and Hanratty couldn't use their credit cards. They'd need the cash until they were settled in under their new identities … wherever they were going.

Hill glanced at his watch. Crowder would've headed back as soon as she found out Finch wasn't flying his aircraft. She'd be there soon. When she arrived, each would cover a door and keep them penned in until the cavalry arrived. Until then the smart thing to do was for him to hide in the woodlands. If Hanratty knew he was there alone, it could have disastrous consequences.

Hill took one last look in the window.

Where was Elsa Larsson?

Footsteps shuffled behind him. He turned. The last thing he saw before his world went dark was the blade end of a shovel.

Chapter 52

Crowder saw Hill's parachute and pointed to where it lay on the ground. "There."

The pilot nodded. "He left it to show us where to set down."

The pilot had radioed for a search and rescue team to intercept the aircraft as soon as he realized it was on autopilot. There was nothing he or anyone else could do to redirect or land the aircraft. The pilot explained to Crowder that autopilots on helicopters were notoriously unstable. The aircraft would gradually lose altitude and crash in the Gulf. The Coast Guard would salvage whatever wreckage remained and retrieve the body.

"Before you land, do a flyover and circle the area," Crowder said. "Not too low. Let's not alert them that we're here."

Crowder saw what Hill had seen. Like him, she figured the house secluded in the forest was the hideout.

When they set down, the pilot called in the coordinates of their location.

"Let's get a tactical unit here as soon as possible," Crowder said as she got out of the aircraft. "I'll find Hill."

The helicopter lifted off and was soon out of sight. She pulled out the GPS tracking device Hill had given her and turned it on. A map of the area appeared on a miniature screen. The directional locator, however, did not activate. The GPS locator on Hill's cell phone was turned off. *But why?*

She headed into the woodlands in the direction of the house.

~

A kick in the ribs brought Hill to his senses. He found himself slumped over on the floor in a corner of the room. Elsa Larsson had done a number on him when she'd clobbered him with the shovel. The entire right side of his face throbbed—pulsating stabs of pain—and his head pounded like a migraine. His cheek was bruised, and above it, his eye was swollen half-shut. He thought his jaw might be broken. The pain from the kick radiated into Hill's chest like electric shocks. It made him forget his other injuries—but only for a moment. He soon had another sore spot to deal with.

He dragged himself into a sitting position and rested his back against a wall. When his dizziness subsided, he saw Hanratty standing over him with Hill's gun in his hand. His cell phone lay on a table in pieces.

The Larssons stood at attention by the door awaiting further orders. Finch sat relaxed in a chair, his legs crossed and his hands on the arms of the chair. The cold-eyed look Finch gave Hill did not bode well.

Finch spoke first. "Where's your other half?" He asked without a trace of emotion. "I thought that wherever you went, your lamb was sure to follow."

Hill mustered the strength to reply. The longer he could engage him in conversation, the more time Crowder had to arrive with reinforcements. "She stayed in the helicopter that was following you," Hill said, grimacing in pain. "It was such a beautiful day, I thought I'd go skydiving."

"A leap of faith on your part, Agent Hill," Finch said sarcastically. "But your beautiful day will not end the way it began."

"The game's over, Finch," Hill said resolutely. "We got to the data on your computer in time to save it."

Finch's eyes shifted to Hanratty as if to signal his displeasure. "It won't matter," he said confidently. "We'll soon be on our way. By the time your body is found, we'll be out of the country."

"We'll find you, the colonel, and his death squad, and there'll be lethal injections waiting for all of you when we do."

"If you do, but you won't be around to give them."

"What kind of monster are you, Finch? Do you even know how many people you've killed?"

"I saw no reason to count them."

"And you, Hanratty, are a disgrace to the uniform you once wore. How many people have you ordered your robots to kill?" Hill sensed Hanratty wanted to answer. And he was right.

"I was trained to kill," Hanratty said icily. "I trained others to kill. We learned how to kill for no reason other than that it was our mission to do so. Did the crew of the Enola Gay equivocate when ordered to drop the bomb?"

"That was different," Hill replied. "Those deaths saved American lives. You …" He stopped momentarily to turn his head in the direction of the Larssons. "… and your Manchurian candidates kill only for the money."

Finch stood, picked up the travel bag that lay by his chair, and walked to face Hill. The colonel stood about ten feet to his left, Hill's gun still in his hand. Hill knew his fate was sealed when he noticed that Hanratty wore latex gloves.

His mind didn't focus on the end of his life, but on the beginning, when he'd met his wife for the first time and fallen instantly in love. He remembered the first time he kissed her, the first time they made love. He saw himself crying tears of joy when she told him she was pregnant, and again when he held his infant sons in his arms for the first time. The scenes came quickly to mind, one after another like slides in a projector.

Oddly, Hill felt at peace for the first time since his heart hardened upon learning that his wife and sons were dead. He'd have no more demons to confront. No more days of drowning his self-pity in bottle after bottle of liquor. No more nights of restless slumber.

"Shoot him," Finch ordered.

The colonel raised the gun and pointed the barrel directly at Hill's face.

Hill felt the pain leave his body.

It was as if his soul had left too.

He felt himself smile.

He saw only the faces of his wife and sons.

Chapter 53

Crowder heard a gunshot as she approached the house. She hurried for cover behind a hedgerow and unholstered her weapon, quickly assessing the situation. Someone had been shot. Probably Hill. It would explain why the GPS on his cell phone wasn't activated. Two persons were needed to drive the vehicles there. That meant the colonel's obedient assassins were in the house with him and Finch. Five of them inside the house.

Her mind reconstructed how it probably ended for Hill. All it would take would be a nod from Finch. The colonel would know what to do. Someone like Hanratty had the moral fabric of a Gestapo agent. He'd want Hill to stare down the barrel of a gun before a bullet blasted a hole in his head, or he might have had one of the Larssons shoot him. Neither would have thought twice about killing an FBI agent in cold blood. Then again, Hanratty might have wanted the pleasure of doing it himself.

Crowder caught herself clenching her jaw. Her heart raced. The gun felt sweaty in her hand, and she felt hot in her core—manifestations of her evolving rage. She hated all of them, but Hanratty the most. The Larssons were the pit bulls he'd raised from pups. They did the bidding of their owner and breeder.

"Sic," he'd say, and they'd be on a target like fleas on a feral cat's ass.

If Crowder had the chance, she'd shoot Hanratty dead without hesitation. No warning to "Come out with your hands up," like Ron Santoro expected her to do. If the opportunity presented, she'd put a couple of bullets in the back of the cold-hearted bastard. And if he survived the gunshots, she'd stand over him and watch him bleed to death with a smile on her face.

But a moment later, Crowder's heart sank. She flashbacked to her liaison with Hill: the way he looked at her the first time they'd met in the gym, their road trip to Hanson, saving each other's lives when their car was about to be blown up, going rogue together at Kratos— risking their careers in search of the truth and for the greater good.

She saw him lying beside her after they'd made love, her head resting on his chest. She remembered how the beat of his heart was rapid but in sync with hers and how gently he stroked her hair. She'd felt connected to him at that moment—a kinship she'd not felt with another man before … ever.

Hill would never love another woman like he loved his wife, and Crowder was content with that. It was enough for her to have shared intimate moments with him, if only for a single evening. For one sweet night, Crowder's rough edges had been smoothed, and for the first time in her life, she couldn't stop herself from falling in love.

Grim reality replaced Crowder's musings. She was outnumbered four to one. Once they discovered she was there, alone, Hanratty and the Larssons would have no trouble getting to her. She couldn't cover the front and back doors at the same time. They'd leave the house from the unguarded door or a side window, one after the other. They'd fan out in the woodlands and triangulate her position. With three guns pointed at her from different directions, they'd open fire while they moved in on her. The first one there would win the prize of shooting her dead.

Crowder needed a better look at what she was up against. She crept to the side of the house, found a window, and peered inside.

She couldn't believe what she saw.

~

Hill's eyes had opened in time to see Hanratty redirect his aim and fire a bullet into the face of Jared Finch. The pain when Hill's jaw dropped returned him to earth. He looked up at Hanratty. "Why?" he asked after a wave of shock passed through him.

"Because Finch was a fool for thinking I was a fool," Hanratty replied coldly.

Hill, still awestruck, said, "I underestimated you, Hanratty. You planned all along to keep the money for yourself."

Hanratty looked down at Finch. The bullet had blown away an eye and was lodged somewhere in his brain. "He thought I was eliminating the others for him. He had his exit plan"—he paused to look at the Larssons—"*we* had ours."

"Bravo, Colonel," Hill said scornfully. "You're a murderer and a thief, and a master at both."

"Agent Hill, I regret to inform you that you are now part of our exit plan." He looked at Elsa. "Put the bags in the trunk and wait in the car."

She complied without delay, but Liam stayed back. Without Hanratty asking him, he busied himself moving furniture and Finch's body.

Hill didn't need to ask why. Once he'd appeared out of nowhere, Hanratty had a patsy. He'd shot Finch with Hill's gun.

Only Hill's prints were on it. The gun Hanratty would use to shoot him would have only Finch's prints on it.

"More staged killings," Hill said, knowing that Finch's death had been a temporary reprieve of his own death sentence.

"We are quite good at such things," Hanratty boasted, putting Hill's gun on the table. He pulled out a pistol wrapped in a cloth from the pocket of his jacket and walked over to where Finch lay on the floor. He removed the cloth and returned it to his pocket. Then for the second time, Hanratty pointed a gun directly at Hill.

Chapter 54

Crowder retreated to the hedgerow as soon as Elsa Larsson received her orders. She waited there until Elsa walked to the car nearest the house and opened the trunk. By the time the lid slammed shut, Crowder stood directly behind her. Startled, Elsa turned and was greeted by the "Okinawan slap," a martial arts strike to the carotid sinus located behind the jaw. When delivered properly, the strike caused immediate loss of oxygen to the brain followed by unconsciousness.

The strike was properly delivered.

Elsa collapsed to the ground.

Crowder did a quick frisk. No handgun. But hidden inside the back pocket of Elsa's jeans was a four-inch-long metal object—a switchblade knife. A small, effective, and potentially lethal self-defense weapon. Crowder slid her thumb against the side of the handle, releasing the three-inch razor-sharp blade, which she used to puncture the tires on the passenger side of both vehicles. She retracted the blade and slipped the knife into her own back pocket.

Elsa lay on the ground unconscious. Crowder had to move quickly before she heard another gunshot—the one intended for

Hill. She dragged Elsa's limp body to the driver's side of the car, pulled out her handcuffs, and cuffed a hand to the side mirror. She then positioned herself on the other side of the car with her elbows on the hood, gripping her pistol in both hands, aiming at the front door. If she had to redirect her aim to the windows on either side of it, her reaction time would be cut in half. If a shooter came out the door, she'd have dead aim on him.

In a shootout—milliseconds mattered.

"Hanratty, it's Crowder," she shouted. "In a very short time you'll be in the middle of an FBI tactical rescue mission, and Liam's sister will be in the middle of any shootout. You know how that will end."

The half-closed shades on the front windows rose to the top, one after the other. Crowder redirected her aim back and forth between windows.

A window opened next. "You know what we're capable of," Hanratty yelled from behind it. "We've been on suicide missions before, yet here we are to fight another day."

"The only chance for you to fight another day is to release Hill. Send him out, and we'll give you a head start. The keys to both cars and the handcuffs are on the hood. We'll be stuck here, and you'll be miles away before anyone shows up."

"So it's Hill you want in exchange for that chance."

"It was Finch I wanted. But he's dead. You made sure of that. I'll have to settle for Hill instead."

Crowder understood hostage situations. Both sides needed to give something to get something in return. She'd give Hanratty a chance to escape. He'd give her Hill. A good deal for both sides—as long as both sides could be trusted.

Elsa groaned from the other side of the car and wiggled her hand in the cuff. She pulled the chain links taut a couple of times, then stood, rubbing the side of her head with her free hand. With a glare at Crowder, she said, "We meet again … for the last time."

Crowder stood, making sure to keep Elsa between her and the front of the house. "I wouldn't bet on it," she said, her aim still on the front door.

"I would. You see there's a difference between us. You kill only when your life is in danger. I kill even when it isn't. That often makes the difference in who lives and who dies."

"Don't be so sure, Elsa. Sometimes my finger itches to pull the trigger so much that I feel like you."

"We'll see." Elsa reached across the hood for the key to the handcuffs.

Just before she reached them, Crowder hit the top of her hand hard with the handle of her gun.

Elsa jerked back her hand and screamed obscenities.

Crowder had been called a fucking bitch on more than one occasion. It didn't hurt her feelings before, or now. "I've been called worse," Crowder snickered. "I'm sure you have too. Now behave yourself, little girl, and let the adults figure out what's best for you."

Elsa's eyes narrowed into a menacing stare. "I'm going to enjoy killing you. And if not today, someday."

"Get in line. There're more than a few punks serving time who'd like to have that chance if they ever get out."

The front door creaked open, and Hanratty called out from behind it. "We're coming out. When we're all outside in the open, unlock the cuffs, and we'll exchange Hill for the woman. Then you and Hill move away from the cars, and we'll get in and drive away."

"Sure," Crowder said. "Come outside. Let me see what I'm getting in the exchange."

Hanratty pushed Hill out the door, holding onto him by the

collar of his jacket, a gun pointed at the back of his head. Liam followed, his gun pointed in Crowder's direction.

Crowder kept Elsa between her and Liam, which allowed her to keep her aim on Hanratty.

Hill looked disheveled and more than a little beat-up, but physically able to defend himself if given the chance. He looked at her with opportunity written all over his face.

She put herself in Hill's shoes. What would he expect her to do? He'd want her to do everything possible to foil Hanratty's escape. Releasing three lethal weapons to kill again wasn't an option. Hill's best chance was to be one-on-one with Hanratty.

The trio stopped after they walked off the porch. The car Elsa was tethered to was about fifty feet from them.

"Okay, cuffs off," Hanratty demanded.

"Sure." Crowder picked the key off the hood of the car and tossed it on the ground in front of Elsa but outside her reach. "Liam, she's your sister; you do it. But before you do, holster your weapon. It will even out the fire power. Fair is fair."

Hanratty didn't immediately respond. Crowder figured he was assessing the consequences of having one less gun ready to shoot. But it was risky to have Liam so close to her. If he pulled out his gun, the slightest hesitation on her part in shooting him could prove fatal.

Liam had police protocols in hostage negotiations on his side. Police were trained to get the hostage back—they didn't shoot first. That's what Ron Santoro believed. But not Crowder. Not all the time. Not now. Not with Hill's life on the line. If Liam reached for his gun, she wouldn't hesitate—she'd shoot him dead.

Crowder put herself in Hanratty's head. What would he do? He'd know Liam would shoot her the first chance he had. Two scenarios played out in Crowder's mind.

In the first, Liam would approach his sister and use her body to obstruct Crowder's view of him. When Elsa saw him reach for his gun, she'd know to drop to the ground and give Liam a clear shot at her. He'd keep shooting until Crowder was dead. Even before he stopped, Hanratty would put a bullet in Hill's brainstem.

In the second, Hanratty would get things rolling by shooting Hill, and he'd use Hill's dead body as a shield when Crowder opened fire on him. In the bedlam, Liam would pull out his gun and fire away.

Either way, Hill and Crowder ended up dead. Hanratty held all the aces. And Crowder was bluffing with a pair of deuces.

Liam looked at Hanratty for direction. He nodded. Liam stepped aside, held his gun up so Crowder could see him place it in his shoulder holster, then walked slowly to where the key lay on the ground.

Crowder kept her aim on Hanratty. She wanted him to know that if something went awry her first shot would be at him.

Liam bent down to pick up the key. Crowder's eyes moved to him. He paused a moment before picking it up—with his left hand. That was the proof she needed. Liam had held his gun in his right hand. If his next act was to unlock the handcuffs, he'd have picked up the key with his right hand. If she noticed it, Hill probably did too.

Crowder couldn't see Elsa's eyes because she was facing her brother. But she could see Liam's. They were opened wide, looking directly at his sister, and blinking unevenly. He was communicating with her in Morse code, telling her to drop to the ground as soon as he reached for his gun.

Crowder did a quick risk-benefit analysis as her gaze shot back and forth between Liam and Hanratty. She noticed Hill's head move side to side as if to warn her that Liam had no intention of opening the handcuffs first.

But who does she shoot—Liam or Hanratty?

To open fire on Liam would mean a bullet for Hill. But if she fired at Hanratty, she'd only have the one shot. A barrage of bullets from Liam's gun into her would come too quickly.

Her life or Hill's life?

She'd have to choose.

Chapter 55

Liam Larsson was within arm's reach of his sister when Hill elbowed Hanratty in the chest and yelled, "Shoot him."

Crowder didn't hesitate. She redirected her aim to Elsa's head and pulled the trigger the moment Elsa dropped far enough to the ground for Crowder to see Liam's gun pointed at her chest. Two simultaneous blasts later, Crowder found herself on the ground bleeding from a bullet wound to her right side. Her gun flew from her hand when the shot propelled her backward. Both hands went instinctively to where she most acutely felt the pain —just below the ribcage.

Blood oozed from the wound. If the bullet had lacerated her liver, she could bleed out. No amount of pressure applied to the site of the wound would help. Her bleeding would be mostly internal. She'd go into shock, and her blood pressure would continue to drop until she passed out.

Crowder had to muster whatever strength remained and find her gun. She rolled over on her side, located the gun a few feet away, got onto one knee and picked it up as she stumbled to her feet. A rush of warm blood went to her head, making her momentarily dizzy and disoriented. She thought she might faint. But the syncope passed. She could now focus on getting control of the situation before her gas tank was empty.

Hanratty and Hill were fist-fighting in front of the house.

Elsa jumped to her feet and used her left foot to kick at the mirror.

Crowder held her left hand against her wound. The gun felt wobbly in her right hand, and before she could aim it, the side mirror broke off. Elsa dropped to the ground, out of view. Crowder staggered back to the side of the car. Over the hood, she saw Liam lying on his back holding his throat with both hands, blood seeping through his fingers and out his mouth. His body convulsed as he lay there bleeding to death.

Elsa dove for her brother's gun, gripped it in her right hand, and with the handcuffs dangling from her wrist, rolled over into a kneeling position and turned to shoot. Crowder's hand trembled as she fired three shots in quick succession, but at least one hit its target. Elsa slumped over on her side. The single shot Elsa got off grazed Crowder's head just above her ear. Blood trickled down the side of her face.

Hill was on top of Hanratty punching him.

She dragged her feet around the front of the car and stepped over Liam's body on her way to Elsa. His body no longer shook. He'd died choking on his blood. Elsa lay there motionless beside her brother, his gun on the ground by her hand. Crowder kicked it away. Blood puddled on the ground from Elsa's gunshot wound to the sternum.

She looked again at Hill. He and Hanratty were wrestling on the ground. It was time to put an end to the fight, and to Hanratty. She raised her pistol and started to walk toward him, but a hand grabbed her ankle and yanked her back. She lost her balance and fell face-first to the ground, the gun dislodged from her hand. She rolled over on her back. In an instant, Elsa was on top of her, punching her repeatedly in the face. Pinned down by Elsa's body weight, Crowder was defenseless. Then the punching stopped.

Elsa grabbed Crowder by the throat with both hands and began to choke her. She dug her thumbs deep, blocking the airway. Crowder gagged and gasped for air. She managed to pull Elsa's hands free, but it only momentarily allowed her to breathe. Elsa soon had a vice-like grip around her throat again.

A neuron sparked in Crowder's mind. She let her right hand drop to her side and rocked her body side to side. When there was enough room under her right hip, she reached into her back pocket. The feel of the metal object in her hand gave Crowder a sudden burst of energy. With only fumes left in her tank, she pressed her thumb against the handle of Elsa's knife and released the blade. Crowder took one last gasp of air and, with all her remaining strength, she thrust the blade into Elsa's chest.

The rush of air into Crowder's lungs when Elsa released her grip was like a shot of adrenaline. She pushed Elsa off her, found her gun, and got up, looking over at Hill.

He stood over Hanratty with the colonel's gun in his hand. Coughing the words between breaths, he said, "Bring … your … cuffs."

She holstered her weapon, wiped some of the blood off her face with a sleeve, and then, after grabbing the key from beside Liam's body, she stumbled her way back to Elsa, who lay there lifeless, the knife stuck deep in her chest. Crowder removed the cuff from her wrist and walked over to Hill.

His face was bruised and bloodied. So was what she could see of Hanratty's, who lay on his stomach spitting out blood. Hill put the gun in his jacket pocket, took the handcuffs from Crowder and planted his knee firmly in the small of Hanratty's back. The colonel arched his back with a groan. Hill yanked his hands together and handcuffed him, eliciting another groan.

"Looks like you won by a TKO," Crowder said through a painful smile.

"The score card had us even for a while, but I knew he couldn't go the distance," Hill boasted, his bright-white, perfectly straight teeth at odds with a battered face. "That was a lot of shooting I heard." His gaze narrowed to focus on the blood on Crowder's blouse and blazer. "Is that their blood or yours?"

"It looks worse than it is." Crowder chuckled and winced in pain for the effort. "The bullet passed through me. I felt some blood ooze through the exit wound. It must have missed my liver because I'm still here."

Hill stepped in front of Crowder and held her in his arms. She nestled her head into his shoulder, and he kissed the top of her head and stroked her hair. A flashback of them in bed after they'd made love made her pain momentarily subside. He'd whispered sweet things to her while he held her tight against his side. She remembered every word he said to her that night. But it was what happened afterward that mattered most.

As he'd done that night, Hill released his grip on her and looked into her eyes. Only the sound of their breathing disturbed the still quiet as, for what felt like a very long time, they let their eyes see into their hearts.

The approach of a helicopter broke the splendor of a bittersweet moment. It circled once and hovered above them. A voice blared on a bullhorn from the cockpit, "Hill, are you in control of the scene?"

Hill smiled, raised his arm over his head, and gave a thumbs-up. It was then that he saw Elsa Larsson standing with a knife stuck in her chest and a gun clenched firmly in her hands pointed at Crowder's back.

Hill's pistol was in the pocket of his jacket. There was no

time to reach for it. He did the only thing left to do. He hugged Crowder hard, picked her up, and swung her around.

Crowder watched in horror over Hill's shoulder as Elsa got off a shot just before a bullet fired from the helicopter blew off the top of her head.

Hill slumped into Crowder's arms, his body limp.

Crowder fell to her knees with Hill still in her arms, holding him tightly … in one final embrace.

Epilogue

Hill and Crowder were medevacked to a trauma center in New Orleans. The bullet that entered Hill's back lodged in the middle of his spine and dislocated two vertebrae. A delicate five-hour surgery removed it, but he remained in the ICU on a ventilator, paralyzed from the chest down.

The bullet that passed through Crowder did so without striking any internal organs, arteries, or major veins. She was hospitalized for two days and released. She spent most of her time in the hospital at Hill's bedside, occasionally squeezing his hand to let him know he wasn't alone.

After Crowder's release, she visited Hill every day in the hospital until he was weaned off the ventilator and had been moved to a step-down unit. Mentally, Hill fully recovered in a couple of days. Physically, he was in for a long haul.

When his condition stabilized, his doctor transferred him to a rehab facility where he received intensive physical therapies. If he'd ever walk again depended on whether his injured spinal cord healed without permanent damage and if his willpower was strong enough to overcome the many obstacles he'd face during his rehabilitation.

When Crowder visited Hill in the hospital, she often went to the non-denominational chapel to reflect on why things came down the way they did. She wasn't a church-going Christian. The narrowmindedness and hypocrisy of organized religions were too much for her to accept. In her mind, the existence of a supreme being was at best a fifty-fifty proposition.

During her chapel visits she reflected on whether her life had any real meaning. Was the world a better place because of what she did? What Hill did? Bringing to justice those whose vile acts harmed innocent people was the noble purpose that had led her into law enforcement. But over the years, with all the violent criminals she'd put behind bars, not much had changed. There were, and would always be, others to replace them.

She thought about the old western movies she'd stayed up late to watch on television with her father when she was a child. How the sheriff would singlehandedly rid his town of gunslingers, cattle wrestlers, and bank robbers.

Only in the movies.

Crowder's idealism waned over the years—replaced by skepticism and cynicism. Too many crime scene photos of dead people had taken their toll on her. Maybe Ron Santoro was right—she'd put herself in harm's way so that she could exact her own brand of justice. Maybe she wanted to confront the bad guys like so many sheriffs did in those western movies—until the bad guy, or she, lay dead on the ground.

Crowder reflected on how she felt after she shot Liam Larsson and saw him in extremis. There was no sense of urgency to go to his aid. It had pleased her that he was dying and would soon be dead. And to have put a blade into Elsa Larsson's chest with her knife was more than poetic justice—it was Crowder's brand of justice. She'd wanted both to die for what they'd done to Cletus Moss, Brian McManus, and so many others. But the collateral damage this time was too much for her to bear.

Alex Hill had taken a bullet meant for her. She should be the one nearly mortally wounded, not him. The guilt weighed heavy on her heart. She'd been careless. She should've made sure Elsa was dead. And to have left Liam's gun on the ground for Elsa to use would haunt her her whole life if Hill didn't recover from his injuries.

During her visits to the chapel, Crowder did something she hadn't done since her mother died unexpectedly when she was a child—she wept. And for the first time in a very long time—she prayed.

Crowder spent the month after her discharge from the hospital working with FBI investigators and Rita Morales, assembling the evidence for the case against Heartland Insurance and James Hanratty.

A federal grand jury returned an indictment against Heartland Insurance for RICO violations and murder. Finch and members of his inner circle could not be prosecuted—Hanratty made sure of that when he murdered all of them. The indictment listed them as unindicted co-conspirators.

A trial of Finch's company was necessary, however. Morales needed the guilty verdict to empower the judge at sentencing to seize the company's assets and the money stashed away in offshore accounts. The money would be used to compensate the families of victims and to locate and treat the remaining persons who had been injected with Litchman's death serum. Some would not be saved. But many would.

As for Moss, Hartman, and Helmsley, Louisiana law prevented Heartland Insurance from recovering the proceeds of their policies because the company had instigated their murders. The proceeds went to their next of kin.

Crowder attended Hanratty's sentencing. So did Hill. By

then he was out of a wheelchair and using a cane to walk. They sat with Brian McManus's sister and Jason Crockett's parents. Hanratty was not prosecuted for his involvement in their murders. But the judge at sentencing stated on the record that Hanratty had arranged them, that Brian McManus had never used illegal drugs, and that Jason Crockett didn't take his own life. That was enough to bring closure for the families.

Hanratty was convicted of the murders Morales could prove beyond a reasonable doubt—Jared Finch and Grayson Gladstone, and the attempted murder of Hill. The jury made sure the colonel would be reunited with Finch and the other members of the inner circle. They sentenced him to death.

Hanratty expressed no remorse at sentencing and, like his grandfather before him, he took the coward's way out. He hung himself that night in his cell.

~

A month later Crowder sat at her desk at district headquarters when she received a call from Hill.

"First day back. It feels great," he said from his office at the FBI Headquarters in Washington, DC.

The good news of Hill's near-full recovery comforted Crowder. He no longer needed a cane and walked with a barely perceptible limp. He'd also received a promotion.

"Congratulations, Alex, I hear you've been rewarded with a new position and office in Washington. No one deserves it more."

"Thanks. I had a lot of help from a homicide detective from New Orleans. Jo, you are one damn good cop."

Hill paused long enough for Crowder to prod him along. "And?" she said, sensing that he had more to say.

"Before I agreed to the promotion, I went to see Morales. I wanted her to know what I'd done. I didn't give her the CD. I left you entirely out of it. Morales told me—"

Crowder interrupted. "Alex, I told my captain that I took the serum and the documents from Litchman's desk and mailed them to you."

Both remained silent for a while.

Crowder could almost read Hill's mind. They were so much alike. The thought of violating laws they'd sworn an oath to uphold scorched their moral fabric. If they could so boldly break the law, what lengths might they be willing to go to—plant evidence, lie about what suspects say to them, force confessions, shoot a suspect and lay a gun near the body? It repulsed Crowder to think of where it could lead, and she suspected it did the same to Hill.

He broke the silence. "Morales told me that there were times when she knew an agent had overstepped his authority. But it was the first time an agent had owned up to it. She opened a drawer of her desk and placed a CD in front of me. I knew what it was, of course. She looked at me and said, 'Special Agent Hill, would you please dispose of this. It's no longer of any importance to anyone.' Jo, she knew what we'd done and did nothing about it."

"And we know better than anyone why she didn't. Like us, she believes that sometimes, when the evil is so great, no rule of law should protect it … that sometimes the greater good demands that someone have the courage to stand up and put an end to it."

When the call concluded, Crowder sat back to reflect on the meeting she had with O'Malley when she confessed to what she'd done at Kratos. O'Malley held a similar view about what she'd done. He told her that the best cops weren't the ones who followed the rules all the time, regardless of the circumstances.

The best cops were the ones who had the courage and good sense to do what was right under the circumstances, regardless of the consequences. Her father had felt the same way.

Crowder reached in the drawer of her desk, picked up her copy of the CD—and tossed it in the wastebasket.

A Note from the Author

Some of us may be taken aback, even offended, that a homicide detective and an FBI agent could so boldly violate the Constitution and laws of our nation. Some of us may be troubled, even angered, that Crowder and Hill avoided responsibility for their misdeeds.

At first, I was too.

Then I asked myself this question: Should the Nazi guard whose job was to secure the gate at a concentration camp do nothing when he suspects that prisoners are being subjected to atrocities inside the camp? Should he be punished if he opened the gate he had a duty to secure, and allowed a prisoner to escape? Aren't there occasions when following the rules and doing nothing are just plain wrong?

Crowder and Hill put their careers on the line to uncover what they suspected were mass killings for profit by Finch's company. They were right in their suspicions. Had they been wrong and the serum had been a groundbreaking discovery for the cultivation of a synthetic grain that could feed the world population, they surely would've been fired from their jobs, perhaps criminally prosecuted, for what they did.

Are Morales and O'Malley corrupt for not exposing Hill and Crowder's misdeeds? In answering that question, consider what would have been gained by doing so. Two careers destroyed. And for what? They broke the law, for sure. But they uncovered a diabolical plot and saved many lives. And those who couldn't be saved had their justice too. The truth came out about Finch's criminal enterprise. Sometimes that's all that matters, for the victims, for their families, and for all of us.

I fear that this will not be the last time Jo Crowder will face this dilemma. I'll try my best to have her walk a path that's straight and narrow. But there's only so much I can do because she has a life of her own. What she does from here on, I have little control over. Sure, I have an attachment to Jo Crowder and want to protect her. I admire her chutzpah, for sure. She is brave, and relentless in the pursuit of truth and justice. But she is impulsive and prone to take risks that put her in harm's way. She resists doing only what's expected of her. She knows she's capable of doing so much more. When it comes to protecting her world from evil, she has no boundaries other than the ones she sets for herself.

I do know this.

Jo Crowder will be there to protect us … when no one else will.

~

If you enjoyed this book, I would be very grateful if you would write a review and publish it at your point of purchase. Your review, even a brief one, will help other readers to decide if they'll enjoy my novels.

And I invite you to read my other Jo Crowder books, *Identical Misfortune (*AIA Publishing, September 9, 2020) and

The Easter Murders (AIA Publishing, May 7, 2021), available in hardback and paperback at richardzappa.com, amazon.com, and barnesandnoble.com.

About Identical Misfortune

When Veronica, a heartless sociopath, learns that her good-hearted identical twin, Ann, has married into a wealthy family, she very cleverly manipulates family members and the police into believing she's Ann, then stages Ann's suicide and makes off with millions. In a duel of wits between a cold-blooded killer and a cop, each brilliant in her own way, Detective Jo Crowder pursues Veronica while she schemes, lies and murders her way in and out of families on both sides of the Atlantic. But can Crowder stop the killing without turning her back on the law she's sworn to uphold?

Here's what the reviewers said about *Identical Misfortune:*

"A grim and engrossing procedural with a stellar cast."

—Kirkus Reviews

"A winding roller-coaster ride of betrayal and intrigue … as harrowing as the journey is, it's worth the effort." — Charles Ray, author and Awesome Indies Book Awards assessor

"Utterly spellbinding crime drama thriller … a well-imagined and outstanding work of fiction." — Online Book Club

"Suspenseful battle of wits … that balances cerebral puzzle solving with vigorous action." — IndieReader

About The Easter Murders

A serial killer chooses Easter week to leave dead pregnant teens in front of Catholic churches in New Orleans. Homicide detective Jo Crowder doggedly pursues a trail of evidence that leads to the arrest of Miguel Diaz, a twenty-year-old Latino nursing student. Crowder's instincts tell her that the evidence against Diaz was planted by the actual murderer. Though directed by her superiors to close the investigation, Crowder suspects Monsignor Rossi, whose connections to the victims are too suspicious to overlook. But can she prove that the clergyman is a cold-blooded murderer in time to save Diaz?

Here's what the reviewers said about *The Easter Murders:*

"Zappa beautifully captures multifaceted tensions that keep the story moving along at an easy clip. A twisty and highly readable thriller." — Kirkus Reviews

"Once you start reading *The Easter Murders*, you'll find yourself compelled to keep on, following clue after clue, red herring after red herring, until all that is left is the inevitable, but unpleasant, reality. Zappa has outdone himself on this one. I give this 5 stars." —Charles Ray, author and Awesome Indies Book Awards assessor

"A thrilling crime/drama mystery … engrossing and difficult to put down … four out of four stars." — Online Book Club

"Zappa's *The Easter Murders* keeps readers entertained with solid police procedural work, tense courtroom drama, and insidious backroom dealing." — IndieReader

About the Author

Richard Zappa is a trial lawyer and novelist. A graduate of the Washington College of Law of the American University in Washington, DC, he was an editor of the Law Review, and Dean's Fellow to Adjunct Professor of Law and former Associate Justice of the US Supreme Court, Arthur J. Goldberg.

During a distinguished career as a top personal injury and medical malpractice lawyer, he has litigated and tried numerous cases in federal and state court, many of which resulted in multimillion-dollar recoveries for his clients. A black-belt martial artist and self-taught pianist, he writes from his homes in Wilmington and Rehoboth Beach, Delaware, and St. Thomas, US Virgin Islands.